VENGEANCE BE MINE

VENGEANCE DEMONS BOOK 1

Louisa Lo

TIN CAN PRESS

Cover Photo: Sara Eirew
Cover Design: Jacqueline Sweet
Editing: Rhonda Helms and Jena O'Connor
Interior Design: Tin Can Press

Vengeance Be Mine/Louisa Lo—1st edition
ISBN: 978-0-9939396-0-0

DEDICATION

To Andrew, the most supportive hubby in the world.

To S.T., whose passing taught me how to live. RIP, my friend.

To Murray, for all the wonderful tales of Saint John.

ACKNOWLEDGMENTS

To every disappointment, regret and heartbreak
that has ever graced my life. Without you there
would've been no need for me to be strong.

To Gina, for sharing the joy of writing
and being a patient sounding board.

To Wendy, for the amazing beta read.

To my parents, who never failed to put food on the
table,
and my brother, who bought my first piece of writing
with his allowance.

To Mr. Ng and Mrs. Anderson, who encouraged my
life-long love for writing.

Thank you all for contributing to my writing journey,
and
in doing so, making this book possible.

ONE

THERE IS A SAYING AMONGST vengeance demons—justice comes slowly, but surely.

Or on rare occasions, it could hit hard and fast, like the waves of contractions my male target was experiencing as I stood over him.

"Make it stop. I'm begging," he groaned, arching his back on the hotel bed. His T-shirt was drenched, like in those bar contests he frequented, revealing the long torso and lean six-pack of an athlete in his prime. He looked up at me, his brown eyes pleading, and his gaze unfocused—the way humans got when they were in pain.

"Mr. Lodge, it's not even midnight yet. We've got another four hours of torment to go, according to my work order." I tried to sound professional, but my nineteen-year-old voice was just a bit on the squeaky side, even to my own ears. The business of vengeance was harder than I'd ever thought possible.

This was my first solo practice session after a year of in-class lectures at the University of Demonic Studies, Faculty of Arts and Vengeance. I needed it to go well.

Problem was, none of my textbooks mentioned how to deal with a crybaby.

A crying *man*-baby.

MVP Jeremy Lodge, aka "The Machine," clutched his

stomach and whimpered. The famous basketball star was known for striking fear in the hearts of opposing teams all over the world, but now the only thing that came knocking was another contraction.

"What's happening?" The Machine panted during a respite, the tranquility of the hotel room clearly lost on him. There was soft light from the paper lantern overhead and a fluffy sand-colored carpet one could sink one's toes into. The sliding doors made of mint-frosted glass added a touch of modern elegance to the five-star suite.

What was happening? What a question.

When I'd fantasized about getting my vengeance demon designation, this was the part I'd found the most satisfying—telling the target how his actions had led to the consequences he was facing.

"A taste of childbirth pain, which is a fitting punishment for cheating on your pregnant wife with the whole cheerleading squad."

I had to pat myself on the shoulder for coming up with *that* particular punishment. Why exact a boring old vengeance when you could spice it up with a cool, ironic twist?

"You little bitch!" The Machine pounded his enormous fist on the mattress.

"Hey, the name is Megan. Not bitch. Not little." I gritted my teeth.

"Fuck you!"

I pushed aside my first instinct—getting mad or, worse, scared. I'd been insulted before, but usually with more subtlety than that. I guess humans weren't exactly subtle creatures. It might also be the difference between having the cuss words tossed at me, rather than learning them in a classroom setting. I forced myself to unclench my fists, my fingernails peeling away almost reluctantly from the imprints they dug into my palms. There was a magical barrier between us, and I was in control.

Even though it was my first time alone with a target.

I straightened. Never show fear, they'd taught us in *Occupational Insults & Threats 101*. "Bad manners will only get me mad and extend your punishment."

"I'm going to kill you," he snarled.

"Alright, an extra ten minutes it is."

Was insisting on ten too harsh? Should I have said five? I caught myself brushing my fingertips over the edge of the pocket-sized training manual currently pressed against my jean-clad bum. This being my first time, I'd packed the mini-bible along just in case. Now I longed to take it out and flip to the chapter on *How to Deal With the Misgivings of Hurting In the Name of Justice*, because every single moan that came out of The Machine hit my guts like ice water. Since I wasn't the target's direct victim, it was hard for me to establish him as the total bad guy in my mind, and part of me felt bad about administrating the suffering to him. Green, green, green—that was what I was.

Come on, Megan. You can't afford a soft heart. You want to help people, remember? Keeping balance in the world is helping them.

I sometimes forgot how annoyingly logical my inner voice could be.

"I swear, I'm going to kill you," The Machine repeated, every muscle on his body taut, his eyes promising death and destruction. Had I been a mortal, I would have been scared shitless.

I sighed. "I heard you the first time. How about you try

not cheating in the future?"

The Machine looked ready to explode into a string of curses when his eyes widened to the size of saucers. Halftime was over, and there was no sitting this round out.

"Alright, listen up." I hastily leaned over. I had under a minute to get him to understand. "Breathe in through your nose and out through your mouth. In for three, then out for three. Come on, I've read these exercises on your Internet and it should help."

Oh boy, it was going to be a long night. At least the target was contained within a dome-shaped energy barrier covering the entire bed. An attack from over two hundred pounds of pure muscle was something I did not need.

And so the labor carried on past midnight. And on. And on.

According to my training manual, I was supposed to stay with the target throughout the entire process. I tried, I really did. But after three hours of his moaning and bitching, I'd had enough. Why, oh why, was my fickle magic able to mute the noise for all humans within hearing range, but not for me?

The grating sound of torment caused my head to pound with the intensity of a full-blown aura migraine, the queen of all migraines that even a supernatural being couldn't escape. First came the offending aura; a whirling circle of flashing light the size of a penny appeared in my visual field. Soon, it expanded to cover most of my vision, pretty much blinding me. When the aura dissipated, that was when the nausea, dizziness, and excruciating pain in my skull started. Fun.

I stumbled out of the bedroom and sank down on the sofa in the dim living room, my temples throbbing. There was still another hour of vengeance to go, but my magic should maintain his torment for a while in my absence. Right now, my priority was to survive until this terrible pain in my skull went away, and that meant putting some distance between The Machine and me.

It was two in the morning, and the floor-to-ceiling window greeted me with a view of the Toronto Harbor. Mercifully, the yachts pushed only feeble light into the surrounding darkness, and the undisturbed water calmed my nerves. I did mention I was sensitive to light in my current state, right?

I hoped it would get easier with each job, like Dad had claimed.

At long last my migraine subsided, but I wasn't ready to face the howling athlete just yet. I was still on the clock, and The Machine was still suffering. Who was there to see that I wasn't actually *in* the room the entire time? I just needed a few more minutes. It was more than fair, considering the occupational hazard.

As if on cue, The Machine's wails took on a kicked-in-the-balls tone, only to change pitch midway into a string of inventive swear words, most of which I'd never even heard before.

I turned on the lights, took out *Renters Weekly* from my backpack and sifted through the roommates-wanted ads. Now that the in-class segment of my demon education was almost over, bye-bye college dorm, hello sweet independence.

As I lost myself in the magazine, The Machine's yowls faded to nothing but ambient noise.

These human females sure were easy to please. Being a non-smoker with no pets that mortal eyes could see and no qualms about living in dodgy neighborhoods, I had my pick of the lot.

At some point, the screaming stopped and there was a distant thud. Huh, I wonder what that was all—

Wow, look at this ad with the most amazing feature ever: "3 meals/day incl. I'm a culinary student and I LOVE cooking!"

My mouth watered. It would be like living on the Food Network 24/7. As a half demon, I might not *need* to eat, but I sure *liked* to. Stuffed mushrooms, seared scallops with pancetta, fluffy soufflés...

"Ahem." Someone cleared her throat from the edge of the sofa.

I jumped, sending the thick rental magazine to the floor with a *smack*.

A slender figure in a tailored, taupe business suit and genuine sea pearl necklace graced the living room with her stern feminine presence.

Crap.

It was my turn to clear my throat. A lump formed at the base of it, the blockage nonexistent just seconds ago. "Hello, Enid. I didn't hear you teleporting in."

A moment of silence.

My heart raced guiltily and I shifted my weight, feigning sudden interest in a spot on my right shoe. The image of The Machine trapped in bed, going through the routine of tears and pain without proper supervision, came to mind. Damn, talk about rotten timing. I suppose that was why they called it a *surprise* inspection. How could I not have realized I'd get into trouble the moment I stepped out of line? It'd been happening since that one time I'd tried to talk behind the teacher's back in grade two history class.

Enid was a middle-age brunette with a tightly coiled hair bun and thick-rimmed glasses. She showed off her maturity not with the tiny crow's feet around her eyes, since anyone could get them with the purchase of a bag of semi-permanent faery dust, but from the well-measured power she carried around. That kind of discipline took decades to hone, and my program mentor was a lady who meant business.

After a year of in-class lectures, students like me were eligible to join the co-op program with Enid's approval. Given the serious expression on her face right now, I needed to convince her I was responsible and reliable, which I wasn't exactly doing by being caught taking this little breather.

"Megan, in our line of work, control is an art," Enid began with quiet dignity. "Making the targets suffer just enough–"

I lifted my head. "I'm so sorry. I got a migraine and stepped out for just a mo—"

"—without scaring them to death." Enid stared at me. "Or pushing them to commit suicide."

I swallowed. "Suicide?"

Shit, what have I done? How could The Machine be dead? I left him for, like, five seconds. I'd painstakingly tested the dome-shaped barriers in the school lab. Was it my flaky magic, failing me when it most counted? Or did I overlook a procedure somewhere along the line? Didn't matter. The guy still died on my watch. Dammit.

Without another word, Enid led me into the bedroom— which was empty. She gestured towards the French doors and the balcony. "Twenty-two stories down. He landed on the concrete, poolside."

I winced. I might not have cared for the cheating bastard's lifestyle, but that didn't mean I wanted him dead. And there was his wife to think about, not to mention his newborn baby. From what I heard, it was expensive to raise kids, no matter what plane they were born into.

"You can reverse it, right?" I asked Enid urgently.

"Of course." My mentor nodded towards the window. "I've already called Reapers 'R' Us to cancel the dispatch. But you get a mark of zero in this practice session."

I wanted to kick something or cry. A mark of zero. After all the group practice sessions and hard work. I didn't realize until now that a part of me honestly thought I'd aced this with no issues. It was demoralizing to screw up in such a disastrous manner.

Alright, chin up and do some damage control. You lost the battle, but not the war. Try saying something contrite and repenting. You can't afford to fail this semester. Not if you want to move out of the dorm and get away from those dreadful girls.

"What does *he* get?" I heard myself ask. I couldn't help it. I might not want The Machine dead, but the idea of him getting off scot-free, with no memory of his punishment, didn't sit well with me, either. Maybe I just plain sucked at the whole detachment thing they valued in school.

"Something a little less...heavy." I could've sworn there was just the tiniest curve at the corners of Enid's mouth. In an instant, the facial expression made my usually austere mentor appear a decade younger.

"Like what?" Now I was intrigued.

"A period."

Two

"BEFORE EXACTING YOUR ASSIGNED VENGEANCE, reconnaissance within reason is allowed under Article 4.3, section E of the IICVD handbook..." Professor Mando shook the said handbook in his hands for emphasis.

It was the last class of the semester in my freshmen year, and three weeks since The Machine made international headlines holding a gun to a convenience store clerk's head for a package of winged maxi pads. The air was scented with late spring flowers. A few hummingbirds dive-bombed each other outside the classroom windows, their rapid flight graceful if one discounted their violent attacks on one another in their ceaseless turf wars. There was just enough of a cross breeze entering the stone structure to keep the students awake as Professor Mando droned on and on about even more rules we'd all one day be regulated by.

Assuming, of course, that we earned our designation from the Interdimensional Institute of Chartered Vengeance Demons. We might have the blood of vengeance demons in our veins, but that did not guarantee being certified as a practicing member of our race. Those who failed the professional exams became support workers, like paralegals to lawyers. Those who failed to become support workers got on an even lower tier, and on and on it went until the worst of the worst simply became outcasts in our society. A dropout two years ahead of me was now living on the human plane, working as a security guard on *Judge Judy*, and nobody ever talked about *him* again.

Clang...clang-clang-clang...clang-clang...

I tried to focus on the lecture, but my mind kept straying to the metallic sound resonating from the floor and what it meant.

It meant somebody was being bullied. It meant that in a school intent on training future justice handlers, someone was deserving of a little comeuppance herself.

Yes, it was a she, and so was her victim. There was only one person in class the sound of iron would be terrifying to.

The target of the bullying was Serafina Anastassia Advocatus, a vengeance demon stolen at birth by changelings and only released a year ago. As a result, she had to learn the ways of her people from scratch, and it hadn't been easy for the pale and mousy girl. The prestigious name of her birth family might've earned Serafina an entrance into the university, but that wouldn't give her decent grades, nor stop the mean girls from targeting her.

The ringleader of the freshman clique, one Madeleine Abrianna Lex, tapped her heels on the floor in front of her seat. Embedded in the heels was a pair of miniature horseshoes. With each tap, the slick blonde hammered out a wave of vibration that would be nerve grinding for the iron-fearing changelings. Not that iron could actually hurt Serafina, who didn't have a drop of changeling blood, but tell that to eighteen years of conditioning. Serafina suffered the onslaught of pulsation in silence, shaking and folding her body in a near-fetal position on the chair, not daring to make a sound.

She reminded me of my younger self, before I toughened up and fought back. That sense of helplessness and isolation had to suck. I should've reached out to the reticent girl at the very start of university, but I'd been too wrapped up in pursuing my own career goal.

Professor Mando favored rubber shoes and didn't feel a thing. Before the start of class, Madeleine had craftily offered him an enchanted cupcake. One tiny bite had ensured the dear old prof couldn't hear the clanging, either.

Nobody else in class seemed inclined to do anything about the blatant bullying, which was playing out right in front of the teacher. They might find the vibration distracting, but nothing worth speaking out about, considering the consequences of doing so. No one wanted to make Madeleine angry, even if it meant approving through silence the re-victimization of someone who'd already been through so much. The whole thing was just so damn high school. Since Serafina had already missed the benefits of going through an adolescent education, she shouldn't have to suffer through the pain of it, either.

I totally got how it felt to be different, to be excluded because of something I couldn't control. There were rumors about Serafina botching her practice session because she'd tried to get her mean drunk of a target help rather than punishing him. Not that I thought we ought to save everybody, but the fact that Serafina *tried* was something.

While the vengeance demon in me protested Madeleine's cruelty, another part of me—the part I inherited from my trickster mother—whispered devious, delicious plans in my head to make her stop. I tended to think of myself as a vengeance demon, but in times like this I was reminded of my dual heritage.

I could make Madeleine sprain her ankle with the next tapping or give her a phantom toothache with a rhythmic pulse matching the one she was dishing out. That oughta stop her. Or, to hell with a good poetic twist, I could simply compel Madeleine to climb onto the table and perform a little impromptu striptease. Videos of the blue-blooded heiress twerking could have a few thousand hits on the DemonTube before Professor Mando even called me to the front of the class.

Too bad I couldn't listen to my naughty side.

If I were seen using my mother's magic, no one would take me seriously in this school. Heck, they thought I was a joke as it was. Knowing my trickster heritage was one thing; seeing it in action with their own eyes would be another.

I loved Mom, I really did. I just liked Dad's profession more than hers, that was all. Tricksters had a bad rep for being impulsive, irresponsible, and lazy. I just wanted to get a bit of respect, build up a healthy credit score, and resist the urge to enchant my prof's chair with a whoopee cushion spell. Was that too much to ask?

Though I must admit, the idea of Madeleine on a whoopee cushion during a hot date did have a certain appeal. Talk about the opposite of being sexy.

Oh, shut up. Not happening.

But imagine the horror on her face. C'mon.

Not. Happening.

The tapping, and the blatantly public assault, continued.

"Now, I'm going to pass around my own vengeance dagger for you to see. You youngsters will get yours when you graduate from this program. Notice the carving on the left side, which originated in the eleventh century when humans were still aware of our existence." Professor Mando went on about the Five Principles of Vengeance, the Six Decrees, and so on.

Madeleine lived on my dorm floor. Opposing her in a public manner would mean certain consequences. I'd gotten crap this past year just for being a hybrid. My stomach tightened with the memories of her past pranks, from curdled rice pudding on the eve of my four-hour final exam, to itching-powder-laced body lotion right before my co-op interview. Each prank had gross and devastating results. Stepping in now would mean taking things to the next level.

Screw it. I'd be damned if I'd sit through the harassment of Serafina and did nothing.

I stared at the commemorative dagger being passed around, an *iron* dagger, and it gave me an idea.

When the person in front of me gave me the dagger, I deliberately dropped it at just the right angle, while sending a temporary shield to encompass Serafina. The blade bounced off the floor with a pronounced *ding*, sending a resonating feedback straight to Madeleine's iron-centered heels, cracking the horseshoes each in half.

"Ouch!" she screamed, rubbing her temple. Poor girl, the feedback must be ricocheting through her head like a malfunctioning human speaker. It would've pained Serafina even more, if not for the protection I'd placed around her.

"Oops." I filled my voice with innocent regret and picked up the dagger. I sneaked a glance at Serafina. She uncurled herself from her fetal position, looked up and around for the first time in class, like a wide-eyed baby owl fresh out of a snow cave, surprised at the abrupt end to her torment.

"What's wrong, Miss Lex? Why did you scream?" Professor Mando frowned at the obnoxious queen bee.

"Nothing, sir. I was caught off guard by the sound of the drop, that's all." Madeleine smiled weakly at our lecturer, then gave me a look of pure venom. She knew I did it on purpose and I'd pay for it later.

"Remember, a vengeance demon should never be so easily startled. It's our job to startle *them*."

Madeleine's flawless face flushed to a crimson color. Alright, maybe the payback would come sooner rather than later.

I squared my shoulders. What was done, was done. Even if I could take it back, I wouldn't.

Towards the end of the lecture, there was a knock on the classroom door. Through the window, we could see that it was Enid holding an envelope. The entire class sat up straight as a single entity, the sleepier ones doing so before their eyes were even fully opened.

It was time.

Professor Mando waved our program mentor in. "I'm just about finished, Enid. Come on in. Now, class, this is the moment of truth."

Enid stopped next to the professor and addressed us, her shrewd eyes roaming around the room, missing nothing. "Congratulations on a successful first year, freshmen. But in life, it doesn't matter if you're a supernatural or a mortal, there will always be competition. The following is a list of those who have been selected into the vengeance co-op program. If you're chosen, you'll get your first assignment in the next few days. If you're not, you can apply again next year or switch to the General Stream."

Oh, the dreaded General Stream. Desk job workers supporting those who went into the field. Like those guys who polish James Bond's cool gadgets or file his travel expense reports. Sexy, it was not.

Nobody found out whether he or she was selected until this moment, not even the ones with family connections. Way to make sure that not a single freshman skips the last class, considering the exams were already over.

Enid took out a single piece of paper from the envelope. "First on the list, Miss Madeleine Abrianna Lex."

Madeleine stood and nodded in an arrogant manner that came from multiple generations of extreme privilege. She wasn't at all shocked that she'd been accepted, and why should she be? To top off her straight A's, her dad was on the Concord Council.

The names went on. With the reading of each of them, there was applause as the successful candidates stood up, took a bow, and sat down again. They were mostly predictable favorites, the ones who, while they might not have powerful family names behind them, had performed well in their practice sessions and won their spots fair and square. Serafina, unsurprisingly, didn't get in. To be frank, the girl seemed relieved not to be picked. Her shoulders became more and more relaxed with every name read that *wasn't* hers.

I could barely prevent myself from biting my knuckles. I willed my name to be read. I deserved to be on that list like the rest of them. I'd gotten pretty good grades, though I didn't brag about it. Well, not that there was anyone non-hostile enough I could do the bragging to. As for the practice sessions, in the three weeks since my disastrous encounter with The Machine, I'd worked like a demon—literally—to catch up on my marks. With the help of a dozen industrial-strength earplugs, I gave a corner-cutting contractor a botched root canal, a corporate air polluter severe asthma, and I kept an insurance fraudster honest by matching his physical conditions with his claims—word for word.

The man had said he had a herniated disk, so he got his disk herniated. My brand of justice was funny *and* fitting. I should get into the co-op just on that alone.

"The final name on the list is..."

I crossed my fingers. Here it came. The last chance. I peeked at Madeleine, who was exchanging smug nods with her two hench-girls. One of their names had already been read, and the other one, from the confidence evidenced on Madeleine's face, was the undoubted candidate for the final seat on the co-op train.

"Miss Megan Aequitas."

Instead of cheering and well wishing, my name was met with stunned silence. Then all hell broke loose.

Everyone was talking at the same time, their collective sound like the buzzing of angry flies over a pile of manure on a hot summer day. The words "cheating" and "trickery" abounded. The energy ripple of a few dozen students drawing on their vengeance magic unconsciously was rather unsettling, considering I was the one with a brand new target on my back.

"Calm down," Enid chided the group.

Madeleine stood. "As the student council president, I demand that the administration reconsider this decision."

Enid's eyebrow rose. "You *demand*?"

Under Enid's stare, Madeleine's face flushed. "No, I mean I...I... But she's a trickster!"

"Fifty percent trickster," I muttered. Not that anyone was listening.

"And a dirty half-breed."

I was the first vengeance demon/trickster hybrid ever born to any of the planes. I knew that. Everybody knew that. But did Madeleine really have to be so rude about it? I didn't like the unique status, but it was something I was born into.

Madeleine continued. "She should never even have been allowed to be here with us. Who's to say she didn't get the spot using trickery?"

"Miss Aequitas' acceptance into this university is a decision made by, and solely by, the school administration. And are you suggesting I was tricked and didn't even realize it?" Enid's tone was as chilly as winter on the Ice Priestess' plane.

That gave Madeleine pause. Enid was one of the most powerful vengeance demons at the university, and the idea of me, a fledgling first year, pulling one over on her was a bit far-fetched.

Ha, take that!

Self-preservation kicked in, and Madeleine tried to backpedal. "No, ma'am, I don't mean that at all. It's just that, well, it's never been done before. She doesn't even have a proper middle name."

Her last line ended like a whine. Taking the lead from her, the rest of the class settled into an uneasy silence. Not a good thing, because in my experience repressed dissatisfaction had a way of blowing up later, when the teachers weren't around.

I hated the sense of foreboding in my gut. This should've been a moment of total triumph for me. And instead of support and congratulations, I was getting dissed for the same old, same old. It made me not sad, but angry as heck.

After the class was dismissed, I headed towards my dorm through the school courtyard. I didn't need eyes in the back of my head to know I was followed by Madeleine, her two hench-girls, and a few other students. And not in a we-all-just-happened-to-be-heading-towards-the-same-destination kind of way. No, their movement was furtive and deliberate, in an attack formation. I was pleased to hear that Madeleine's footsteps had a limping quality to them, thanks to the broken horseshoes. It was a testimony to her drive to hurt me that the fashionista didn't even bother tending to her footwear first.

I sighed, took a deep breath, and slowed down. In my experience, there were two options when it came to bullies. It was either fight or flight. In my high school years I'd tried both, to varying successes.

I wasn't in high school anymore. And the ship had already sailed for anything but the fight option. It'd sailed the moment I'd refused to be a bystander in Serafina's plight, and the co-op placement was the final nail in the coffin.

I assessed my surroundings. From the glaring daggers I'd gotten from everyone who crossed paths with me, it was a good bet that word had already spread like wildfire on campus. I'd made quite a few enemies with the simple pronouncement of my name from Enid's lips. I had to do something before somebody suggested a mob lynching.

So fight it was.

However, I did have some leeway when it came to

choosing *how* to fight. And I chose to turn the imminent ambush into a direct confrontation. I was a straightforward kind of girl.

I pivoted and coolly locked eyes with Madeleine. Seeing the highborn heiress in full fury was quite something. She placed her hands on the hips of her black leather pantsuit, her long, bony fingers tightened with tension, as if she longed to close them around my throat.

Well, no "as if" about that.

"You'll pay for what happened this morning, Megan," she spat out, and her flock of hench-girls crossed their arms, pouted, and snarled, then pouted some more.

I rolled my eyes. The posturing and insults were really getting old. "Paying for what, breaking horseshoes or breaking tradition?"

I couldn't keep the pride out of my voice. Now I had the ability to decide where I wanted to live during the work term.

"Both. I heard you're not going to stay at the dorm for a few months," said Madeleine, as if reading my mind, her voice suddenly dripping with honey. That was never a good thing. "Have you started packing yet?"

Leaning into my personal space, she pulled out a family photo of my parents and me on our vacation last summer. It had gone missing from the top of my dresser around a month ago, and I'd assumed it had fallen into the disarray that surrounded it. With my messy habits, I had no idea where half of my stuff was most of the time. Turned out, Madeleine might've had it all this time.

"Here you go." She handed the photo back to me. Before letting go, she dug her thumbnail into the glossy layer printed with my mother's image, pressing in with a small push of magic so my mom's face peeled off. "Oops. Sorry."

My blood boiled and my eyes saw red, literally. Madeleine was insulting my mom by using an old human superstition, which said that destroying an image of someone would cause that person harm. With the right incantation and tools, that wasn't exactly an old wives' tale. It was a grave insult, if not an outright threat.

I tightened my fists. I didn't have a lot of pictures with just Mom and Dad and me, and the opportunities to take more grew fewer with the increasing demands in my life, given my chosen career path and the exhaustive venture of growing up.

"You could always mend it with magic." Madeleine suggested, her mocking tone burned like acid on raw skin.

I reverently picked up the peeled-off piece of my mother's image from the ground and concentrated. Nothing. I tried harder, squinting my eyes and almost giving myself early wrinkles in the process. Still nothing. The small scrap of glossy paper refused to reseal itself onto the photo. Madeleine's more cunning magic blocked me at every attempt.

I could feel blood rushing to my cheeks and the air becoming as thin as if I was standing on top of the Himalayan Mountains. Guilt and frustration gnawed at me. Here I was, missing time with family in pursuit of a profession full of the Madeleine type, the sort who'd never accepted my own mother.

"What's the matter?" she jeered. "The dirty little half-breed's too weak to give Mommy a hand? You're a pretender, Megan. Never forget that. I don't know and I don't care how you managed to get into the co-op, but you're not one of us, you hear me?"

Of its own accord, my mind started creating scenarios of getting to the brat through trickery, and ironically that was what slowed my pulse down. Action was always more calming than inaction. How about putting a progressive shrinking spell on her tight pantsuit and a time-released rip of the seam during her next student council speech? What about an illusion spell so she kept reading an extra ten pounds on her scale? If I was really careful, she would never find out what I'd done...

Watch out, Megan. You're in a public area. This is exactly what she wants. She wants to catch you tapping in to your trickster side in front of the whole school. Then there would be no dispute that you could've used trickery to get placed.

I looked around. The school courtyard had indeed gotten more crowded since I'd last checked. Students had started congregating around us, watching our every move, hoping to catch a good fight.

So I would give them one. But not the one they wanted.

"Why don't we take it into the ring?" I gestured towards a designated combat practice ring in the courtyard.

I turned and headed in that direction, knowing Madeleine would follow suit.

A light rain started to drizzle as the elf manager of the ring greeted us.

Martial arts and other combative training were a part of our vengeance education, not because we used it very often—with vengeance magic backing us up and all—but because the administration believed it was a great way to develop discipline.

But for students, the practice ring was a way for them to settle personal scores while staying under the school's radar. We were prohibited from using our powers on each other within campus, but whatever happened in the practice ring was fair game.

Madeleine and I were even civilized enough to put our names on the sign-up sheet, blocking off a slot of exactly one hour.

The random game selector, a wheel that depicted over ten types of combative sports, started to spin.

Please let it be staff fighting. I'm good at staff fighting. There are plenty of soft organs to hurt with the dull end of a stick.

The tiny black arrow spun around the colorful pie-shaped wheel, stopping on a bright yellow wedge labeled *wrestling*.

"Are you serious?" I shook my head.

"What's wrong with wrestling?" Madeleine smirked as the elf blew faery dust on her shoulder, changing her outfit into tank top and shorts in an instant. Then he proceeded to do the same for me. "You scared?"

Nothing wrong, just two college girls with wet tops rubbing skin to skin, grabbing at each other, that was all. I decided not to point out how porn-like the scenario would be for an average human male. For one, males in the vengeance world got more turned on by ball-busters—both on and off the job—than a pair of sweaty girls. Second, I didn't need to share the fact that I was a human pop culture buff. I already had enough strikes against me.

And wrestling might actually work out better than I thought.

Madeleine took off her shoes. Doing so seemed to have reminded her of what I'd done to them, and that only got her madder. I passed my mother's photo and the bits of paper that held the image of her face to the elf manager. "Keep it safe, will ya?"

The next hour was broken into three twenty-minute rounds of the girls each taking their turns pushing me around. There was only one of them in the ring with me at any given time, so it was technically fair, and that was the kind of fairness the administration could live with. Whenever the elf manager turned his back, the girls cheated, using vengeance magic to make their pounces faster, their shoves harder.

More and more students gathered around the ring, pointing, jeering, and making wagers. There were those who mistrusted me, those who feared me for what I was, and those who were downright jealous, though I doubt any of them in their heart of hearts believed I'd cheated. And then there were a few who didn't seem quite comfortable being there, who regarded me with a measure of sympathy. I wasn't moved. Pity was cheap when one refused to act on it.

Tears were cheap too, I told myself as one threatened to make its way out of my eye. I ought to have gotten used to the hostile treatment by now. After all, it had started in kindergarten.

Nobody said anything when vengeance power was illegally used.

I used none. I couldn't afford it. I was running pretty low, since I'd been throwing every bit of vengeance power I had towards the practice sessions.

Nor would I use my trickery power, regardless of how much I had on reserve. I'd worked too hard to be here. There were over two dozen witnesses around me.

In general, it was the source of a magic that provided its distinctive flavor. Vengeance magic stemmed from cold logic and a sense of duty, while trickery came from a love of fun and mischief. One had the bitter aftertaste of Earl Grey tea; the other, margarita and pineapple.

This lot around me could definitely tell the difference.

Halfway through the hour, I heard a gasp and turned toward the sound, leaving myself open for a scratch across the lower half of my face. The coppery taste of blood filled my mouth as I brought the horrified face of Serafina into focus. She was standing right at the edge of the ring. I had no idea when she'd gotten there.

"Everyone, please stop." She struggled to be heard over the racket.

"Get outta here!" I shouted at her. The crowd was wild, and the nasty mood could easily shift from me to the former changeling kidnappee, which would defeat the entire point of trying to stop the bullying in the first place. "Go!"

"But—"

"I'm just enjoying a good workout, that's all. Ouch!" My opponent wrapped a lock of my hair around her fingers and pulled hard. I returned the favor by elbowing her right in the breast. "Now GO!"

Serafina stared at me with an unreadable expression and left the courtyard without another word.

I was sore from head to toe from the "workout". The girls weren't as much into beating as they were into cat scratching, pushing, and tripping. So tons of bumps and bruises, not to mention some broken skin, but not exactly life-threatening injuries. The visual effect of blood and floor kissing was a crowd-pleaser though, so after a while, I just tuned them out.

My sweating slowed to a trickle, as if my body had figured out there was no point, and I was grateful as I was starting to stink. My defensive blocks felt like they were done underwater, and my eyes grew heavy with fatigue.

When the one-hour timer sounded off, I slumped to the floor on my stomach, not bothering to make sure my opponent would honor the cease-fire and resist giving an extra kick to my head.

And that was how Madeleine and her cronies left me, defeated on the floor of the ring, content that they'd taught me a lesson. The crowd dispersed as many finally remembered they had to pack for the short break before summer courses began. The courtyard was soon deserted.

I took my time getting up.

And found Serafina standing next to the elf manager. She took a handful of faery dust from him and blew it on me once to get rid of all the sweat and bruises on my body, and twice to change me back to my original clothes. All my pain was gone in an instant.

"Thanks." I mumbled.

"No, thank *you*."

His shift ended, the elf manager turned and left, but not before throwing one last pitiful glance my way. Serafina, on the contrary, was grinning ear to ear, her eyes dancing with mirth.

"You figured it out?" I asked her.

"About halfway to the dean's office. I kept thinking about the way you said you were *enjoying* it." She glanced down at the pearl pendant hanging around my neck. At the top of the hour, the pearl had been semi-transparent; now it was glowing with a healthy luster. "I never would've thought to get charged up this way."

That was the real reason I'd brought the fight to the ring. I was doing more than rubbing skin with those girls.

My pearl, a depository and amplifier of power, was robbing my attackers of their vengeance magic every time they thought they were hurting me. During the last hour, my body might've been exhausted, but my pearl was quietly storing up power, waiting for me to tap into it once the crowd was gone.

"I did give something back as a parting gift, you know." I grinned. In another month, the girls would suddenly sprout hairy pig's tails, and they wouldn't even notice them at first. The tails would poke out of their pantsuits, bouncing as they tried to incite terror in their co-op targets, or better yet, while they were flirting with hot guys.

I even took the time to give the one that was pre-set to go on Madeleine an extra curl. All with the girls' own magic.

Serafina took my family photo and the curled-up paper bits from the elf manager and handed them to me, "There's one more thing you can do with that magic."

"You read my mind." I touched the paper bits gently against my pearl pendant. The ruined parts unfolded themselves and leaped back into the photo where they belonged, restoring it. I put the picture in my bag and grinned at Serafina.

"Hey, you want to go for a fire and brimstone bubble tea?"

The only thing worse than standing in the dorm parking lot with three gigantic pink suitcases and snobbish girls smirking from the upstairs windows was to do so with the designated getaway car MIA.

After what felt like hours, a familiar purple sedan came into view.

"Esme, over here!" I waved at my half-sister, who swung the car into the space next to me, precisely fifteen inches from the white line on both sides. Somehow, though the car window was open and it was a windy day, not a wine-red hair was out of place.

With one manicured finger, Esme pressed the button to pop the trunk. As a senior and a TA, she dressed head to toe in black, similar to Madeleine. The difference was, the pantsuit gave the impression that Madeleine was trying too hard, while Esme pulled it off with sleek curves and subtle confidence. Esme's pale, freckled skin and green eyes made a stark contrast with the leather that covered the rest of her size-zero body, and her chiseled cheekbones were sharp enough for her to get a part-time job cutting magic mirrors for goblins.

I sighed. My own mud-colored hair, brown eyes, and olive complexion were quite different from Esme's classic redhead look. It didn't take a genius to tell we weren't full sisters. And unlike her, I inherited my trickster mother's body type—more on the plump and jolly than super skinny. Except I didn't want to be jolly. I wanted to be light-footed and graceful and terrifying.

Esme got out of the car and walked towards the open trunk. She started helping me put the suitcases in.

"What took you so long?" I complained.

"Sorry, Megan. I was delayed by a target. He tried to bribe his way out of vengeance by kissing me."

I whistled. "Kissing on the job. Somebody is finally having a life."

"He's a slime demon." Esme stroked one of her pearl stud earrings and shuddered. "I had to go home for a complete scrub-down."

"Ouch." For someone that gorgeous, the girl sure had bad luck when it came to men. I glanced at the clock on my smart phone and swore. "Oh no, we gotta hurry. I'm fifteen minutes away from losing my freedom."

"What do you mean?"

"If I don't show up with the cash by three, the landlord will give the room to someone else." When I left after having bubble tea with Serafina two days ago, I headed straight to my dorm and dug up the outdated *Renters Weekly*. I'd never quite stopped thinking about that culinary student's ad since I'd first read it. To my delight, the room was still available for immediate occupancy. Yes, the landlord was slightly eccentric, but that was more than made up for by a live-in chef, not to mention escape from the dorm on such short notice. If he wanted cash by three, he'd have it.

Besides, it wasn't like I was allowed to make the man more accommodating with my magic.

"What's the money for?" She frowned.

"It's what the humans call the first and last. They're big on insurance because they can't employ Hire A Hellhound to chase down their debtors." I'd exchanged most of the magical credits from my Becoming, the demonic version of the Bat Mitzvah, into human currency for the down payment. Thank Hades the co-op was a paying gig, or else no way would I be able to afford the rest of the rent for the four-month work term.

"Do all humans like to deal in cash?"

"I'm not sure. The landlord mumbled something about never trusting the banks and how it's better to hide it under the bed." I lugged the last bag into the trunk and closed it. "Alright, we're all set."

Esme turned her head towards the freshmen dorm in longing. Two years my senior, she'd enjoyed her time there and fit in like I'd never been able to. "Are you sure about this? Living off campus, amongst humans? I can't recall if it's ever been done."

I chewed my lower lip, unable to put my need to move out into words. Esmeralda Kassandra Aequitas, a full-blooded, got-a-proper-middle-name vengeance demon, from her shiny red-scaled wings down to her effortlessly executed glamour to camouflage them, would never understand. Esme's path was set and her future certain.

She wasn't a socially unacceptable half-breed demon-wannabe, like me.

"Yes," I said with as much firmness as I could without being rude. It would be nice to have a place where my mother could visit without dirty looks and jeers. I'd missed her easy and infectious laughter in the past year.

I used to laugh like that, embracing Mom's heritage, finding sheer delights in all things trickery, from sending the mailman running with illusion of salivating bulldogs, to enchanting the ATM machine to display zero account balances for my neighbors. Complete random victimology was a trickster's trademark. No targeted justice. No reasoning of merits. No guilt. Just the pure joy of pranking. Part of me missed that simplicity in my life, even though it was the exact thing about tricksters that had driven vengeance demons crazy since the beginning of time.

Esme considered me for a moment. Something on my face must've convinced her. She nodded. "Let's go then."

As the car zoomed off, the early summer breeze drifted through the rolled-down windows and kissed my cheek with the sweet scent of new beginnings. I leaned out and grinned like an idiot. After all this time, I was finally free. Well, for a while anyway.

Living with humans was going to be a gamble, but it beat sure misery. There was even a chance that being amongst mortals might help my control issues. Since they had no magic to speak of, they wouldn't be tempted to overuse what they never had.

The way I was tempted, every moment of my existence.

"Woo hoo!" I couldn't help but chortle as we passed a group of witch majors. The broomsticks they were on jumped back on autopilot. I snickered.

Esme gave me a puzzled look. Guess she never quite got the concept of unadulterated joy, since it wasn't exactly a vengeance demon trait. Clearing my throat, I made as if I was calling a bird.

She hesitated, then said, "Congratulations on getting Enid's co-op approval."

I straightened on my seat. I could feel the impression of her thoughts in my mind. And they reeked of reservation and doubt. "You're wondering if I won it fair and square, aren't you?"

"I didn't say that." Her fingers tightened around the steering wheel.

"But you *thought* it." I crossed my arms. "I. Didn't. Use. Trickery."

Esme's shoulders relaxed. "You didn't?"

"Gee, thanks for the vote of confidence." I shifted my weight and drummed my fingers on the side window panel. Now I was getting a bit annoyed. My former lightheartedness vanished like dew drops in the first morning rays. True to my trickster nature, my mood could change like quicksand sometimes.

Face reddened, Esme said nothing.

Seconds that felt like minutes went by.

"Tell me when you see the portal entrance, alright?" Esme asked quietly, cutting through our awkward silence with a subdued gentleness that vengeance demons generally looked down upon. I slowly released the breath I didn't even realize I was holding. My half-sister might not have believed in me a hundred percent, but here she was, giving me a ride for the move, ignoring the nasty things her friends had no doubt said about me. It meant something. And I should stick with that.

"Maybe a bit farther down. I think it's shifted again."

"Okay."

The University of Demonic Studies was located in a dimension parallel to the University of Toronto on the human side. Cross-dimensional transport could be done either through an existing free-of-charge portal or a temporary one opened for a fee of magical power. Since the control of—and by extension, the frugality towards—one's power was prized in a vengeance demon's upbringing, the first option was the way to go for non-emergency travel. I already figured out a passage to use for my future travelling back and forth between dimensions, but it was for walking only and too narrow for a car to fit through.

Once we got out of the campus area, the not-so-pretty part of downtown greeted us with overflowing garbage bins on the sidewalk and thick layers of dust covering the windows of the rundown shops lining the street.

"There, that's it." I pointed at a payday loan store with a banner that said *Why wait? Get your magic today!*

"Are you sure that's the entrance?" She squinted. "It looks innocent enough."

"Trust me."

"But how do you *know*?" Esme insisted. Great, gotta hand it to Miss Top-of-Her-Class to not settle for anything but a proper answer.

"Today's Friday," I pointed out, baring my teeth.

"So?"

"Do you see a line-up of drunken unseelie faes and gambling tricksters cashing their employment insurance cheques?" I shuddered, not exactly proud of the frivolous spending habits that were the signature of my trickster blood.

"Good point," Esme conceded, turning her car around. She drove it right into the front of the store and came out in a quiet alley on the human side.

I directed Esme to Parkdale, a once-prominent west end neighborhood that suffered "death-by-highway" in the fifties. Now, run-down Victorian houses accommodated young students, druggies, and low-income immigrants alike, with trendy cafes gentrifying the outskirts of the neighborhood wherever more upscale parts of the city were attached.

My new home wasn't on the outskirts of Parkdale.

As Esme turned the purple sedan into the residential street with large maple trees, I was glad at least it was too early in the day for the hookers to come out. She would've told Dad, and hell hath no fury like an overprotective demon father. Never mind that I was perfectly capable of taking care of my supernatural self. In his eyes, I'd always be his little girl. He would find out about my new neighborhood soon enough, but hopefully not today. Call me selfish, but I wanted today to be perfect.

We parked on the street in front of a red-brick duplex,

but before I could even open the door, a petite blonde in a white apron ran out of the house and towards me, holding a rolling pin with a smudge of dough still attached to it. She looked just like the chefs I'd read about on the Internet, my sole information source for everything human-related.

"Whew, thank the lucky stars you're here," Rosemary breathed. "Mr. Lochte is showing the room to someone else right now. A *guy*. I don't want to live with a guy."

I jerked the car door open and marched towards the duplex, Rosemary falling into step beside me. "That neurotic, untrusting, grumpy old man. It's only two fifty-seven. We got here in record time."

Mr. Lochte emerged from the front door with a bespectacled guy about my age. *Hands off, Mr. Just-In-Case, the place is mine!* I marched up to Mr. Lochte as I reached for the cash envelope in my pants pocket. Totally ignoring my competition, I handed the landlord the cash. "Here, a thousand dollars, and not a penny less."

I almost felt sorry for my rival when Mr. Lochte counted the money, pocketed it, then turned to the younger man and said, "The place will be available again in four months. Can you wait?"

After getting rid of the bespectacled guy and Mr. Lochte, I went upstairs to unpack. Esme tried to help but was soon frustrated by my organizational style, which was a polite way to say that I was a slob who hated hangers and binders. Neither of us could hide our relief when she got the call to handle an ad hoc vengeance request.

In a few hours, the delicious aroma of burnt fat and meat drifted through the closed bedroom door. Rosemary must've fired up the barbecue for that early dinner she'd promised.

Then I heard her scream.

I raced downstairs, taking two or three stairs in every stride. Rosemary was by the patio door, holding a stainless steel spatula and pointing at a large man with broad shoulders, crouching over a corner in the kitchen. Fear was apparent in her voice. Being a defenseless human living in a dodgy neighborhood, fear probably came with the territory. "This guy just barged in and starting doing...whatever it is he's doing over there!"

The imposing figure straightened and turned towards us. He was a tall man, and he loomed over the tiny room with his size as much as his menacing presence. In his hand was a trowel; its sharp edge gleamed when it reflected the late afternoon sunlight. Rosemary made an involuntary squeal.

I breathed a small sigh and laid a reassuring hand on my roommate's trembling arm. "Don't worry, I've got this."

I put as much authority in my voice as possible. Though to my human roommate's eyes I was as defenseless as she was, my confidence made her relax. She allowed me to push her across the threshold to the walkout patio, but she held onto her spatula.

I closed the door and turned towards the man. "Hey, Dad."

Dad's face split into a brilliant smile, and he pulled me into a hug with a wealth of affection, shoving the trowel into his back pants pocket. "There's my little pumpkin."

"How did you know where to find me?" I'd already figured out the answer.

"Your sister texted me the directions. You're serious

about living all alone, outside the protection of the vengeance plane? I still can't believe it."

I didn't bother to point out that such *protection* came with a high cost. Like Esme, Dad wouldn't understand. Heck, he'd been the valedictorian when he'd graduated from Demon U.

Dad gave the house interior a suspicious once-over. "Is this place defendable? I heard a gang of organ-smuggling ghouls has escaped from prison."

I rolled my eyes. "That just happened yesterday, three planes over. They can't travel that fast, even if they're heading this way."

"What about gremlins? Humans have too much of this technology thing."

I snorted, "Said the guy who's just got the latest iPhone."

"What about banshees? Brownies with a grudge? Weak spots for cross-dimensional stalking? Did you check for all that before signing the lease? You know how we demons feel about contracts."

It was almost comical, seeing my dad, the arch vengeance demon, fussing over imaginary threats against his little girl. My eyes suddenly zoomed to the corner of the kitchen my dad was bending over earlier. There were patches of white all over the base molding. "Dad, what have you done?"

"What?" Dad tried to appear nonchalant, but I wasn't fooled.

"What's in the inner pocket of your coat?" I eyed the bulge by his left ribs and raised a brow. "And what was the trowel for?"

Almost sheepishly, Dad pulled out a small plastic tub, the type humans put cream cheese in. "It's an all-purpose sealer that blocks out every magical creature imaginable. I enchanted it to make an exception for Sassy, of course."

I couldn't help but feel touched. Here was my dad, a legendary bringer of justice notorious for his mighty vengeance against war criminals and mass murderers alike, slathering sealant over tiny cracks in his daughter's new digs. If an average demon caught wind of this ridiculous DIY project, Dad would lose street cred fast.

It was sweet, if slightly overprotective.

Dad finished with the rest of the cracks at top speed, then left for a strategy meeting with the other arch demons. To appear inconspicuous, they were always meeting on the human plane, and this week it was at Chuck E. Cheese's.

Before he left, Dad gave me a large Hellhound-grade pepper spray. I knew better than to argue. I wanted him gone before the hookers started hitting my street corner—he'd freak out.

I braced for Rosemary's reaction to all this, but when I explained that the "intruder" was my dad, she took it really well. She said something about having an Asian roommate before who had a tiger mom. I had no idea there were shape shifters amongst humans.

After making sure that Rosemary was okay with it, I invited Serafina over to the human plane for my very first dinner since independence. Well, as independent as someone who relied on others' cooking skills could be. Ever since that fire and brimstone bubble tea, I'd developed a friendship with Serafina. I liked her, not just because we had the common ground of both being outcasts, but also because her nature was much sweeter than the average vengeance demon.

We shared a relaxing meal of barbecued pork chops,

roasted corn, and peach cobbler. After dinner we cleaned up together, and by that I mean Serafina and I pretended to know what we were doing as Rosemary showed us the wonder of dishwasher loading.

With a pork chop doggy bag in one hand, Serafina gave me an awkward hug at the front door. "Thanks for having me. It was fun."

"No problem. We should do it more often. And you should seal this before you get back home." I pointed at the doggy bag.

"Huh?"

"You'll hurt the house brownies' feelings if they smell the food," Serafina didn't live on campus. After a lifetime of being away, her family insisted she stay with them through the school year, and it was common knowledge that brownies from those old estate houses were as skillful in the kitchen as they were prideful.

"Oh, right."

After Serafina left and Rosemary insisted on staying in the kitchen to prepare the batter for tomorrow's breakfast, I went upstairs. I closed my bedroom door and shut the heavy-duty curtains, blocking out the flooding streetlights and the muffled sound of a couple bickering in the next house.

For the first time in my life, I was in a world reserved only for me, and it felt good.

And lonely.

And exciting.

And scary.

And then not quite so alone. Sassy, my pet feline shade, passed right through my blanket and settled in for cuddling, digging her claws into my ribs. She must've finished the first patrol of her new domain, pity the poor unsuspecting mice and B&E guys. Laughing, I kissed her furry transparent head goodnight.

THREE

*T*ZEEEEEEE...TZEEEEEEEE...

"What the hell?" I flopped over on the mattress and pressed the pillow to my ears. No use. I could still hear the ringing of the morning breakfast bell by Ms. Morris, the hag who served as our dorm mistress. The old witch took delight in tormenting me at every crack of dawn.

Tzeeeeeee...tzeeeeeeee...

Hold on, that didn't sound like Ms. Morris's bell. The sound through the wall was a lot more metallic.

More human.

This must be the morning drilling routine of Mr. Lochte that Rosemary had warned me about when I first came to check out the place. At the time, desperate to escape the dorm, I was hoping she was exaggerating. Guess not. Great. Bye-bye, demented dorm mistress. Hello, crazy mortal landlord.

There was an unforeseen downside to having a landlord who lived right next door.

Bang, bang! Bang, bang, bang!

Here came the hammer.

My fingers twitched and I itched to snap them. Just one snap...a little push of magic that would cause an accidental slip of Mr. Lochte's hammer. A tiny ding on the thumb never hurt anyone much. My dear landlord would be done for the day, and I could get some much-needed beauty sleep.

"That's violating the guidelines, as you're well aware," a voice said from the foot of my bed.

I bolted upright. The voice belonged to Enid. Stupid, quiet-as-a-mouse teleporting. I could never manage it with such stealth. Enid stood with utmost dignity amongst my semi-unpacked suitcases and yesterday's wrinkled clothes-slash-impromptu floor mat.

"How did you know that's what I was thinking? I thought you were only a partial mind-reader," I asked curiously.

"I am. But your desire for violence, small as it was, sent out a dissonance in the Concord that I could detect right away. Remember, we carry out violence, but we don't use it for our own convenience or pleasure. Control is of the essence."

"I'll keep working on it." Enid had risked the wrath of most of the school, and probably some of the staff, in giving my effort a fair chance in the co-op application process. The last thing I wanted to do was to fight with her over the small stuff.

She tilted her head. "Do you want to talk about that wrestling match I've heard so much about in the teacher's lounge?"

"Nope."

"Alright."

The silence stretched until I blurted, "The teacher's lounge?"

"They were taking bets." Enid shrugged off-handedly, as if we were discussing the weather. "Most of us lost."

That would mean most of the teaching staff was putting the money on me to win the match. Which was flattering in a way, though a bit disturbing, since wagering was illegal within campus for both students and facility.

"Wait a minute, *us*?" Us, as in Enid was a part of it?

Instead of answering, Enid placed an envelope on my lap. "Your first official co-op assignment."

She'd just avoided answering me, but I was pleasantly distracted and didn't care. It wasn't like she'd say anything further on the matter anyway. I combed my fingers through my disheveled hair and opened the envelope with great eagerness. What was it going to be?

Unlike the vengeance demons in that *Buffy* show I watched online, who took on clients and fulfilled their wishes of retribution, in my world we were the guardians of the Cosmic Balance—commonly known as the Concord—the balance between right and wrong, good and evil. Until I became well-tuned to the mood of the Concord, Enid collected injustices off it like spun sugar from a cotton candy machine and put them in nice little office envelopes for me to fix up.

I spilled the contents of the envelope onto my bed. There was a photo of a distinguished, elderly gentleman, a brochure for an assisted-living home, the layout of a building, and a standard vengeance order form. According to the form, the name of my first co-op target was Dan Pillar. He was human, which wasn't surprising since I didn't have the clearance level—not to mention the strength—to tackle the supernatural wrongdoers yet. Dan Pillar had fifty-eight women listed as his victims in a two-decade-long career of broken hearts and stolen life-savings.

An image of Benjamin Theodore Judicium, a transfer

student in my high school senior class, appeared in my head. He was handsome and smart, and I'd thought he genuinely cared about me. Turned out I was just an entrance fee for him to join the "in" group. To make a long story short, we had sex, he stole my panties to show his new friends, and I got back at him by posting pictures of his Hello Kitty collection on the student online forum. But I'd never forgotten the anger and hurt of being played.

I didn't let Benjamin get away then, and I wasn't going to let Dan Pillar get away now.

My eyes continued down the vengeance order form, and I frowned, noting that the scamming had stopped on August second, nineteen ninety-six. The halt was sudden, abrupt, and permanent. That was strange. In general, a criminal's rap sheet didn't just end. The nature of the crimes might change, but no one simply stopped unless the person was in jail or dead. Dan Pillar was neither.

Enid nodded. "I see that you noticed the date."

I chewed on the inside of my jaw. "Why did he stop?"

Enid shrugged. "Not sure. Sometimes they claim to have found God. Sometimes the last job scared them so much they went straight. Whatever the reason, it doesn't excuse what he did to those women. We caught up with this guy a bit late in the game, but since no amends were ever made, the procedure is the same."

"Got it." If amends had been made, the quality of the remorse and rectification would have to be examined by an independent tribunal, and the level of vengeance would be downgraded by the determined value. In my target's case, the lack of amends made it much more straightforward.

Ready or not, here comes vengeance.

I crossed the lawn of my latest target's residence with a spring in my step. I had my first paying gig, a room of my own, and freshly baked blueberry muffins for breakfast. Plus, my pearl pendant was still pretty charged up, thanks to Madeleine. Life was good. What was there to complain about? Yes, the landlord's drilling was annoying, but there had to be a way around that.

I chose to be an optimistic demon. Half-demon. Whatever.

The garden of the assisted-living home, beautifully landscaped, had a gazebo and a fountain. The three-story building was a stucco structure with French balconies and graceful columns. And was that a uniformed doorman? The place resembled a high-end spa more than anything else.

It seemed Dan Pillar had invested the money he bilked well. I narrowed my eyes as I thought about what that financial security could've meant for those women he'd taken money from. Asshole. Now, what would be a just dessert for him? There was his age to consider, so I couldn't go too wild. I swear, my co-op's no-kill policy was such a killjoy.

I entered the lobby with a cool nod to the doorman, acting like I had every reason to be there. I'd taken care to dress in smart business-casual and to brush myself with faery dust designed to temporarily age me around five years. I'd found the dust on sale, which made sense because who would pay full price to make themselves appear older anyway?

With the help of the faery dust, my youthful skin dulled a shade or two and the corners of my eyes creased with the earliest signs of wrinkles. Let the staff think I was a young lawyer here to discuss a will with one of the building's well-to-do occupants. Better that than to be cast in the role of a salivating, greedy relative, looking for a handout.

The marbled lobby gleamed under a soaring vaulted ceiling. To the left was a stone fireplace, to the right a concierge desk with a couple of staff. As I approached the desk, both receptionists smiled at me.

"Hello, I'm here to see Mr. Dan Pillar." I nodded at the receptionist with the nametag "Kristi." I laced a compulsion into my words to make her more obliging and less likely to ask inquisitive questions.

Kristi beamed. "Mr. Pillar is at the spa for his massage appointment. Would you like to wait at the bistro?"

"Sure." I fought to keep my voice neutral. Spa, huh? He'd need a lot more than a relaxing massage by the time I was through with him.

"It's upstairs, miss, just past the entertainment lounge. Feel free to help yourself to the refreshments. I'll notify you when Mr. Pillar becomes available."

The elegant bistro, with lace linen tablecloths, gleaming silverware, and expensive china tea sets, treated patrons to the magnificent view of Lake Ontario. Soft piano music played in the background. A pair of chefs in starched white aprons were on standby in the open kitchen, a wild array of fresh ingredients from asparagus to salmon on display behind them, ready to create culinary delights on demand.

I ground my teeth. Daily fine dining for the bastard in his twilight years, and what about the poor women he'd stolen from in *their* dying days? How many of them had been forced to live on day-old bread and bruised vegetables from the discount grocery aisle?

There was a station at the front of the bistro full of cut-up fruits, coffee, and fancy pies. These must be the refreshments Kristi had been talking about. Well, I was never one to let free food pass me by, even though my stomach, still full from Rosemary's truly awesome muffins, was a bit queasy over the upcoming encounter. Not that I hadn't done vengeance before, but this was the first time I was earning marks that actually counted towards the co-op.

Maybe the refreshing taste of key lime pie was just what I needed. I cut a small piece, lifted it, almost dropped it back to the tray, and rescued it just in time. Stupid, unsteady fingers. Finally, I settled down on a dining chair and placed the pie in front of me.

Just as I put a forkful of citrus delight into my mouth, a shadow loomed over me. "You're here to see my grandpa?"

I munched on the treat, looked up, and narrowed my eyes on a guy standing over my table in a white T-shirt and jeans. So this was my target's grandson, huh? Funny, somehow I never figured the con artist to be the family type.

"Yes, I'm here to see Mr. Pillar." I tried my best professional smile, the my-business-is-my-own kind of detached politeness.

"What do you want to see him for?" Suspicion was evidenced from the downward turning corner of his mouth.

"I have an appointment." *Be vague and bluff your way through.*

"No, you don't. I already checked his Google calendar."

Damn.

"So why are you *really* here?" the guy persisted.

"None of your business." Alright, that sounded fresh out

of tricks, even to my ears.

The guy's jaw hardened. "Anybody coming to see my grandpa is my business. We've got a lot of scammers hanging around here, hoping to make a quick buck off the seniors. So if you can't give me a good reason why you should be here, then I'm going to have to ask you to leave."

I wondered if this guy, so protective of his precious grandpa, was aware of the irony of calling *me* a con artist. I crossed my arms over my chest, and he mirrored my stubborn stance.

The guy breathed out exasperatedly and ran his fingers through his hair, "Listen, you shouldn't even be here. I left specific instructions at the reception to block unwanted visitors."

I realized that if it hadn't been for that compulsion I used on the receptionist, I would most likely have been barred from entry. But now that I was in, there was no getting rid of me. Vengeance demons were like termites in that way.

The guy was still standing over me. I disliked the height difference, and the psychological disadvantage it placed me at. I also didn't like how he looked me up and down like I was a bug. A money-grubbing bug.

"Sit down." I gave the command almost before I realized what I was doing.

The guy sat with a smack as his bum hit the chair. Oops, I might've been a bit too heavy-handed with the compulsion.

"What's your name?" I asked him. While under my spell, he would tell me the truth. All truth.

"Will Pillar," he obliged in a flat voice.

"Is your grandpa free now?"

"Yes. We're done for the day."

I frowned. "I thought he was having a massage."

"He was. With me."

"Why you?"

"I'm studying to be a massage therapist. This way he gets a free session, and I get to practice."

I noted for the first time that Will Pillar had a white towel over his shoulder.

He continued talking. Sometimes I gave off tiny, unconscious magical outbursts, and the subjects offered information beyond my questioning. I guess I just had a knack for making people loose with their tongues. "Mr. Harrison claims I pinched a nerve that one time, but Grandpa doesn't mind. He keeps letting me practice on him."

If the elder Pillar could afford to live here, he could afford to pay for the most experienced massage therapist money could buy. So finances was definitely not the motivating factor behind his participation in these free sessions. I had a sudden mental image of an indulging grandfather risking bodily injury to let his rookie of a grandchild work on him. It seemed so contradictory to the heartless bastard I'd pictured in my mind. Could people change over the course of a few decades?

I wished my paternal grandma was that good to me. The Aequitas matriarch hadn't even come to my Becoming, nor did she send along the traditional gift of a pair of pearl stud earrings. The two tiny lustrous spheres, custom-sculpted by the Baltic mermaid-witches, were a means to enhance and control one's power. My grandma had sent me a store-bought pendant on a chain instead, the humiliating single pearl dangling on my neck for everyone at the party to see.

A slap in the face, mocking my hybrid status.

Half the vengeance power times half the amplifier. Any wonder why my magic sucked? This Dan Pillar might be a shady character, but at least he seemed to be treating his grandson alright.

On a hunch, I leaned over and locked eyes with Pillar Junior. "What is your date of birth, Will?"

"Nineteen ninety-six, August the second."

Now I understood why Dan Pillar had stopped.

I felt a pang of sympathy for him. Somehow, the harm my target had caused got lodged in the Concord and took decades to come back to haunt him. But come back, it did, even long after the wrongdoer started to love.

I was certain now that was exactly what had happened. Somehow, the birth of his own child's flesh and blood had woken the older man's conscience.

Never mind. All the love and conscience in the world couldn't take away the mass suffering of Dan Pillar's victims, and I still had a job to do.

Gently putting my unfinished key lime pie on a neighboring table, I got up, leaving Will Pillar shaking the cobwebs out of his brain. He wouldn't remember our meeting.

As I went downstairs and walked across the marble lobby floor, the clicking sound of my heels bounced around the hallway. I kept clear in my mind an old medieval expression I'd learned in my high school history class.

Justice arrives on a wooden leg.

As in, it would come slowly, but surely. In the absence of a wooden leg, my pair of leather kitten heels would do.

Kristi the receptionist gave up Dan's room number without a fight. In less than five minutes, I was taking the elevator to the top floor and knocking on my target's door. "Mr. Pillar?"

"Come in."

I opened the door and my jaw dropped. This wasn't a "room." This was a penthouse suite done up with a ten-foot ceiling, a mahogany library on the left, and a contemporary kitchen on the right that was larger than my entire living space at the duplex.

Dan Pillar was sipping brandy in an armchair in the library, a leather-bound volume on his lap, appearing every inch like his photo. Even as an old man, the senior Pillar was one handsome fellow. His angular face and brilliant eyes bespoke decades of fine living, his hair a steely shade of grey. The large ruby ring on his slender right hand seemed right at home.

I closed the door quietly and, before I turned, I activated the magical noise muffler for some much-needed privacy.

Dan lifted his head, saw me and smiled. "Hi, there. Are you here to deliver the cupcakes for this afternoon? Well, don't close the door. Just bring the whole cart in. The gold leaf red velvet was quite the hit last time."

Huh, I wasn't even wearing a caterer's uniform. Guess when you were used to a certain social position, you assumed everyone worked for you in one manner or another.

I cleared my throat. "Are you Dan A. Pillar, of Hamilton, Ontario, born to Sophia and Robert Pillar?"

The smile fell from his face and he clutched his hands

together. He glanced at the door and finally seemed to realize why I'd closed it. His jaw set, he nodded.

"Mr. Pillar, it's time to pay for your past sins. By the power vested in me by the Concord Council, you're hereby sentenced to Vengeance. May you endure it with grace and contemplation."

My plan came in two stages. First, I'd force him to experience what his victims felt. All the heartbreak, shame, and despair in one fell swoop. Then I'd redistribute his wealth to those he'd hurt.

That sounded pretty fair to me.

Next thing to do was to give him his Belinda, the vengeance demon version of the Miranda rights. "You have the right to remain silent. Anything you say or do may offend the assigned vengeance demon and lead to a more severe punishment. You have the right to—"

"Thanks, but I have no intention of keeping silent, nor being punished, for that matter," Dan said softly. His demeanor changed from easygoing to chilling in less than a second, and every ounce of warmth left the apartment. With his hands held together, he began to rub his blood-red ruby ring against his thumb, muttering something under his breath.

The hair at the back of my neck stood up in attention.

"I knew your kind would come one day, so I'm prepared at all times," he continued.

Wait a minute. It wasn't just my imagination; the temperature in the large penthouse had indeed dropped by a few degrees. A vortex of light and energy formed in the space between us, and there was no mistaking the shockwave of power filling the room.

Oh shit, Dan was calling magic. The dark and brutal

variety.

He was not *of* magic, that much I was certain. But there were magical objects in the world that could be dangerous in the wrong hands, mortal or otherwise.

I would've tried to stop him, to reach for my pearl pendant necklace—weak magic against such an unnatural force and all—but from the moment he'd started the muttering, I'd been unable to move. In a my-body-is-in-a-block-of-invisible-cement kind of way.

I tugged at my arms, then tugged some more, all to no avail. It was like those sleep paralysis episodes I'd had when I was a child. My eyes darted from side to side, seeking a way out, and all I saw around me was expensive carpets and oil paintings. Beautiful, but useless. I had to get out of here. This was not the way things should be going down.

At least when I'd experienced the paralysis as a kid, deep down I'd known I was still safe in my bed. The present-day me didn't have that comfort. I was alone, helpless, with no access to my own power and completely at the bad guy's mercy.

I didn't want to die.

I tried to kick out, my legs more than willing to give it a shot, but I was unable to move even an inch. I wanted to do something. Anything but stay still. The nervous energy building up inside me ricocheted across my cold and tightened muscles, assaulting my senses with its feral need to be released.

I pressed down my rising panic. If I couldn't move, maybe I could talk my way out of this one. It always worked in those human movies.

"Where did you get that ring?" I croaked. Was that really my voice? Coarse and weak, it held none of the authority I was desperately trying to project. My galloping heart threatened to jump out of my chest, and the bitter taste of bile was on my lips.

Dan's lips curved. "As I said, I've got...friends."

"I bet it cost you more than a few gold leaf red velvet cupcakes." I spit out.

"It was worth every penny to stop a vengeance demon in her tracks."

How did he know to do that? The average human went through life without ever hearing of my kind's existence. Except Joss Whedon, and people just thought he was super-brilliant at making shit up.

Dan rubbed harder at his ring, and some sort of bubble materialized. It expanded to the size of a small elevator, then came toward me and enveloped my body. Inside the bubble was a mini universe of intense high temperature. My body, which had been freezing until that point, heated up.

My skin was scorched and my hair began to singe; the aging faery dust on my cheek melted away as if it was never there. Next was my vengeance magic. The ring neutralized it with frightening efficiency.

The bastard intended to burn me alive. And to think I'd been feeling sorry for him. If, no, *when* I survive this, all bets were off.

"You won't get away with this." He wouldn't. If he realized that, maybe he'd hesitate. "My handler knows where I am."

"Let me worry about that." Dan waved his hand. "*Think*, my dear, if I have friends who could help me destroy you, then I have friends who could help me survive. Bye-bye, my little vengeance demon. As they say, it's not personal."

But it was.

The soles of my kitten boots began to melt. The acrid smell of rubber invaded my nose. Instinctively I closed up my airway, which only served to make me dizzy from the lack of oxygen. With dark spots swimming in front of my eyes, it finally sank in. I was going to die. In a few minutes I would be burned to a crisp.

I wasn't ready to die. Not by a long shot. My life had barely started, and there was so much I wanted to see and experience. Mom and Dad would be devastated if something happened to me. Heck, *I* would be devastated.

Mom.

Wait! There was one thing that might help.

The very reason why I only had half the vengeance power was because I also had half the trickery power, and I had plenty of *that* on reserve, dormant and not affected by Dan's spell.

For a trickster, the simplest trick, first learned and last forgotten, was how to play dead.

I closed my eyes, the gleeful face of Dan Pillar the last thing I saw. I pulled the long-neglected trickery magic around me, fueled it with the raw energy stemming from my fear. I darkened my skin with a messy layer of ashes, dried blood, and raw flesh, simulating the visual effects of a third-degree burn. Then I shut down my organs, froze my veins, and stopped my lungs from taking another breath.

I set my internal timer to wake up in one hour, and sank into oblivion. I would've sent up a quick prayer if I could've, but ya know, being a demon and all.

Four

WHEN I CAME TO, THE first thing I noticed was the revolting mess of rotten meat and vegetables covering every inch of my body. My shoulder was wet, and there was the distinct stench of alcohol in the air. My best guess was that there was a beer spill in the lot and my top had conveniently absorbed most of it. Luckily I could hold off inhalation for minutes on end, because the one breath I got into my lungs almost made me gag. Wherever I was, it was pitch black.

I stretched my legs and gave my surroundings a tentative kick.

Pang!

Damn, my foot hit metal. I kicked harder.

Pangggg!!!

Make that *very* solid metal. Wait, a large dark metal enclosure with moldy mushrooms and animal fat galore? That could only be...

A lid opened above me, and someone swore, "Shit, I knew it!"

The sudden transition from total darkness to high noon was blinding. I lifted my hand to cover my eyes, only to remove it just as fast when I realized I was smearing slime all over my eyebrow.

I could make out a person—I think a woman—with one hand holding up the lid, a black plastic bag of trash in the other. She scowled, though whether from the bright sunlight or the way I looked, I didn't know. She was in her mid-forties, plump, and wearing some sort of human service worker uniform. Not a janitor though. A member of the cleaning staff, maybe?

"I *knew* I heard something." She shook her head. "Are you hurt?"

"I'm alright." As alright as someone could be after being taken out like the trash. I flexed my fingers and toes. I could use a shower, or ten, but all my limbs seemed to be in good working order.

"Can you get up?"

I pushed myself up to a squatting position, not daring to move too fast. Ouch, I think a few of my toes were caught in one of those plastic beer can rings. Yep, there was definitely some fermentation going on in this enormous metal box.

"Here..." The woman leaned in and offered me her hand. I didn't hesitate to take it.

It was a bit of an awkward climb, getting out of the dirty dumpster full of sharp and oddly shaped objects. In the end, it took me three tries and the help of two pizza boxes, one broken office chair back support, and the shell of a humidifier.

The woman kept bitching while she pulled me out. As I needed her help, I decided to keep quiet.

"What are you doing in *there*?" she demanded. Then she sniffed when I got my beer-drenched self closer to the edge of the box. "Oh hell, did you get drunk and fall in? It's not even past the lunch hour yet. Is this over some guy? Trust me, hon, it ain't worth it. You're like, not even twenty. You'll find someone else."

Not even twenty? Oh, right, the aging faery dust was long gone. But even with it on, I doubted it would stop the woman's lecture. She seemed to take it upon herself to give me some worldly advice.

"Now you listen to Hazel, and you listen good. No man's worth it. I kicked my no-good husband to the curb in nineteen ninety-eight and haven't look back since. Repeat after me: no man's worth it."

"No man's worth it," I obliged. Yeah, this was over some guy, alright, but it wasn't a matter of him being worth it or not. I had a job to do. And I had to finish it.

But maybe not today.

As I jumped down from the edge of the metal box, the momentum carried me forward and I slumped over Hazel's body, smearing tomato sauce and who knows what else onto her uniform. The landing wasn't at all as controlled as I intended. Just that little leap out of what would've been my coffin took most of what I had left. I was seriously out of juice.

At least I started the day with clean underwear, I thought as stars swam in front of my eyes. Next thing I knew, I was in the tearoom of the Fainting Goats Palace, a favorite destination for demonic souls during a loss of consciousness.

I barely got down two cranberry scones, three cream custards, and four lemon squares before the mortal plane called my soul back. Might as well; the herd of resident fainting goats, who also served as pastry chefs for the spiritual getaway spot, were starting to give me the evil eye.

Cheapskates.

Pearl pendant digging into my neck? Check.

Deep and long breaths mimicking sleep? Check.

Trickster blood flowing through my veins with glee, exuberant from my recent calling of it? Check. I'd work on reining in that naughty impulse later. For now, I needed it to sharpen my instincts.

I'd woken up a full minute earlier, but I dared not broadcast that fact until I got all my ducks in a row. Jerking up from a bed after fainting was all nice and good in those human movies, but in real life, losing one's capacity to control one's body was not a thing to be taken lightly. I had to make sure there were no unfriendlies around.

No matter how nice Hazel had seemed.

Yes, I was definitely in a bed of some sort. Lying on my stomach, I could feel the too-hard mattress cutting into my ribs and the cotton sheet pressing up against my nose. It smelled clean but stale, as if it hadn't been used since its last wash.

My stomach growled. I missed my dream-scones and orange pekoe tea served on the finest bone china. It really sucked that no matter how stuffed one got in the Fainting Goats Palace, the feeling never got carried back to the world of the conscious.

Confident that I was alone, I was just about to get up from the bed when I heard footsteps, so I stayed put.

The door opened.

"Hey, are you up?" Hazel asked.

If she'd remained silent or tried to walk in unannounced, I would've leaped up and ran out of the bedroom. Or at least tried to. But I was weak, so weak, and a more diplomatic route was preferred.

"Yeah, I'm awake." I opened my eyes.

Hazel was standing at the doorway with her arms folded. "You were out for hours and hours, girl."

Wow. That long? My body must've taken quite a hit and needed the down time. Was being out this long natural for mortals? Not willing to say anything that might reveal myself, I simply looked at the human female at the opposite end of the room.

She continued, "I brought you here because I didn't know who to call. You don't have any ID on you."

While it was true that I never carried any human ID when I went on vengeance, there was no reason not to take me to a hospital. Every TV medical drama I'd ever watched revolved around people landing themselves in such an establishment.

"Why didn't you just call an ambulance?"

"A dozen middle-grade kids came down with a mysterious flu. It's causing wide-spread panic, and the ERs all around the city are swamped. They're advising people not to go there unless it's an absolute emergency."

"Oh." My heart sank. A mysterious flu and wide-spread panic? Sounded like the handiwork of one of my half-brothers. My *trickster* half-brothers.

"Believe me, being here is way better than what you'd get if I dump you at an ER."

I looked around me. "And here is..."

"The employee infirmary room at the Parkington Inn. I work here."

Parkington Inn. I remembered now. It was across the street from the retirement home. How arrogant of Dan

Pillar to dump me right in his own neighborhood. But then, who would ever suspect an elderly man with a fondness for gold leaf red velvet cupcakes of committing murder in his private library?

"Thank you," I said formally. I noticed for the first time that I was wearing a shapeless cleaning staff uniform. A spare, no doubt. My body wasn't what I'd call powder-fresh clean, but most of the stink was gone.

"Don't worry about it. I found you, so I thought it was my responsibility to bring you here and give you a wipe down with a wet towel." She shrugged. "Look. I don't mean to pry, but getting drunk like that, that's not cool. If I hadn't found you when I took out the trash, you'd be in the back of a dump truck heading for the landfill, without anyone noticing."

I'd bet my formerly trash-covered ass that was what Dan Pillar was counting on.

I didn't know how to respond to Hazel. I could've asked her to mind her own business, except something told me that she genuinely meant well. I lowered my head in the pretense of shame. It was best not to correct her assumptions. If I was a drunk who just happened to wander into the neighborhood and collapsed there, then there would be no point in mentioning me to anyone at the surrounding businesses. In that case, Dan wouldn't hear about my survival. The bastard might even be arrogant enough not to skip town right away, giving me a small window of opportunity to catch him.

Figuring my bowed head was pretty much the most she could expect from me, Hazel gestured towards a small closet in the corner. "I put your clothes through the wash."

I got up from the bed and started for the closet.

Hazel turned to leave then faced me once again, "The closest AA is just two streets down."

I had no idea what the humans were doing with Angels Abound, a group of demons who were into the alternate lifestyle of cross-dressing as heavenly beings. But as it turned out, humans weren't as out of touch with the supernatural as I thought. Who knew?

Tired as I was, I couldn't hail a cab to take me home. Aside from not having any money on me, I couldn't trust my trickery side not to be tempted into messing with the GPS direction or enchanting the human cabbie into a rousing chorus of "Born to be Wild." Yes, the resulting chaos would be as inconvenient for me as it was for others, but trying to repress trickery using logic and self-preservation was like trying to convince a scorpion not to sting.

The walk home, across downtown Toronto with low magical storage, was excruciating. My kitten boots weren't meant to be walked in for long distances. And there was the fact that they were half-melted. My leg and thigh muscles ached in protest with every exhausted pound onto the hard concrete.

I forgot to take my cell with me this morning, nor did I think to ask Hazel to let me use the phone before leaving. So I couldn't call for help, either.

It wasn't until I was halfway home that my muddled brain figured out there *was* a way for me to seek help. I could channel my trickery magic through a minor, single purpose spell. I focused my energy on the No Good Deeds enchantment, a spell that would summon someone who'd benefited from a kind gesture of mine in recent memory.

The spell was very specific, only usable if the good Samaritans ended up having bad things happen to them afterward. Hence the name. But even with the spell as restricted as it was, I had to be careful not to overdo it, otherwise it could go sour and call forth someone I'd taken from instead. I so did not need to come face to face with the likes of Madeleine Abrianna Lex right now.

Serafina popped into an empty bus shelter ahead of me, her right hand holding onto a wet paintbrush on a downward stroke. She blinked as she took in her surrounding, aware that she'd just been yanked across the planes. For a moment she looked almost...wistful. Then she saw me, dropped the paintbrush and hurried over. I must've imagined that look of disappointment on her face, as if she was hoping to see someone else.

"What happened?" She asked, grabbing hold of my elbow as I swayed.

I explained in the briefest manner possible. My new friend opened a portal in the next deserted alley and saved me the rest of the walk home. Luckily with her being a full-blooded vengeance demon, my trickery magic couldn't disrupt her power—otherwise we could've ended up in the zombie plane or something.

By the time she dragged me up the steps of the duplex at nine in the evening, I was drained, feeling as if I had no substance at all and even a little breeze could blow me away.

The surrounding area of the house felt...right. Balanced, in harmony, and at peace—in a demonic kind of way. I realized my half-sister must be here already. I wondered how she knew to come.

When I walked in the door, a worried-looking Rosemary

got up from the living room table along with Esme. It appeared they'd been waiting up for me. While Rosemary seemed relieved at the very sight of me, Esme's brows burrowed deeper. It was clear from her face that she immediately saw through the very weak glamour I'd thrown up just before I approached the entrance.

If I were a cell phone, my battery indicator would be at the last bar. In red.

Esme glared at Serafina, assuming, I suppose, the latter had something to do with my current status. I shook my head and gestured to Serafina, "She helped get me home, that's all."

Esme's shoulder relaxed.

"Sorry, Megan." Rosemary approached, kneading at her apron. "When you didn't show up for my veal chops dinner—you sounded so excited when I quoted you the menu this morning—I assumed something was wrong and called your emergency contact."

Yeah, little did she know the phone number I'd given her was enchanted to dial across the dimensions to reach Esme on the demonic side.

"Enough talking." Esme cut Rosemary off. Miss Not-Used-To-Human-Interactions began tugging at my hand, leading me to my room and ignoring my roommate and the fellow demon who'd brought me home. To my half-sister, I was having an emergency, and she was tending to that emergency. Vengeance demon minds could be a bit one-track sometimes.

"Thanks. You did the right thing." I turned my head to assure Rosemary as my sister dragged me away. Serafina nodded in understanding.

"I'll see myself out." She muttered.

"Megan, you don't look so good." Turned out the token glamour wasn't enough even for my human roommate. Maybe it was the instinct of a chef, a provider of nourishment. "Sure you don't want to go to the hospital? They cleared up that flu panic. Turns out the kids were all in the same free dental clinic and there was something about breathing in too much laughing gas—made it look like a mystery flu. It didn't make a lot of sense to me."

Esme muttered under her breath. "Blasted tricksters going to be the death of us all."

Vengeance demons always complained that the chaotic nature of tricksters was going to destabilize the Concord one of these days. Couldn't blame them. Vengeance was all about being exact, logical, and reasonable, while anything went for trickery as long as the fun factor was high. The sheer randomness of the prank victims was enough to give a vengeance demon a stomach ulcer.

I pretended I didn't hear Esme's complaint. I wouldn't share my suspicion that the mischief was the doing of one of my half-brothers even on a good day, and this was anything but. Besides, while I always cringed when I saw an over-the-top trickery antic ending up in the human media, considering how I owed my life to my mother's blood just hours ago, it seemed rather ungrateful to be ashamed of it.

I'd wait a day or two.

"So, no hospital then?" Rosemary followed us, refusing to be dismissed by Esme. Rather than those happy singing Italian chefs on TV, it would appear she had more of a Gordon Ramsay in her.

"I know what she needs," Esme said simply.

Rosemary shook her head. "What she needs is some food, at the very least."

"Later," Esme snapped.

With a look that said *let me handle this*, Serafina hurried over and blocked Rosemary's way. She started ushering my roommate toward the kitchen without looking like she was herding her. All the while, Serafina inquired about seasonal illnesses to look out for and general nutrition information. For all her potent though untrained power, Serafina used no magic on my roommate, relying instead on distraction and persuasion. I got the impression that the use of vengeance power still felt quite foreign to her.

Esme closed the door.

"Hey, be nice to Rosemary," I chastised Esme. "She's just trying to help."

"She was in the way. I need to tend to you as soon as possible." Esme frowned. "And she doesn't seem to realize the urgent nature of this matter."

"She *does*. That's why she suggested the hospital. She's a human. That's how they get help."

Once we were alone, I dropped the glamour, useless as it was, and flopped onto the single bed unceremoniously. Esme leaned over, traced my pearl pendant, then gasped in horror. I forced my tired eyes to focus on what she was looking at.

My pearl was translucent to an almost clear color, as if it was nothing but a tiny glass globe.

Uh-oh, I was almost completely out of power.

Without another word, Esme put my hands in hers and let her magic flow into me. It was a ticklish feeling, but not painful, like a thousand kitten whiskers brushing up against my palm.

Vengeance demons didn't share power unless it was a dire situation. Enid would, now and then, help out her charges, but it was mostly due to her position. My half-sister and I had never shared power before. As I received the gift of her magic, I felt her love and worry rushing over me, warming me up from the inside out.

I closed my eyes and allowed myself to be surrounded by the life essence that was uniquely Esme—logical yet loving, ruthless yet vulnerable at the same time. I always knew that she cared about me, but experiencing it firsthand was quite another thing. Between her standoffish nature, the differing ways we were treated by society, the inherent conflict of interest between siblings, and my own insecurity, there was plenty to keep us from being close. But at this moment I felt so connected to her that I could catch glimpses of her soul in my mind's eye. That closeness felt good, and I hugged it to myself as I touched my forehead lightly against hers.

Despite our difference in status, worldview, and temperament, we would always be sisters. Nothing would change that.

Esme didn't stop the recharge until the milky-white luster returned to my pendant and her own earrings became semi-transparent. Only then did she pull away in exhaustion and slump over the squeaky folding chair I'd borrowed from the landlord.

"Thanks," I whispered after a long moment.

"You're welcome." Then her face hardened. "What happened? Was this on a job?"

I told her, sparing no details. "Did you tell Dad?" I asked Esme.

"No, but I was going to if you didn't show up in another hour or so. He called earlier in the evening and wanted to visit. He had leftovers from the Annual Veteran Vengeance

Demon Picnic," Esme said guiltily. "I told him you were out with your sorority sisters."

I snorted. "When hell freezes over."

"From the look of it, you fared better with them than with your target. And yes, by that I meant I heard about the little fight in the ring." Esme frowned. "And the man who did this to you was a human? Who would've thought?"

"I swear, he looked totally like a run-of-the-mill mortal. There was nothing to tip me off about him."

"I believe you." Esme chewed on her lips. She looked like she was about to say something I wouldn't want to hear, and I got a good idea where she was going. "It sounds like you wouldn't have been able to beat him even if he hadn't had the element of surprise. Look, you can't go back to Enid empty-handed. She might like you, but she still answers to the Concord Council, and you know how they are."

"Yeah. A bunch of old-school, judgmental jerks who are just waiting for an excuse to kick me, the abomination, out of the vengeance program. I know." The Council members also served on the Board of Governors at the university, so there was no escaping them if I wanted a career in this field.

"We have to find a way to match your power to Dan's, so you can complete your assignment. You know what we have to do, don't you?"

"Let me see, kidnap a magic-sucking mosquito fairy and squeeze some juice out of her?"

"Megan, this is no time for jokes." Esme gave me the dirtiest look she could manage, which was a tough job. Despite her devilish good looks and a budding reputation in the field of vengeance work, on a certain level she was still very much an innocent. The blood and gore of the job was a part of her as much as a meal of torn-up zebra was to a cute little lion cub. It didn't turn her cruel, and she gained no pleasure from the target's suffering. Her way of life was just that—life.

That was where, deep down, I feared we might be different. Trickery was all about the joy of the ruse, and the temptation to go full throttle during vengeance was in my very genetic code.

My very messed-up, confused genetic code.

Speaking of genetics...

"Alright." I sighed. "We'll go see Gran."

I hated my grandmother because she was never shy about what she thought of me, and who knew, she might just be right. I hated her even more now because she was my best bet for beating Dan.

"She's throwing a ball tonight to raise money for a sanctuary for retired golden lost-soul retrievers."

"Good. Because I've got something I need to retrieve from her."

"What is it?"

"My other pearl!" I paused and sniffed myself. "Well, shower first."

FIVE

SERAFINA WAS GOING TO THE same event. Her socially conscious family had insisted on her attendance, whether she wanted to go or not. So she left to prepare for it, promising to meet up with me at the ball later. Just as well, Esme and I had some preparation of our own to do.

Some kids sneaked a beer from their father's basement before heading off to a big party. We opted to go to our parents' place for a little magical pick-me-up.

My grandma's world was all about appearances. If we showed up looking like we were on the verge of running out of juice, it would be rudeness equivalent to dressing like a hobo for a Hollywood red carpet event. You know what they say, you have to have magic to get magic.

I managed to convince Esme to go behind my dad's back. I didn't want to worry him, and I didn't want him to take over my assignment, either. It was my mess to fix. Besides, what I needed was beyond even his pay grade.

But we could definitely use a Blue Unicorn from Dad's mini-fridge. The energy drink, sprinkled with ground-up pearl, was the supernatural version of Red Bull. Useless in a real magical battle, it was nevertheless helpful in pumping us up for the glitzy party.

If Red Bull gave a human wings, then Blue Unicorn

fluffed up a vengeance demon's already existing ones. Well, for Esme anyway. Her wings were a pair of dark red beauties, an intricate masterpiece of smooth and cool-to-the-touch scales. What did I have? Well, let me put it this way...

In a family of birds, I'd be the flightless chicken.

In a group of human internal organs, I'd be the useless and easily infected appendix.

In *Hell's Kitchen*, I'd be the one Chef Ramsey told to f— Well, you get the picture.

We entered a working-class, mixed race neighborhood on the outskirts of the vengeance plane. The area was home to a variety of supernaturals, from single income bogeymen with piecework jobs, to retired goblin goldsmiths.

Esme parked the purple sedan two blocks away from the suburban home my parents lived in. That was right, Nicolas Bartholomew Aequitas the second, the arch vengeance demon specializing in the punishment of war criminals and mass serial killers (don't bother calling if the body count is below thirty), lived in a matchbox bungalow with a bird bath and a pink plastic flamingo on the front lawn.

Alright, to be fair, the flamingo was more my mother's touch. So was the swan-shaped birdbath, as a matter of fact. It gave Miss Neringa, the nosy giantess next door, quite a fright every time the stone swan burped out feathers.

My dad put his foot down when it came to the randomness of the trickery, though, so the easily startled Miss Neringa only saw the burping when she was gossiping or up to no good. In my parents' house, order and chaos formed an offbeat kind of harmony, held together by a steadfast love.

Esme and I got out of the car and headed towards the bungalow. Less than ten yards into our walk, we stopped abruptly.

"You going to tell me how you plan on getting us past that?" She nodded doubtfully towards the boundary beyond which our dad could sense our presence. With advanced magic, it was possible to hide from a vengeance demon. But not from an arch demon, and definitely not in our current state.

I held my hand out to Esme. With a raised eyebrow, she took my hand.

"Ouch." Esme pulled back when a spark jumped from my fingertip to hers.

"Sorry. But hey, we can go in now." I put one foot inside the invisible boundary and the other one outside. I could sense my dad, but I just knew he couldn't sense me.

"How?" For once, my half-sister sounded awed by me. Tough gig, considering she was top of her class in everything.

Well, everything vengeance anyway.

Second to playing dead, hide and seek was a talent near and dear to a trickster's heart. I sighed. Not that I was a big fan of calling on my mother's blood, but in for a penny, in for a pound. The reckoning would come soon enough, when I had to fight the urge to invest my rent money in a pyramid scam or reanimate a Council member's pet rabbit. For now, I might as well enjoy the perks.

With a nod to Esme, I led the way, approaching the bungalow's basement entrance through the interconnecting backyards of the neighborhood. Even with the shield, a certain amount of creeping around was involved, since we had to avoid triggering the alarms of our neighbors.

The door to the basement was unlocked. My parents never really worried about anyone trying to get in, because people generally couldn't get away from them fast enough. Once inside the house, Esme and I made a beeline for the mini-fridge behind my dad's bar.

I grabbed two Blue Unicorns and passed one to Esme. Without ceremony, we drank them down. A delicious warmth enveloped me, rejuvenating in its caffeinated energy. It automatically repaired my glamour, much like a microdermabrasion unearthed a fresh layer of skin in a human spa.

The skin appeared great for a few days before peeling like crazy, but for a little while there, it looked amazing.

I was on my last swallow when I heard my dad's voice booming from the very back of the bar, "What do you think you're doing, Meg?"

I choked and then coughed, spilling the energy drink down my front. Damn, just my luck that Dad was here...

Oh, wait.

I glared in the direction of the voice. "Hi, Fir."

Fir, my trickster half-brother, stepped forward. I always thought his name was quite fitting, since it was seventy-five percent of the word "fire." He was all spiky ginger hair and freckles, with a fierce yet sneaky personality to match. Though both redheads, Fir was as bright and carefree as Esme was composed and sultry. Oh well, I had no more control over my family members' appearances than their natures.

Disappointment was apparent on Fir's face as he grumped, "How did you figure it out? I nailed that mimicking."

"You did, but Dad wouldn't have called me 'Meg.'"

"Damn." Fir shook his head. "So close."

While vengeance demons were all about elaborate and illustrious names, tricksters were the exact opposite. Tricksters carried no last names and favored given names with only one syllable, such as Fir, Clef, Boone, and Ty—which happened to be my older siblings' names.

And yes, that was right, I had one half sibling on my dad's side and four on my mom's. Before meeting my dad, in the typical flamboyant style of the tricksters, my mother was very, um, social.

"Don't be so disappointed about the mimicking." I snorted. "You managed to see through my shield."

"Nah, that was easy. Same trickster blood and all."

True, one didn't trick a trickster.

"So dare I ask? What are you doing raiding Dad's fridge, Little Miss-I-Just-Wanna-Be-A-Law-Abiding-Boring-Old-Vengeance-Demon?" Fir folded his arms across his chest and smiled evilly at me.

My enrollment at Vengeance U had long been an object of ridicule, good-natured or otherwise. Fir, my other half-brothers, and all the trickster relatives just couldn't wrap their heads around the idea of me not wanting the easygoing, fun-filled life they'd taken for granted. If I'd wanted to become a full-time trickster, there was no university to attend, no professional hours to accumulate. I would just *be*. Reaction to the news of me trying the vengeance route had ranged from utter puzzlement to feeling downright insulted.

I sighed. To a vengeance demon I was too trickster-like, and to a trickster I was too vengeance-demon-like. You just can't please everybody. Though I had to be fair, the tricksters in my life had always loved me with open arms. They had a child-like ability to live for the day, and they gave and forgave. Couldn't say that about the vengeance demons.

Sometimes, like my trickster loved ones, I wondered what the heck I was doing, wanting to have a place in the vengeance world. Maybe because it was something I had to work for, and after a lifetime of being an outcast in that society, I had something to prove.

But that didn't mean I wasn't aware I was disappointing a lot of people I cared about by not taking up the trickster lifestyle of eat, drink and be merry.

Deep in thought, I didn't raise to Fir's bait. That only got him more interested. He winked at the empty Blue Unicorn bottle I'd gotten caught red-handed with, making sure not to spare Esme a single glance. "Oh, I'm so going to tell."

Esme pushed me aside and stepped in front of Fir. The energy drink was making her a little tipsy, and she cared far less about manners than she usually would. "Hey. Don't talk and act like I'm not here."

Fir finally looked at Esme. His eyebrow rose. "I can talk however I want."

Esme scoffed. "Why, you little fiscally irresponsible, live-at-home—"

I had to stop her before she said something she might regret later. True, one was more likely to find a trickster writing bad checks than saving to move out, but in this particular instant, Esme might've let her prejudice blind her just a little bit.

"Er, Esme, I think Fir here is actually trying to be *nice*."

Esme frowned. "By ignoring me?"

"According to his Twitter update, his latest calling is to

prank the super serious. You're like an early Christmas present to him right now, and the only way to resist pranking you is to avoid direct contact."

"Oh."

Unlike vengeance demons, tricksters didn't go to college to be educated and find job placement. Instead, they goofed around until inspiration struck, then picked the calling of the week and wreaked some havoc.

Fortunately, the humans on Twitter thought all these weekly updates were for laughs.

If I was correct, Clef's latest calling was blind spots (Miss Neringa overlooked her winning numbers at the Lady Luck's Scratch & Win lottery), Boone's was panic (mysterious kiddy flu, anyone?), and Ty's was the old switcheroo plus illusion (for twenty-six minutes during the royal visit to Toronto last Saturday, people were bowing and curtseying to a goat rather than Her Majesty the Queen of England).

I made a point of keeping abreast of these things because I'd been the victim of way too many pranks in my life.

"See?" Fir fisted his chest with a loud *thump*. "I'm the good guy here."

"I wouldn't go that far," I mumbled.

"So, back to my original question, what are you doing raiding Dad's fridge?"

I winced, knowing I had to give Fir some parts of the truth if I didn't want him to hound the whole thing out of me.

Think Fast, Megan.

"We're going to Grandmother Aequitas's charity ball. It's raising money for the, um..."

"Retired golden lost-soul retrievers," Esme filled in primly.

"Right. Just boosting up for the party." I gave him what I hoped was a convincing smile.

"Well, come on up and say hi to everyone then." Fir started walking towards the stairs. "I'll create an illusion so it looks like you're coming through the garage door, not the basement. The two doors are next to each other anyway, so it's a simple trick."

That was a bit too easy. Maybe it was the Blue Unicorn or the trauma of the day making me careless, because the glimmer of mischief in Fir's eyes should've been a fair warning.

In hindsight.

I'd read *Romeo and Juliet* in high school—not even enrolling in the demonic education system could save you from Shakespeare. In the play, the death of Romeo and Juliet reconciled their feuding families.

But what if Romeo and Juliet hadn't died? And they each brought children from previous relationships into the marriage, and then went on and had a kid of their own? What if their prospective families weren't so much feuding as freezing each other out with quiet disdain and mutual distrust?

Yep, that would describe my extended family.

When my parents met, Dad had just gotten a divorce from a vindictive vengeance demon specializing in scorned women and severed male sex organs—guess he should've seen that one coming, eh? Mom had just kicked Ty's father to the curb. It was just as well that tricksters in general didn't believe in marriage contracts, or it would've been impossible for her to get rid of that no-good leech.

During an assignment on an international arms dealer, Dad found Mom in the grenades storage, pulling the old switcheroo. They saw each other over a box of stink bombs, and that was it. Though one never believed in marriage and the other had had his faith badly shaken, they fell in love and got hitched, much to the chagrin of both sides of the families.

Why the opposition? Well, the vengeance demons saw Mom as an opportunistic slut hoping to climb the demonic social ladder, and the tricksters thought Dad was a boring old killjoy who was going to make the supernatural world take them far too seriously. Both groups looked upon the marriage in utter disgust and horror.

How my parents managed to get together amongst the outcry and social pressures I'd never know, but there sure was a lot of excommunication and dung throwing in the early years.

But in the end, things settled down. The Concord Council came to realize that mushily in love or not, Dad was still the most fearsome arch vengeance demon they had, so they made everyone back off. As for the tricksters, well, they were creatures of intense but short-lived passions and just couldn't stay mad at anyone for long.

By the time I was in grade school, all the doors had re-opened for my parents on both sides, reluctantly or otherwise. But that didn't save me from the nasty whispers or being the last chosen in every game in gym class. Things were always simmering just below the surface, the disdain evident in the dirty looks that came from young classmates and adults alike. Not to mention every birthday party I wasn't invited to.

I knew about those parties, though. Through Esme. She was always invited. Just like she was invited to this charity gig for the bloody soul-grabbing retrievers.

I must admit, I liked the tricksters' more straightforward style. They threw all the dung they could at ya, and then they were good. None of this decades-long cold-shoulder crap. So I stand corrected, the aforementioned quiet disdain and mutual distrust were mostly from the vengeance demon side.

As I reached the top of the stairs to the main floor, the smell of delicious cookies filled my nostrils. Mmm, chocolate chip cookies, Mom's favorite recipe. The woman made horrible main courses, but her cookies were the stuff of legends.

My tummy growled, and I realized I'd drank a whole bottle of Blue Unicorn on an almost empty stomach. I'd eaten the four mini cucumber sandwiches Rosemary left at my door, but my deprived system had digested that almost immediately. Oh, delicious cookies...nothing like washing a strong drink down with some homemade baked goods. Wait, I think I got that in reverse. Oh well, it was a good excuse to eat.

The basement staircase opened into the kitchen, which was empty. All the noise seemed to be coming from the living room. I felt almost sorry that Fir wasted a good illusion, but then I remembered the more energy he used, the less trouble he could potentially get himself into.

I grabbed five cookies from the tray on the cooling rack and walked into the living room.

Mom and Dad were kissing on the couch. They did that a lot, but the "ewww" factor never went away. Dad was in black pants and a dress shirt with his tie loosened up. I bet he just came from work and didn't even bother to change before settling in with Mom. She had that kind of effect on him. With her long, black, curly hair, radiant skin, and voluptuous figure, she was one gorgeous woman—never mind what the vengeance demons and their harsh beauty standard said.

Clef, Boone, and Ty sat on the carpet in front of my parents with their eyes glued to the television. Their clothes were made of small patches of rags inclusive of every color under the rainbow, as any self-respecting male trickster's wardrobe would be. When I came into view, all three of my half-brothers straightened up and looked at me at the same time, reminding me of a group of meerkats.

A group of beer-bellied, hair-losing meerkats in their mid to late twenties. Weight gain and early baldness had always been a trickster's bane. That was why court jesters—which were really medieval tricksters in disguise—always had those silly pointy-tipped hats on in paintings. All the better to hide their bald heads with.

As for weight issues, let's say that the most popular insult I got in high school was pounds-related, not magic-related. I was always on the more...er, curvy side of the scale.

Mom pulled away from the smooching and greeted Esme and me with a beautiful smile. Dad hastily tugged down the front of her top to cover her exposed lower belly, and gave us a sheepish grin more fitting to a teenager than a fearsome instrument of vengeance.

Mom patted the unoccupied part of the couch. "Megan and Esme. What a surprise. Come and join us. We're just about to start a movie marathon. A four-part comedy, actually."

I picked up the DVD cases on the coffee table. *Scream*, *Scream 2*, *Scream 3*, and *Scream 4*. I guess to a trickster it would be the stuff of comedies, since the ways people got killed in those movies were pretty lame.

It would be kinda fun to sit back and enjoy the show, but with the entire Aequitas clan in the same room, I had to get out of there before one of them figured out what Esme and I were up to. The fact that all my half-brothers were home and not off making mischief meant only one thing.

They were between gigs.

And nobody was as inquisitive as an out-of-work trickster. I did mention Esme was a terrible liar, right?

"Sorry, Mom, I'm just here to pick up a few things," I said quickly.

I regretted the matter-of-fact words as soon as Mom's smile dimmed. Dad was better at hiding it, but he was disappointed just the same. To the rest of the world he was Mr. Tough Guy, but he was always a teddy bear to me. It'd been a year since I'd moved out for college. I missed him, and I missed Mom. I missed the simpler times of taking shelter in their home, safe from the meanness of the outside world. I'd spent so little time with them in the last year, my entire focus on getting the co-op position.

But that position was the exact reason why I had to go. Pronto.

"It's alright, love. Our baby's all grown up and she's got things to do," Dad muttered, pressing a light kiss on Mom's hair.

It wasn't a guilt trip. That wasn't my dad's way. But I felt guilty nevertheless.

Aid came from an unexpected corner. "She can't stay.

She's going to a fancy ball at Grandma Aequitas'," Fir piped in. Since when did he ever call her *Grandma Aequitas*? More often used by him were names like the Wicked Witch of the Venge.

Dad seemed puzzled. "You got invited?"

Sounded like Dad already knew about the ball, had probably received an invitation himself. And like typical Dad, he'd decided to stay in with Mom.

"How?" Clef and Boone asked at the same time. "You never get invited. *Ever*."

"Madeleine Abrianna Lex," I blurted.

"That stuck up? Why? What does she want?" Ty crossed his arms.

I was digging myself into a hole, and I knew it. Damn, I had no idea why Madeleine's name came out of my mouth. I panicked, that was why. "She...she invited me. The house of Lex is helping with the ball's decorations and she wanted me along. We've become friends this semester. She's actually not that bad. We even work out together." Could someone kill me to stop my babbling, please?

"This is wonderful news. You must hurry then." Mom nodded in joyful enthusiasm. She was forever encouraging me to get involved with vengeance society. "I always knew she'd come around."

"I don't know." Dad hesitated. "It might be a bit too stiff for our Megan."

"Don't be silly, Nick. It'll be good for her to spend time with her friends and family on the vengeance side."

My trickster mother was one of the happiest people I knew because she didn't hold a grudge. Despite the cold way she was treated by the entire Aequitas clan, she never ceased to want me to have a good relationship with

Grandma.

But her being treated in a crappy manner was a big part of the reason I didn't want to play nice.

Hearing about my attendance at the ball, my other half-brothers were all making gagging gestures when my parents weren't looking. But Fir gave them a long I'll-tell-you-later look, and they stopped.

"So what is it that you're here to pick up?" Dad asked, sounding resigned. He knew the futility of disagreeing with Mom in the long-standing matter of Megan vs. vengeance society.

It was a good thing that I already worked out what to say in the event of being asked. "Our dresses and hair combs." The Blue Unicorn had given us the instant makeup transformation, so all that was left was the hair, clothing and accessories.

"Come on, girls. Let's go to your rooms." For the second time that night, Fir led us towards a staircase, this one with only two risers, effectively avoiding further questions from my parents.

Whew.

Six

THE LAST TIME I WAS at Grandma Aequitas' mansion, I was eleven and it was her birthday.

As per tradition, Grandma gave vengeance practice dolls to all her granddaughters to celebrate the occasion. Humans gave their little girls Barbies to try out hair and fashion on; vengeance demons gave theirs practice targets to test out the various torture methods. The dolls were enchanted to give off the appropriate screams and curses and stuff.

Everybody got a proper doll except me. Instead, I got a G.I. Joe. Not only did Grandma give me a *human* toy, she didn't even bother to find out that it was a human *boy's* toy.

I told my daddy right then and there I'd never return to the mansion unless I was being dragged by a dozen hell stallions. And I'd stood by my words.

Until now. Funny what desperation could make a person do, I reflected dryly as I stood in front of the mansion with Esme. The estate was so vast it would've taken us a full five minutes to walk to the front door from the lot where cars were being parked. Fortunately there was valet parking. The mansion's lawn was manicured to within an inch of its life, and the looming Jacobethan structure would've put Downton Abbey to shame.

The widowed matriarch's main residence was located in the parallel dimension of Rosedale, an affluent Toronto neighborhood of old money and social connections. The demonic version was pretty much the same, except in here the gloom-and-doom talk was all about the bailout of the spending fairies, and nobody thought that the hellhound teacup Chihuahuas were cute.

"Come on." Esme gave me a nudge. "It's not going to be that bad."

"Ha, walk a day in my outcast shoes, Little-Miss-Grandma's-Pet." I snorted.

"No, I'm not her favorite. She doesn't play favorites because it's against the rules," Esme protested. "And you might want to watch your manners once we're inside. No more unladylike sounds coming through your nose—it's like you're a bleating goat."

So the social norms in these events hadn't changed at all since I was last here then. I expected as much. The men and women in the magnificent lobby were dressed in black, or off-black, as if they were attending a funeral. All those serious and haughty faces—it was like being in the *Addams' Family*, but without the humor.

There was a reason why tricksters thought vengeance demons were killjoys.

They were.

Esme wore a dark purple gown that complemented her wine-red hair. Her comb was bejeweled with dark amethysts that accented her carefully coiled hair bun.

I was dressed in the same color as Esme, but as a sign of quiet defiance, I chose a hair comb of brilliant yellow topaz. Granted, it was completely hidden by my oversized bun, but it was a statement done for my benefit, not anybody else's.

My thick hair threatened to escape even under five million magically enforced bobby pins, but I admitted it was fun having Mom doll me up. We didn't do that very often anymore.

Aidan, the stone-faced butler, announced Esme's name in a grandiose tone, then blew through mine like an embarrassing afterthought.

Upon our entry into the gilded ballroom, the sound of live orchestra music greeted us with classical tunes from a variety of planes. A dozen giant crystal chandeliers, each flicking with real candle flames, added to the majestic feel of the whole place.

Guests milled around the ballroom, exchanging pleasantries in low murmurs. The guest list tonight was full of supernaturals of the "respectable" type. There were vengeance demons from other large houses, reapers, representatives from the four major witches' unions, and M.A.D.D., Monsters Against Drunk Demons.

I even spotted a few banshees, reporters of breaking supernatural news. Even in the demon world, it was imperative to be on good terms with members of the press.

The Three Fates—retired auditors of regulated destinies—sat on a satin bench with Death and Fairy Godmother, sipping elven wines and reminiscing about the good old days when both happily-ever-afters and tragic ends were pre-determined and guaranteed.

Not everyone preferred to live in the past though, as there were plenty of opportunities to wheel and deal in the present. At a pillar close by was Santa Claus, chatting with a colleague of Dad's. Santa's annual naughty list was worth a fortune to the vengeance demons, since it served as an early indicator of future wrongdoers. Desperate for funds to buy gifts in this generation of iPhones and tablets, Santa was known to sell his precious list, very much like a human dentist might sell his clients' personal information to telemarketers.

All in all, it was a ballroom filled with movers and shakers, but no actual dancing at all. Wild party this was not, but at least "O Fortuna" from *Carmina Burana* had just started playing. Yes, it was popular in supernatural high society too. Though hearing it always reminded me of those silly human beer commercials. Tonight they even had the forty-plus-member male choir wearing full monk costumes for the event. If I didn't know better, I'd say they were paying homage to the ads.

Esme tilted her head. "Strange, the choir doesn't sound right."

"What do you mean?"

"The singers aren't evenly distributed in skill."

I shrugged. It sounded just fine to me, but then again, I wasn't the one who'd minored in Cross-Dimensional Music.

As we walked through the ballroom, the guests parted like the Red Sea for me, not out of respect, but as if I had the latest human bird flu. There were appalled faces, dirty looks, and plenty of whispers behind closed hands. Among the crowd, I saw Enid raising her glass in a tiny salute of acknowledgement.

My first instinct was to duck, thinking that Enid had found out what happened with Dan Pillar. Silly, really, as students had a few days before a co-op assignment was due, and mentors generally left us be until then.

My second reaction was to feel a little touched. Enid was the only one here who didn't look unhappy to see me. I gave her a small nod before moving on.

Esme and I found a spot at the farthest corner of the ballroom, away from the crowd that soon forgot about me.

"Wait here. I'll go ask Grandma for an audience," Esme said before dashing off.

I got comfortable on the burgundy silk settee and took in the surroundings that I'd become all too familiar with as a pre-teen loner.

Every physical detail was the same as before, from the two-story French windows, to the *Gone-With-The-Wind*-style staircase, all the way down to the fresco on the ceiling depicting the forty-nine classic methods of vengeance. The only new things were the six golden lost-soul retrievers on display in the corner closest to the entrance.

Due to their location right in a blind spot, guests wouldn't see the dogs upon their entrance unless they turned their heads ninety degrees to the side. That was smart, as the animals were better observed from afar.

Confined in a circle of hellfire, the retrievers were playing tug-of-war with the balled-up soul of a serial rapist. All of these shiny-coated beauties were barely past their puppy stage. Guess they didn't want to depress the patrons with sad-looking, tired, and close-to-retirement dogs, even though such animals would be the real beneficiaries of the donation. It was no different from human models in their twenties doing advertisement for anti-wrinkle creams they didn't need. Public image was important, no matter what plane one was on.

My quiet tranquility, watching the rapist's soul being ripped up, didn't last long.

"Megan, is that you? I was so sure I misheard the announcer. Didn't think you'd get an invite, or have anything other than rags to wear to this type of event." A guy around my age with blond locks and wearing a dark grey dress shirt approached me with a smirk.

Yep, the pre-teen memories were most certainly coming back, including Cousin Fred's jabs. Mister-I'm-So-Popular was as annoying as ever.

"Hello, *Fred*." I smiled in defiance, knowing how much he hated having his name tricksterized.

Fred's lips pressed into a thin line. "Very funny. Hey, a little bird told me you failed your first co-op assignment. Run, Megan, run, before Enid hears about it."

My heart rate began to increase like a galloping pony. How did he know about the assignment? Had Esme said something?

No, I decided. Esme might be stuck up, and she looked way better in a paper bag than most people would in a red-carpet gown, but she wouldn't betray me like that. Up until a day ago, I would've been tempted to doubt her, but that little bit of herself she'd left behind when she'd recharged me made me *believe*.

"No, your info is wrong. I'm doing pretty well, thank you very much." If I asked Fred about his sources outright, he'd play coy and milk this for all he could. If I simply denied the truth, maybe he'd feel the need to prove himself right.

My little strategy worked.

"No, you aren't. Grandma said the Council is still waiting to hear from you. If you'd succeeded, you would've reported back already."

Ah, so that was his source. Our own Grandma dearest. Great.

"The assignment isn't due yet," I reminded Fred. "Some of us like to do proper recon before going in, guns blazing."

Fred laughed, seeing through my lie without effort. "Did the human prove to be too much, or did our favorite little trickster run amok, foam at the mouth, and burn down the target's home?"

"I'll foam *you* at the mouth..." Stupid Grandma and her honorary member status on the Council, and her tendency to complain to others about my failures. I was in the middle of getting up from the silk settee when Fred was joined by Madeleine Abrianna Lex. Great, now I had two of them to handle.

Madeleine was in a little black cocktail dress and in full networking mode. She didn't come over to socialize with me, though. "Frederick Maximilian Aequitas, you must leave our Megan alone. The poor dear is one of the most pathetic wallflowers I've ever seen, and she doesn't need any more grief from you." Madeleine's sugary voice purred.

"Technically, nobody's dancing. So everybody is a wallflower," I countered.

"Keep telling yourself that, you dirty blood."

"Wrinkle-winged," Fred added.

"Flickering light bulb." Madeleine did a one up on Fred, throwing him a flirtatious glance. Great, two nasty people in my life bonding over insulting me. Gag.

"Miss Lex and Mr. Aequitas, I'm sure you're aware that our university has just implemented a zero-tolerance policy on verbal assault and bullying." I had no idea how long Enid had been standing behind the two banes of my existence, but there she was.

Madeleine and Fred jumped guiltily. Fred opened his mouth to argue, but one frosty look from Enid and he thought better of it. So long as they were in the vengeance co-op program, they were under Enid's management and dared not cross her.

A string of mumbled excuses and hastily retreating footsteps later, I was left standing alone with Enid.

"Thanks," I said wholeheartedly.

"Don't mention it." That was strange. Enid's voice sounded so...young. Young, cheerful, and familiar.

I did a double take. Enid winked at me, and the voice of Serafina came through. "Payment for the horseshoe incident, my friend."

"How did you do it?" I was impressed. Serafina's skills were on par with any trickster worth his or her salt. The glamour she executed was precise to absolute perfection, I could've sworn the person before me was indeed Enid.

Except the voice, but only because Serafina allowed me to hear the difference.

"I didn't grow up with changelings without picking up a thing or two." Serafina smiled modestly. "Now I'd better go. The real Enid just came out of the powder room."

I looked in the direction of said powder room. "How did you know? The entrance is blocked from view by a spell of privacy."

Serafina giggled. For tonight at least, gone was the harried, shy girl who was dodging from one embarrassment to another. I had a feeling this was a Serafina more in her own skin, though she was wearing somebody else's. Or maybe she was more comfortable for precisely that reason. "The changelings have this spell that acts like a human GPS tracking device. How else were they able to perform the ultimate switcheroo, century after century without the parents intervening?"

"My brother Ty would kill to have a date with you," I called out as Serafina walked away, then I was horrified when I realized what I'd just done. To the rest of the ballroom, the lady I just tried to set up was the straight-laced middle-aged Enid, who happened to have the power of pass or fail over me. Ouch.

Esme appeared by my side. "Grandma will see you now."

Great, now it looked like I was being called upstairs for the offence just committed.

"No," Grandma said in utter, devastating simplicity. A woman of short stature, she was only a few inches taller than me, even though I was sitting and she was standing. Nevertheless, her commanding presence always made vengeance demons forget her size the moment they met her.

"But you didn't even hear the whole story." My voice sounded a bit whiny, even to my own ears. My chest tightened and my jaw clenched despite my best effort to relax them. I was starting to get rather pissed off, to be honest. I'd walked into her private study less than thirty seconds ago and already the old crone had refused me.

"I don't have to know the whole story, Megan. I know what matters." Grandma turned her aristocratic nose up in disdain. "One, you failed at your assignment. Two, you came to my event stinking of human and Blue Unicorn, with your trickery urges recently sated. Three, you *have* the said trickery urges. What more do I need to know?"

"But—"

"Aidan will show you out."

The butler held open the door pointedly. I thought I saw a tiny hint of sympathy in his eyes, and somehow that cut me deeper than his indifference. Not that I'd foreseen a positive result. In fact, Grandma's response was pretty much expected. Then why was I feeling so shitty?

"Fine," I bit out, knocking my sofa chair back with a loud screech as I stood.

I headed towards the entrance of the private study with a straight spine. *Play it cool, Megan. Just put one foot in front of the other and keep walking. She could make your life miserable if you shoot your mouth off. Well, more hellish than now, anyway.*

At the threshold I turned around and opened my mouth, then shut it with a snap.

Good girl.

I slammed the heavy oak door. It felt good. For only about five seconds, but it shouldn't be discounted.

Bad girl.

The walk from the private study to the grand staircase was less than twenty feet, but it felt much longer than that. My heart was heavy, my spirit crushed, and tears threatened to spill from my eyes. That was strange. If I didn't know better, I'd say I was seriously bummed out. But I couldn't be, because there was never any love lost between Grandma and me.

Then why was every snub from her such a surprise, every single time?

As I started down the grand staircase, I saw something else that was surprising.

Esme. Semi-hidden in the shadow of the floor-to-ceiling curtains by the French windows. Kissing a boy.

I repeat. My murderously brilliant, romantically inexperienced half-sister was kissing a boy. Like, five seconds after meeting him. I knew that with absolute certainty because I'd never seen him before, and she would've mentioned him had she met him before this evening.

This was so unlike Esme. Did some of my trickery tendencies get transferred into her, or was the Blue Unicorn to blame?

I paused at the top of the stairs, ignoring the butler's not-so-subtle cough to ask me to move on. There was something off about that boy. Granted, everything about him fit right in this place, from the dark grey tailored suit to his jet-black hair, a trademark of a vengeance demon from an old family. But something was off, nevertheless.

I didn't have the chance to figure it out, though. There was a sudden flash of light, then every candle on the crystal chandeliers exploded like fireworks. Little rockets of fire rained down on the dance floor.

I squinted. They weren't rockets at all. They looked like large cookies in the shape of milk bones, just like...dog biscuits?

The six golden lost-soul retrievers howled, then jumped over the circle of hellfire in their bid to get at the dog biscuits, their toy of rapist soul promptly forgotten. There must've been a potent dose of enchanted dognip in the biscuits, because the retrievers grew more unruly with each one they ingested, ignoring a lifetime of discipline training.

There was shocked silence amongst the supernaturals, but they soon sprang into action. Each supernatural used the weapon that was most natural to them, from stun spells to scythes to wands, but the effort was largely unsuccessful. The problem was, lost-soul retrievers were not only ferocious and fast, they were also bred to be cunning to the bone. Combine that with the defiance of almost-puppies, and it was impossible to contain them.

It would seem that the dog biscuits were also bewitched

to stick to the supernaturals' bodies. Once the hyped-up hounds finished the treats on the floor, they proceeded to jump up on their hind legs in an attempt to lick the stuck-on biscuits off their supernatural masters.

In hindsight, the older, calmer dogs would've been a better choice, huh?

Before anyone could shake off the smell of dog breath and salvia, the candles on the crystal chandeliers exploded again, this time sending down buckets of crimson-cultured liquid.

Thoroughly soaked, the respectable and dignified members of the supernatural world did the only thing they could.

Screamed and ran like little girls.

Complete chaos and pandemonium. It was like *Carrie*, except that liquid wasn't blood. Please tell me it wasn't blood, because now I had a pretty good idea what was going on.

As if to confirm my suspicion, Fir chortled as he swung 'round and 'round the ceiling on a rope attached to the central chandelier, taking in all the mayhem with sheer delight.

Boone was enchanting the floor to be extra slippery, causing Santa Claus to glide across it with his legs up in the air. Ty created the illusion of the exit being surrounded by fire, and Madeleine screamed, thinking her little black dress was ablaze. Clef stood at the corner of the ballroom, muttering under his breath, and somehow my confused Cousin Fred kept banging into those around him.

Oh, no.

The super serious guests.

Fred's strange blind spots.

The panic.

The illusion.

Fir, Clef, Boone, and Ty weren't interested in gourmet chocolate strawberries or the sheer thrill of getting into an exclusive event. They were after a career-launching, put-your-name-on-the-map kind of trickery.

And it worked. I'd be happy for them if I wasn't so busy being horrified.

My cell phone vibrated with an incoming tweet. To lower my chance of becoming victim to my half-brothers' pranks, I made sure I got regular updates by following them, and every trickster organization imaginable out there, on Twitter.

I glanced at the tweet. It was from Fir, typed with the spare hand currently *not* holding the rope:

@trickstersunite @mischiefrus BREAKING: All #hell broke loose at #vengeancedemonsball. Calling all #tricksters 2 come & play! Sorry @v4megan couldn't resist.

Oh, no, no, no. With this tweet, every trickster within the next three planes would show up and join in the fun. Sorry? Sorry wasn't nearly enough.

So much for trying to get on Grandma's good side.

Madeleine drew my eyes again, this time in a dilemma I would've found funny under any other circumstances. From the back of her little black dress poked a thick, hairy, and curly pig's tail that wasn't supposed to show for another few weeks, but no doubt had been induced to premature arrival by her heightened stress. Sweat and tears marred her face, though her tail remained bouncy as she zoomed from one side of the room to another, as if she thought she could outrun her newest body part.

All around the ballroom there were mini-tornados forming, signifying the arrival of the trickster party crashers. Enid ran around the room, doing this wave thing that seemed to stall the tornados' spins, but there were simply too many incomings for her to stop them all.

Still midway down the stairs, I heard the heavy oak door of the second floor swing open. Uh-oh.

Thud, thud, thud.

The overexcited, teeth-baring retrievers gave a great big yawn and promptly lay down on the dance floor. They were snoring before their heads hit the ground.

Thud, thud, thud.

The crimson-colored liquid was lifted from the surfaces where it had landed and gathered itself back into the buckets it came from.

My grandmother, the matriarch of the Aequitas clan, one of the oldest families in the history of vengeance, stood tall and proud at the top of the stairs. In her hands was a bejeweled, wicked-looking staff. She banged it on the floor again.

Thud, thud, thud.

There was a hush as Grandma's stern voice rang over the ballroom. "Be gone, children of Loki."

Every trickster in the room was ejected from the demon plane, back to wherever they came from.

And though technically I wasn't a pure child of Loki, I was ejected just the same.

Except I didn't go straight home like the rest of them.

SEVEN

ONE MINUTE I WAS ON the grand staircase of Grandma Aequitas' ballroom, the next a mini-tornado wrapped itself around me, taking me away and depositing me in...the exact same spot I'd been moments ago.

"What the—" I slumped and gripped the railing in an effort to prevent myself from falling. I looked around. My surroundings were exactly as they should be, from the chandelier with a broken rope, to the sweeping staircase, to the vengeance fresco on the ceiling. Yet everyone and everything around me looked washed out, discolored, as if there was a thick layer of fog between us.

Grandma was making some sort of announcement in front of the gathering crowd at the center of the ballroom, but I couldn't make out her echoed words. It was like I was underwater and the sound was muffled.

That was strange. Within the mist enveloping me, I swear I could make out various locations in multiple realities overlapping the ballroom. There was what looked like my bedroom on the human plane, and another room with oddly familiar carpets.

I squinted, and that particular reality came into sharper focus. The inside of a suburban home was a juxtaposition to Grandma's mansion. My parents' living room. Dad was standing over the sprawled figures of Fir, Clef, Boone, and Ty, an arch vengeance demon in full fury. I didn't have to have the volume on to know what *that* conversation was all about.

"Dad, can you hear me?" I called out, but he continued to lay into my half-brothers without a single glance my way.

"Hey, Dad!" I screamed as loud as I could. No response from him. With racing heartbeat, I called out to Grandma down in the ballroom. "Grandma Aequitas!"

She didn't give any sign of acknowledgement, which wasn't entirely out of the ordinary, except not a single person from the gathering crowd looked up at me, either. Curiosity was universal, supernatural or not.

Unless they couldn't hear me. Nobody could. Not even Grandma.

I scrambled to get up, almost slipped on the polished wood, and started making my way down the stairs—

And ran right into Cousin Fred, who was making his way up, pressing a handkerchief against a broken nose.

I mean, I ran right *through* him, like I was some disembodied lost spirit. Cousin Fred didn't even blink in the moment right before our bodies should've impacted. He could no more see me than he could feel my physical presence.

I patted my body with shaky hands. It felt real enough to me. That ought to give me some comfort, but I was feeling anything but comforted. If I was real, yet nobody could see me, then where the hell was I? How could I be in different places at once, yet not really in any of them? Was I going to be stuck like this for all of eternity, existing, yet not?

An old legend popped into my head, cutting through the growing trepidation. According to the stories, there were barren spaces, realms of emptiness between planes. Maybe due to me being a product of two worlds? Grandma's ejection didn't quite send me back to my room on the human plane, but landed me in the shadowy boundary between the worlds instead.

I took a few deep breaths, tightened my grip on the railing, and tried my best not to freak out. But I was.

I couldn't stay here. But how was I supposed to go home? All portal openings required an originating address. I had no idea where *here* was.

A low chanting began in the distance. Initially I thought it was Grandma's male choir starting up again, but a glance down the ballroom confirmed that she was still fuming and gesturing. It would seem a less than opportune time to restart the music. Also, the chanting sounded much louder than anything else I'd heard since arriving in Shadow World.

I paused and listened hard. The chanting was indeed male, though it was coming from far fewer than four-dozen chanters, the standard size of a choir suitable for an event like tonight's. The style was Gregorian, and when the art form was created, it was indeed done by monks. The sound originated from within the Shadow World itself.

And the chanters were getting closer. Their voices were getting louder, and I could make out faint shapes from within the fog.

Three hooded figures in long, flowing, dark robes emerged from the mist, prayer beads in hand. Due to the thickness of the mist, their materialization came as a shock. One minute they sounded like they were still far away, the next they were merely a few feet from me.

The figures glided the rest of the way to me. On closer

inspection, what they had in hand weren't prayer beads at all, but the tiny skulls of some unfortunate rodents strung together. The monks, for lack of a better name for them, surrounded me; their chanting rose to a crescendo then fell silent.

The monk in the middle of the group had a prominent pointy chin. He extended a talon-like index finger towards my face, one sharp fingernail tracing my cheek. If my nerves weren't so frayed, I'd have laughed at how cliché it all looked—a mysterious realm, larger-than-life hooded figures, a menacing caress on a frightened girl's cheek...but I was too busy leaning away from the creepy touch. Yet a part of me also wanted to lean forward, mesmerized by the single brown fingernail pressing against my flesh; like a car crash, I couldn't look away. It was long, ugly, and curled, similar to a witch's. My stomach churned.

Don't move. Don't even flinch, or that nail will cut you like a razor.

When Monk in the Middle lifted his hand and struck it down toward me, I couldn't help but squeeze my eyes shut. I knew it was cowardly and un-vengeance demon-like of me, but I couldn't help it.

Then I heard the sound of shuffling; something dropped onto the ground and bounced down the stairs. Someone cursed profusely.

Eyes still closed, I touched my cheek tentatively and felt no smearing of blood on it. There was that, at least.

I opened my eyes and looked down. I had no idea what drew me in that direction first, but something told me it was crucial.

At the base of the stairs was the talon-like hand, but what was more interesting was the area where the hand should've ended and the wrist began. There was no savagely severed wound, but a plastic handle. In fact, the whole damn thing looked plastic, what with the index finger still pointing outward in a rigid fashion and the very absence of blood.

The hand wasn't cut off, it was dropped, like the prop that it was. Come to think of it, the skull necklaces looked fake too. I was reminded of the Halloween accessories human kids would get from novelty shops to jazz up their costumes. What kind of supernatural would buy from mortal stores, when there should be plenty of horrors at their own disposal?

I took a deep breath and rolled the scent of my surroundings around on my tongue, something I should've done right from the beginning, had I not been so freaked out. There was no trace of magic in the air that I could taste.

I rounded on the three creatures. Whatever they might be, they were in trouble now. And they would've realized it too, if they weren't so busy arguing amongst themselves. Monk in the Middle seemed to be the leader, so I mentally labeled the other ones Sidekick Number One and Sidekick Number Two. They had the heavier build and strong facial features of dwarfs, though not the height, as they were only a bit shorter than me. Now that I wasn't busy being scared to death, I could see their not entirely monk-like pot bellies.

It was hard to tell what manner of creatures these three were based on mere surface appearances, due to the huge amount of intermarrying between brownies, gnomes, hobgoblins, dwarfs, and elves since the medieval period, the last time humans had documented their looks. If I were to guess, I would say they were some form of elves, judging not from any specific physical attributes, but from the odd sense of grace in their micro-movements.

Even if not graceful in speech.

"I told you it's too heavy to cart around." Monk in the Middle turned to Sidekick Number One. When the leader had chanted during his entrance, before he'd ruined his badassness, I'd thought he was a deep baritone. Now his voice went up an octave to what I suspected was his natural voice. "Why did you have to pick up something so big?"

"Told you it was too bulky to maneuver," Sidekick Number Two chimed in. He was just a bit bigger than the others, a bit rougher looking.

"But it's so nice and scary," Sidekick Number One complained, looking at the fallen hand longingly.

"Well, it's not so scary now. And I would've been fine." Monk in the Middle poked Sidekick Number One in the shoulder. "If you hadn't stepped on my robe and made me lose my balance—"

Sidekick Number One held up his hand. "It's not my fault. Our robes are too long."

"And why is it too long? Who got us those robes?" Monk in the Middle folded his arms.

"I did, but only because they were on sale. Buy two, get one free. You're the one who said we should always try to get a deal—"

"Er, guys." I cleared my throat.

"Yeah, but I didn't mean cutting corners and making us trip all over." Monk in the Middle bristled, totally ignoring me.

"Yeah, I almost tripped too," Sidekick Number Two added helpfully.

"Fellas." Pissed that earlier these cheap losers had

managed to reduce me to a shivering mess with a pathetic fake hand, of all things, I flared my nose and went into full vengeance mode, pulling my power around me like a blanket. It wasn't much, being borrowed and everything, but I was betting it was more than what these guys had.

The three faces around me bleached, then Monk in the Middle took a good look at me and did a double take.

"You're not her," he blurted. He turned to his sidekicks. "She's not her."

The sidekicks looked at each other and shrugged.

"Didn't you check the picture?" Sidekick Number One asked his counterpart.

"I thought *you* checked it."

I rubbed my temple and felt the beginning of a migraine.

Then I thought about what Esme had said about Grandma's male choir.

The choir doesn't sound right. The singers aren't evenly distributed in skill.

I now knew what that must have meant. The three guys in front of me had infiltrated the ball by hiding in the male choir. Their singing skills might be on par with each other, but they didn't match the rest of the choir. Did they come to the ball just to follow me here? But why?

Their bickering continued.

"Are you sure she's not the same girl? They all look the same." Sidekick Number One scratched his head.

"They all look the same to *you*." Monk in the Middle rolled his eyes.

"Enough!" My voice boomed in the substanceless world, thanks to an extra kick of power fueled by annoyance.

The three jumped. Monk in the Middle looked at me

again. "You're not her."

"I thought we'd already established that." I rolled my eyes.

"Then where is she?"

"Who is *she*? What are you up to? What is this place? What's going on? Did you come to the ball to target me?" I fired off my questions in quick succession with a less-than-subtle compulsion. I had to get home, and these assholes were going to help me do it whether they liked it or not.

The three looked at me, eyes glassy as they came under my spell.

I took that opportunity to ask in a firm voice, "Who are you?"

"Bonaventure the Third," Monk in the Middle said.

"Wistari," Sidekick Number One replied.

Sidekick Number Two didn't answer me. Instead, he shook his head like a wet dog and blinked rapidly until his eyes became clear again. I'd heard of some giants having natural immunity to vengeance magic. Maybe an elf with some distant giant blood in him? That would explain the tougher appearance. It would be just my luck to bump into one, tonight of all nights.

Looked like I still had the attention of the other two, though. They just stood there with their jaws hanging, their postures relaxed and passive. But before I could get another question out, Sidekick Number Two grabbed their hands and made all of them fall backwards, down the staircase.

Into the portal he'd just conjured in midair. He'd opened it through his sheer will. His own damn *sheer will*.

The portal closed before I could follow. Oh crap, there went my only lead.

I didn't know how long I remained on that staircase. My

sole point of reference was "watching" Dad yell some more at my half-siblings and Grandma answer questions from the press with a grim face. Both instances could last either five minutes or thirty, though.

Chanting started in the distance again.

The same Gregorian style, three part harmony, faint shapes from within the fog.

An encore, seriously? Why were they back? Wasn't once quite enough? When did they find the time to recover? When they popped out of the fog once again, I was ready. Whatever game they were playing, this time they weren't getting away.

Monk in the Middle once again extended a talon-like finger towards me. I grabbed his hand and tugged hard.

The hand refused to drop to the ground.

I tugged again.

The hand refused to come off. It stayed on as if it was actually attached to his body. Then his fingers wrapped around my wrist, and he flung my body across what would've been the space above the ballroom, had I been on that plane.

Some kind of invisible web caught me, pinning me to what would've been the ballroom's ceiling corner. I couldn't move, couldn't scream.

I realized too late the bearer of the non-fake hand couldn't have been Monk in the Middle. Not only was my current attacker at least five inches taller, I could also taste the bitterness of heavy dark magic in the air. If the first three losers I'd seen had had that, they'd have had no need for the fake hand at all.

The hooded figures started chanting again; the consistency of their skill level confirmed there was more than one trio of imposters in Grandma's choir tonight.

A bubble began to form in front of them, growing in size and temperature. It moved towards me in menacing slowness.

This bubble looked just like the one Dan Pillar had employed to nearly fry me alive. It seemed too big of a coincidence that another person was trying to attack me using the exact same move as my target.

To face the possibility of death twice in less than twenty-four hours was too much. I froze up and weirdly, the only thing going 'round and 'round in my head was how mad Sassy was going to be when I wasn't around to warm up the bed for her. It was silly, but that was the thought that got stuck in a loop in my mind. I suppose it was easier to deal with than the bigger picture.

The bubble moved closer still.

Thud, thud, thud.

Barely able to move my eyeballs, I nevertheless glanced towards the source of the sound. Grandma Aequitas was at the center of the ballroom, which was now cleared out of both guests and press. The place looked swept up. In front of her was a single row of chairs, filled exclusively with members of the Concord Council.

The Council? In general, they wouldn't show up as a pack to any social events, their combined presence considered too politically concentrated. Though no longer actively involved in the day-to-day running of the Council, Grandma was still an honorary member, and if she'd called a meeting, it meant that she was royally pissed. In a way, I couldn't blame her. If my life weren't in immediate danger, I'd be plotting my trickster half-siblings' murders for dragging me into this mess.

Though I couldn't hear Grandma when I'd first gotten to the Shadow World, I could hear her fine now. I soon realized why. The summons was broadcast in the full-spectrum supernatural public channel, and even the Shadow World could hear it. "Nicolas Bartholomew Aequitas the second, arch vengeance demon of my clan, hear me. I hereby summon you to answer for your daughter's behavior this night."

Ouch, talk about being embarrassed across all planes.

In the overlapping reality, Dad paused mid-lecture to my half-brothers and tilted his head, listening. He glanced over at Mom on the couch and gave her a reassuring smile, though it didn't quite reach his eyes. Then he snapped off the command to teleport to the ballroom.

The monks tensed and stopped chanting. The bubble dissipated two inches from my skin. With a slight nod to each other, they summoned a portal and vanished.

Why were they turning tail? My question was soon answered by the sudden appearance of Dad.

He seemed as surprised to land in the Shadow World as I was. He looked around the greyed-out world in confusion. "What the—"

Then he spotted me just as the invisible web dissolved, sending me plunging towards the dance floor.

At least Dad found me and knows what happened to me. That was my last thought before I passed out.

"Is she going to be okay?" My dad's anxious voice floated to me across a sea of nothingness.

"She'll be fine, Nicolas. You broke her fall," came my grandma's haughty voice. She might be a healer, but Ms.

Bedside Manner she wasn't. "Are you sure she was attacked? I still couldn't believe anyone would do that to her. The girl doesn't even have enough raw talent to tempt a succubus."

"Mother, she was trapped by a silver web." Dad kept his voice to a whisper, and though my eyes were closed, I could sense his caution against potential eavesdroppers.

"You only saw it for a split second." Grandma was clearly annoyed.

"It was a silver web," Dad insisted. "Spun with the finest silk of uni-spiders from the Grimmian Forest. Do you think I wouldn't recognize it?"

There was a warning in Dad's tone, as if Grandma *ought to* know exactly what he was talking about.

When she remained silent, Dad muttered, "My subconscious must've somehow sensed that she was in trouble and sent me to the Shadow World when I teleported."

"Well, she's got luck on her side then." A rustling of clothing suggested Grandma was getting up. "That's something, at least."

I cleared my throat and started to open my eyes. Judging from the chandeliers overhead, it looked like I was lying on the dance floor at Grandma's ball, away from the Shadow World. I knew I'd had real physical contact with the dance floor, and was no longer merely existing between planes, because the white marble floor was cold and hard against the back of my head.

My achy head. In fact, every bone in my body hurt.

"I already know you're awake, Megan." Grandma said as she pressed a finger to my temple. "Now go back to sleep. I'll have you delivered back to your little human home while your father answers to the Council."

"But why should Dad..."

That was as much as I could get in before I sank back into oblivion, as per my grandmother's command.

"Kill the wabbit! Kill the wabbit! Kill the wabbit!"

The sound of Elmer Fudd singing to the tune of Wagner's "Ride of the Valkyries" filled my bedroom. I moaned. The alarm clock had seemed fun and whimsical at the time of purchase, but after the night I had, it just added to the pounding of my head.

I sandwiched my head between the pillows. Maybe if I stayed in bed, I wouldn't have to remember the nightmare that was Shadow World.

"Get up, Megan." Enid teleported a few feet from the side of my bed and snapped her fingers. My pillow disappeared and my head hit the firm mattress with a thud. Ouch. It wouldn't have hurt at all if my head hadn't gone through that fall last night. Sighing, I sat up on the bed, my eyes slightly unfocused.

"Why? What's going on?" I asked, squinting at my mentor. There was a slight alarm in her voice, just beneath the surface. I vaguely remembered being carried home by her. Maybe. I couldn't be one hundred percent sure. I was pretty drugged up on Grandma's compulsion. Judging from the first light coming through the curtain though, I couldn't have been in bed for more than a few hours.

"Your father has given his statement to the Council. Now it's your turn."

I swallowed. "My turn?"

"You're due at the Council's Court in twenty minutes."

Enid referred to her watch of captured faery vapor, a swirl of dense eternal mist, which shaped and reshaped in order to depict the time across an assortment of major planes.

"What?" I jumped out of bed and went into the communal bathroom I shared with Rosemary. I was relieved when all was quiet in the hallway. From the bathroom mirror, a girl in a torn-up ball gown stared back at me with dark circles under her eyes. Her large hair bun was mostly undone, with a few surviving bobby pins clinging on for dear life. The jeweled hair comb was long gone. My face had taken on the greyish hue of faded glamour left behind by the Blue Unicorn. I looked like hell, and not in a good way. I closed my eyes and willed myself not to think about how close I was to *going* to hell. I scrubbed my face hard and did the best I could to smooth out my hair.

I went back to my room and started fumbling through a large pile of clothes lying on top of my suitcases. I changed into dark jeans and a blue top. It was the closest thing I had to courtroom wardrobe.

I didn't know how I managed it, but in less than ten minutes I was ready to go. All without the help of magic.

Enid touched my arm and halted my teleporting attempt. "Before we go, I want you to understand what you're up against."

"Look, I didn't even know about my half-brothers' plan, and my dad knew even less than me." I protested.

Enid's face softened. "Megan, you have to see this from their prospective. In the Council's eyes, you led your trickster kin to the ball, and they got exactly what they wanted at our expense."

"Oh, come on, they're just a bunch of jokers wanting a

bit of street cred." I was mad at them, and I'd deal with that later. But to be fair, tricksters would always be tricksters. And deep down, I knew that my fun-loving, irresponsible, annoying half-brothers would lay down their lives for me, if it came to that. Folks of trickery were stubbornly loyal in that way, despite their reputation. So I had a bit of a soft spot for them.

"And *street cred*—" Enid said the two words in disgust, "—they've got."

She tapped her watch, and the ever-changing faery clouds in it projected a motion picture outward, much like a human 3-D laser display device. Wait, was that a video of Santa Claus slipping on the ballroom floor, knocking people over like they were bowling pins?

"One of your reckless family members had a camera strapped onto his body and it filmed the entire fiasco. The video received over five billion hits on the DemonTube across all planes within the first hour," Enid sighed.

I winced. Oh, crap. The DemonTube was popular amongst witches, fae, and other demons. Tricksters weren't the only ones who thought that vengeance demons had a stick up their collective butts, so I could see how the ballroom fiasco could go viral. The sight of the grand Aequitas mansion being trashed by tricksters would be a guilty pleasure even for some less socially advantaged vengeance demons.

I, of all people, knew how important dignity and image were to the Concord Council. They'd see the chaos as a humiliating loss of control, and having such embarrassment being multiplied by five billion times...wow, this was much worse than I originally thought.

And no, they weren't holding the tricksters responsible.

To them, tricksters were uncivilized savages anyway. They were holding me and my dad, members of their own kind, accountable. Great.

Enid cut off the video just as Cousin Fred banged the union rep of the migraine fairies on the forehead and sent the tiny fae flying across the room. "Now that you're aware of this, let us hurry."

She and I teleported right into the courtroom of the Concord Council five minutes before my scheduled hearing.

The court was located just off the campus of the University of Demonic Studies. I did mention that the Concord Council and the Board of Governors at my school were one and the same, right? In other words, a single organization controlled every step of my career, and its prejudice toward me carried over year after year. Talk about having the chess pieces set against me.

Despite the sunny day just outside the window, the court itself was quite dark due to its espresso wooden...well, everything from its paneled walls down to the court gavel.

When we arrived, the courtroom was already full. There was my dad in the public seating at the back, his eyes cautioning me to watch my temper, and the entire Council lined up along the right side of the wall. Most members I knew by reputation, but I had never dealt with them in a direct manner. Enid was generally the go-between.

Not today.

The court was in session. There was a girl at the defense table with her back to me, without the presence of counsel, her head downcast and shoulders slumped. It looked like this was part of an earlier, unrelated proceeding. *Whew, so I'm not late.* I breathed out in relief.

Edbert Llewellyn Advocatus, FCVD, the Fellowship Chartered Vengeance Demon and high judge who headed the Concord Council, droned on, "...we found the result of your first solo practice session unsatisfactory. The target hardly suffered at all. He's a child molester, and you only managed to get him fired from his camp counselor job."

"I'm sorry," the accused mumbled. "I panicked. It won't ever happen again, sir."

"That's 'It won't ever happened again, *your honor*.'"

"Yes, your honor," the accused echoed in a low, meek voice.

A child molester? When had something like that ever been a freshmen gig? First years dealt with cheaters and petty criminals, and seniors dealt with negligence and progressively violent wrongdoings. But in general, a vengeance demon wouldn't tackle gross cases like child molestation until he or she was close to being designated. Of course the accused screwed up the project—she'd been set up to fail.

I realized who the accused must be. It was Serafina, the high judge's very own niece. When we hung out, she didn't talk about her home life, and I left it be. But it didn't take a genius to figure out that it was hard joining an old family of high achievers after a lifetime away. In the high judge's bid to appear impartial in dealing with kinfolk, she hadn't even been provided with a proper counsel. Asshole. No wonder the lively girl I saw last night was now all but gone, her spirit deflated and her eyes downcast.

"You'll do another two practice sessions. Every failed one will result in double the work, so on and so forth."

The high judge sounded the end of the session with a bang of his gavel. As Serafina headed for the exit of the courtroom, she saw me and flushed. Couldn't blame her for being embarrassed. I nodded slightly to convey my support. She smiled back, her face strained, and left.

Guess I was next.

Enid led me to the same table Serafina had been sitting at just moments ago. I supposed Enid was serving as my defense counsel or something, assuming I was actually on trial.

Who was I kidding? Of course I was.

Grandma Aequitas entered the courtroom and seated herself on the left side of the wall, opposite the regular Council members. Her face was regal and expressionless. She wouldn't even look in my direction.

Things had gotten a little heated the last time we'd met, hadn't they? Damn, it all seemed like a very bad dream.

High Judge Advocatus called the court to order. "Now, to the real matter we're gathered here today to discuss, and the reason that brought us out of our beds last night. Miss Aequitas, this council has tolerated your unfortunate origin, your less-than-stellar disciplinary record, and numerous complaints from your classmates. Instead of gratitude, you brought shame to not only your own house, but also our entire race. We've been more than generous. What have you got to say for yourself?"

Yeah, they were being real generous. If I were a full vengeance demon, I wouldn't be here right now. Esme, for one, wasn't.

I stood and looked to Enid. She nodded encouragingly. I cleared my throat. "Your honor, I didn't have anything to do with what my half-brothers did. I went to the ball so I could talk to my grandmother, that's all."

High Judge Advocatus looked to Grandma Aequitas, and

she said tonelessly, "She did come to me with a ridiculous request, but I have no way of knowing if that was the true reason she was at the ball."

Thanks for vouching for me, Grandma. The woman could sure hold a grudge. She saw the state I was in just hours ago, right? Couldn't she cut me some slack?

High Judge Advocatus appeared curious. "And what was this request?"

"She had the gall to ask me for extra magic." Grandma's lips curled back into a snarl. "I turned the too bold girl down, and she left. Next thing I knew, her trickster brothers were bringing down the house."

Oh, I sure sounded guilty when she put it that way. Really guilty. The rest of the Council seemed to think the same way, as they whispered amongst themselves and nodded to each other. Total sheep mentality.

Demonic, powerful, grown-up sheep.

High Judge Advocatus turned back to me. "And what were you asking the additional magic for? To sell it like a common trickster thief?"

My hands fisted at my sides. Yeah, as if he didn't know why I needed the boost. He just wanted to give me enough rope to hang myself. "I needed the magic to finish my co-op assignment, your honor," I answered.

"You require help to complete your first assignment? But it was just a simple one with an elderly human—"

"My target is not helpless. He tried to kill me. With magic."

The high judge glared at me. He was not used to being cut off. "There's no evidence to suggest that Dan Pillar has any knowledge of supernatural nature."

"Then the record is outdated."

High Judge Advocatus's nose flared. "There's no evidence to suggest that our record is outdated." Shoot me, the high judge was a living, walking bureaucrat. And he wasn't done. "So as I was saying before I was so rudely interrupted, your first assignment is a simple one with a human of advanced age, and you failed to complete it. You didn't inform us of your failure in a prompt manner. Instead, you went behind us and sought to increase your magic to fix the matter yourself. Did I get that right? Miss Aequitas, are you sure you're suitable for this program?"

By the end of his little speech, Judge Jerkface had dropped all pretenses of neutrality and practically gloated at me.

I'm no more unsuitable for this program than your own niece, your honor.

I bit my tongue on that one as well. Even I could see this was the perfect storm. The Council had had it in for me since birth. Given my sins as listed by the high judge, my half-brothers' troublemaking was just the icing on the cake.

Never mind that I was innocent, never mind that Dan Pillar was a special case, and never mind that I almost lost my life in the Shadow World.

Judge Bias continued, not expecting an answer from me. "I now call a second witness, Miss Madeleine Abrianna Lex."

My heart sank. Madeleine walked into the courtroom in a pink lacy full skirt, one of those that looked like it was layered over a heavy petticoat. She looked more like a Gothic Lolita than a vengeance demon. The choice of clothes was such a far departure from her usual fanfare that I couldn't help but notice, despite my present dilemma.

"Your honor," Madeleine bowed. "I heard Megan

threaten Frederick Maximilian Aequitas just before disaster struck. She has to be in league with the trickster criminals."

I groaned, not just because of the negative testimony, but also because I told my dad she was a friend. And now he'd know that I'd lied to him.

"What did she say?"

"She said, *I'll foam you at the mouth*. And the next thing we knew, poor Frederick had a broken nose and banged up head for his trouble. Megan had to be involved. This is all her doing."

"Thank you, Miss Lex. You may sit."

Madeleine's face reddened. "I'd rather not, sir."

"It's alright, you can sit. I'm allowing it." The high judge encouraged.

"I mean, I *can't*." She smoothed down the back of her full skirt, and for the first time I noticed something uneven poking out. The pig's tail. She still had it. She was wearing what she was wearing for practical reasons. Just like last night, it would've been funny if it were any other time.

The high judge turned to me and scowled. "The Council will now vote on a verdict. Your senses will be muted as we discuss this matter."

As I stayed rooted to my spot, in a semi-aware trance to prevent me from eavesdropping, I was left with nothing to do in my mental fog but to confront the two opposing emotions swelling up deep within me.

Hope and anger.

Hope that the Council would see past their own wounded pride and prejudice and give me a fair ruling.

Anger that they'd put me through this whole drama to begin with.

After five minutes, but what felt like an hour, High

Judge Advocatus released me from my mental prison and addressed me. "We, the Concord Council, hold you responsible for what happened last night at the Aequitas ball. You are found guilty, and by extension, your father as well."

Wait a second, I thought Dad was only here to give a statement. I had no idea he was on trial as well. Dammit, the last thing I wanted was to drag him into my mess.

"For Nicolas Bartholomew Aequitas the second, the arch vengeance demon." High Judge Advocatus went on and named a minor fine Dad could easily afford.

Plus a grueling punishment ordered out of pure spite— three months of being on call for the most crappy work assignments in remote planes. Mom was not going to be happy. Actually, chances were she was going to sneak off and join him. Human wives went shopping while accompanying their men on business trips; my mamma went mischief hunting instead. Nobody did a disguise better than her, and she knew enough not to blow my dad's cover or to be detected by the Council's spies.

So maybe not too bad in Dad's case, then.

"As for you, Megan." High Judge Advocatus didn't even bother to use my full vengeance demon name, which was not a good sign. "You're suspended. From both the co-op program and the university until further notice."

I struggled to breathe as hot blood boiled through my body, threatening a lifetime of disciplined training. Suspension? Seriously? I'd smash their heads together and show them *suspension*...

Calm down. There was no use getting angry. Try convincing them with logic.

"What about Dan Pillar? He's getting away."

"The target is no longer your concern. You're off the case."

EIGHT

ENID ESCORTED ME TO MY rented room in the human dimension. Once she left, I flopped back onto my bed in sheer mental exhaustion. To be suspended over something that was out of my control...the unfairness of the situation made me punch the mattress, earning me a hiss from Sassy as she jumped off the bed.

What was I thinking, trying to approach Grandma for magic? None of this would've happened if I hadn't gone to that damn ball.

Never mind the ball. Why the heck did I bother fighting for a place in this blasted vengeance world, when its very governing body had had it out for me from day one? There was no winning with that crowd.

Maybe I should just give up.

As soon as that thought entered my head, I bounced right out of bed. Feeling sorry for myself and admitting defeat was not an option. I'd worked too hard for that. There had to be a way out of my current dilemma. I just had to figure it out.

I quickly identified two goals I could set my sights on: rejoining the co-op program and figuring out who my attackers were in the Shadow World. I supposed some would say I wasn't getting my priorities straight if I didn't put investigating the threat to my personal safety above all else, but the idea of someone trying to hurt me, or even kill me, was so hard to wrap my head around that I needed something a little more tangible to start with.

The first trio of monks had said they'd got the wrong girl, but the second group said nothing at all, and they were the ones who got right down to business. Was I the true target? Who knew?

There was the third goal of bringing Dan to justice, but that was off the table until I could achieve goal number one. But I will get him, I vowed.

I forced myself to scrub my face in the bathroom, then changed into a T-shirt and faded jeans. With one leg inside the jeans and the other out, I stumbled on a running shoe lying on its side and landed face first on the floor.

I caught sight of the pocket-sized vengeance training manual at my eye level. During the unpacking, it must've fallen under the bed. Suddenly, it occurred to me that I'd only ever read the sections on practical vengeance procedures and skipped over the opening chapters on the university's general policies.

What if there was something there I could use?

I grabbed the training manual and sat back on my bed. I flipped to the thick chapter called Co-operative Policies & Guidelines and started reading.

Alright, let's see. The selection into the co-op program was solely at the discretion of the Concord Council, blah blah blah, and so was the decision to suspend one from said program. There was a whole section on the suspension itself, from just cause to proper documentation of the procedures.

I squinted at the very last sentence of the entire

segment. There, in the smallest font possible, was a superscript that read *189.2.3A-V.*

I looked up the footnote at the back of the manual, then I left a message asking Enid to come and meet me at her convenience.

After that, there was nothing to be done except head downstairs and start my day. Enid would come when she came. And when she did, I'd sense it no matter what room in the house I was in, as long she allowed me to do so.

First order of business: breakfast. Then...well, I had no idea, but I wouldn't be moping in my room anymore.

I sniffed the air. Was that the smell of fresh-baked goods?

I followed my nose to the common kitchen and found Rosemary humming over a tray of steaming buttery croissants with her back to me.

"Hey," I said awkwardly. I'd been here a few days now, but I'd pretty much been an absentee roommate, despite the verbal agreement that I'd be picking up some slack around the place.

Rosemary had no idea I was busy doing vengeance, avoiding getting hurt, surviving a pointless ball, then called to trial, more often than not in another dimension. From my poor roommate's perspective, I'd either stayed in my room for a long period, out for a long period, or come home looking rather worse for wear. On top of that, I'd been eating a lot of her food. Heck, I even brought a friend along to mooch on my very first night here. What would Rosemary think of me?

I decided right there to pick up some responsibilities, starting this second. It was the just thing to do.

Besides, I wanted to get to know her. What was the

point of living amongst humans if I didn't take the opportunity to understand them outside of vengeance? There had to be more to human-demon conversation than "ugh, get away from me, you monster!"

Rosemary didn't seem to have heard my greeting, so I repeated myself, much louder this time.

She jumped and put a hand to her heart. "Oh my God, Megan! I didn't hear you."

I repressed a wince over the use of the G word and shrugged, pretending that my supernatural ability to be as noiseless as a mouse was no big deal. "I have really quiet feet."

"I must be losing it." Rosemary shook her head, put a croissant on a plate and handed it to me. I accepted with gratitude. I'd have to wait another few minutes before putting the hot baked goods in my mouth, but boy, I could enjoy the divine smell. "Last night I swear I heard someone break in, but turned out it was just my imagination."

"Oh?" I said nonchalantly. I had a feeling it wasn't just her imagination, so I added a little push of compulsion into my single word.

She obliged with more information. "After I got into bed, I heard a loud crash downstairs. I ran down. But there was no one here. And the windows all seemed fine. I guess I've gotten jumpy, living in this neighborhood. But to be fair, it's gotten a lot better in the last little while. I should thank my guardian angel."

As if on cue, Sassy the feline shade roamed in and without ceremony sat down on the kitchen floor, put one leg over her shoulder, and started licking her fur. I narrowed my eyes. Sassy's tummy was getting quite round. She'd been eating well. A soul devourer with an appetite for bad guys—the more violent the tastier—she was the perfect familiar to a vengeance demon.

And the best invisible guardian for my fragile human roommate. I'd asked Sassy to look out for Rosemary the first night I moved in. Rosemary would never know about it, but *I* knew and that was enough.

Rosemary seemed nice, and not the type who'd release incubus bush babies onto my bed.

I realized Rosemary was looking at me expectantly. Oh right, I should be making a comment on her observation about the neighborhood crime rate. It wasn't like the human could read my feelings on the subject. "Yeah, sure, a good neighborhood is good news."

I groaned inwardly. Did I just use the word "good" twice in one sentence? I blurted before Rosemary could bounce the reply ball back to my court, "Sorry about my sister yesterday. She isn't very good in social settings."

Well, apparently I wasn't, either.

Was an apology too strong for "small talk"? This whole human-interaction thing was harder than I thought.

Rosemary shook her head. "Don't worry about it. She was just concerned about you."

"Thanks for understanding." *Whew.*

"No prob."

Another stretch of silence. Now what? Wait, humans liked talking about their daily endeavors. Those online articles were always advising men to ask about their wives' days. The same trick should work for roommates, right? "So, Rosemary, what are you doing today?"

Rosemary smiled. "You can just call me Rosie. I told you that already."

Yes, she did. And I wouldn't. In the vengeance demon

world, it was considered very rude to shorten another's name. Even though Rosemary wasn't a demon, a lifetime of habit died hard.

I repeated the question minus the name. "So, what are you doing today?"

"Getting some more baking done, then I'm off to the shelter."

"The shelter?" The only shelter on the human plane I knew of was the bus shelter.

"The animal shelter," Rosemary clarified.

Was that like a bus shelter for animals? Did animals take a separate bus than their respective owners here? Maybe an animal shelter was where husbands went when they got sent to the doghouse? This was really confusing.

I decided to draw attention away from my ignorance by firing another question. "What do you do there, at this animal shelter?"

Rosemary's eyes shone. She was generally a high-energy kind of girl, but this pushed her enthusiasm to a whole new level. She pointed at two cookie sheets on the side I hadn't noticed before. On them was unbaked dough cut out in the shape of tiny dog bones. "You see, I run a side business making gourmet dog biscuits. I give back by offering free treats to our four-legged friends in the pound."

I thought of that sanctuary for golden lost-soul retrievers. "I'll come with you," I volunteered.

"You sure?" Rosemary looked surprised but pleased.

"Yeah." At the very least, I could help her carry the cookies. That way I'd make up for the last few days. I had no idea what kind of regular contribution she needed around the house, but right here in front of me was an opportunity to help with a cause she was into. I could also get to know her along the way.

Most important of all, by keeping busy, I wouldn't get obsessed over the traumatic events of last night, and the things I planned on saying to Enid.

"How many more batches are you doing?" I eyed the bag of flour on the table and the clean bowls she was putting out. I'd never played with cookie dough before. We could bond over food, a shared passion. Well, she was passionate about cooking it, and I was passionate about eating it, but surely it counted.

"A couple more. They're popular."

"Can I help?"

"Sure. Finish the croissant first, though. Don't let it get cold."

She didn't have to worry about that. I wolfed it down in two seconds.

"Er." Rosemary leaned over the mixing bowl with a horrified look on her face. "What is that supposed to be?"

"The dog biscuit mix." I was assigned the task of combining the ingredients for a new batch while she rolled out the already prepared dough and cut it into little dog bone shapes.

"I don't think I'd be able to roll that out. Why is it so runny?" Rosemary frowned, pushing my slushy dog biscuit mix around with a spatula. The clumpy parts of flour and egg whites stayed together, and the watery parts ran through them like spring rain over a muddy country road.

"I might've added some extra water," I confessed.

Rosemary's eyes widened. "How much more?"

"Two cups. Otherwise, the biscuits are going to be so

hard." I kept thinking about how every cookie I'd ever tasted was so moist, so there had to be more water. So I added more. It seemed like a good idea at the time.

"They're dog biscuits. They're *supposed* to be hard."

"Oh."

Rosemary squinted. "And why is the mix so dark in color?"

I brightened and puffed my chest up in pride. "I added chocolate."

It was a brilliant touch, if I must say so myself. I saw the dark chocolate chunks in the kitchen cupboard and just couldn't resist. I hoped the dogs loved chocolate as much as I did.

My roommate paled. "Chocolate is deadly to dogs. In fact, one of the dogs in the shelter had kidney failure after eating chocolate. This could've done him in."

Deadly? How was I supposed to know that? The golden retrievers in my world were used to having evil souls for breakfast. A little chocolate wouldn't have been an issue at all.

"Sorry," I said sheepishly.

"Megan, you're supposed to perfect a recipe before altering it." Rosemary looked like she wasn't sure if she should laugh or cry. Or both. "And you should be cracking the eggs, and using a mixer to avoid flavor bombs."

What was a mixer? The only mixer I knew of was the Soul-Mixer, the eternal ritual of mixing a soul with a new personality right before reincarnation, so that every lifetime had its own distinctive flavor. I doubted that was the flavor Rosemary was talking about, though. Damn— everything I'd learned about humans, I'd learned from academic books, TV, and movies, and none of those sources had gone into the logistics of real, everyday mortal lives.

"Let me try again," I offered, flipping over the notes I'd taken from her earlier. "Wait, after you crack the eggs, where do the shells go?"

Just then the doorbell rang, and Rosemary pushed herself off the counter she was leaning on just a little too fast. "Let me go and get that—" She began to turn, then froze. Like, actually motionless on the spot, her eyes staring, unseeing.

"Enid." I nodded as my mentor materialized near the breakfast bar. I knew what had happened. My mentor had made the doorbell ring to capture Rosemary's attention, then temporary froze her to have a private conversation with me.

"Megan." Enid sighed. "Look, I know you're upset, but I have to deal with the fallout from last night. I don't have the time to—"

"Did you know?" I asked her, pulling the training manual out of my pocket.

"Know what?"

"This." I flipped to the page I'd bookmarked and read from it, "'The suspension may be lifted if the student is able to obtain ten freelance markers.'"

If Enid was surprised that I'd been able to dig up that obscure little rule, she didn't show it. "Yes, I'm aware of that stipulation."

"Then why didn't you tell me? You know what this would mean to me."

"It's not something we advertise." Her tone hardened. "Performing freelance vengeance is hard and dangerous work. I didn't want to give you false hope."

"Shouldn't I decide whether or not it is a false hope?"

"There are protocols—"

"This trumps protocols." I waved the training manual for emphasis.

Enid tightened her jaws and said nothing. I got the feeling this was as close as she was going to get to admitting defeat, which meant the Council would be forced to accept the said freelance markers as academically legitimate.

I wondered what battle I'd just won, and if it was more trouble than it was worth. For all I knew, freelance could be way out of my league, given my failure with Dan. But I had to try, right? Just about anything was better than inactivity.

"Now, tell me how it works." I grinned at my skeptical mentor, grabbed the recipe notebook from the counter, and proceeded to write down the procedure for freelance vengeance, right below the instructions on how to make the world's best dog biscuits.

NINE

A FEW SECONDS AFTER ENID left, Rosemary came out of her magic induced brain-freeze. As far as she was concerned, she'd just heard a doorbell and was on her way to investigate.

I waved her off. "I'll get it."

On my way out of the kitchen, I reached for my second croissant of the day from the batch Rosemary had made earlier and finished it before I reached the foyer. Hey, cooking and plotting my way back to co-op was hard work, you know. I had to reward myself.

I didn't actually expect anybody to be at the door, of course. So I was the one who was startled when the doorbell rang again. Had Enid returned to provide more information on the whole freelancing business? Was it Esme, coming to check on me? No, I felt no magical disturbance from behind the closed door. Whoever was standing on the other side was human.

I opened the door, and there stood a guy in his mid-twenties with olive skin and large glasses.

"Can I help you?"

"Is Rosemary here?"

"Jordan!" Rosemary came rushing out of the kitchen and beamed at the newcomer, wiping her hands on her apron self-consciously.

"Hey, Rose." Jordan's attention was so focused on my roommate, I might as well have not even been there. "I thought I could give you a ride with all those dog biscuits."

"You shouldn't have come," she protested. "I'm fine rolling it along in my shopping cart."

This must be what humans meant when they described saying one thing but meaning another. Despite Rosemary's verbal objections, she seemed rather delighted by Jordan's presence.

I cleared my throat.

Rosemary turned to me, as if suddenly remembering I was there. She blushed. "Jordan, this is my roommate, Megan. Megan, this is Jordan, our volunteer leader from the shelter."

With everything Enid had told me about vengeance freelancing, I almost forgot I'd promised Rosemary I'd help out at the shelter. As much as I itched to start on the freelancing ASAP, a promise was a promise. After I paid my debt to Rosemary, I'd search out pockets of untended injustices and create my own assignments.

The next hour was spent doing more baking and packing. Well, Rosemary was baking, but Jordan and I were only allowed to pack.

"Don't worry about it." Jordan winked at me. "I had a little accident in her kitchen too. So I'm as banned as you are."

I laughed. Nice to know that even humans could screw these things up.

Together we transferred the cooled dog biscuits into plastic containers and stacked them up in the trunk of Jordan's beat-up car. But there was only so much of that we could do, so we ended up talking quite a bit while we waited around in the kitchen.

That must be what "hanging out" was all about. Since I'd gotten neither prank nor insults from my fellow hangee yet, I'd say it was so far so good.

"So if you don't bake cookies, what do you do for the shelter other than organize volunteers?" I teased Jordan.

Jordan's expression became guarded. Not wary, per se, but closed off, like he wasn't sure how much he should tell me.

Rosemary looked up from her cookie trays, saw his face and sighed. "Jordan's got one of the toughest jobs in the shelter."

"What is that?"

"Helping the vets with the new arrivals," Jordan said.

"Some of the animals show up in really bad shape. From neglect and abuse," Rosemary explained. "Hypothermia, malnutrition, broken bones...you name it."

I gaped at the two humans in horror. "People don't get caught over this?"

"Some do. But even in cases when we know who the culprit is, most of the time they get away with a slap on the wrist."

"What?" I was outraged, and yet the vengeance demon in me sensed opportunity like a shark smelling blood.

Jordan fisted his hands. "The arcane animal laws haven't been updated since the horse and buggy days, and they don't always protect the animals. Truth is, most of the time they don't. I've seen some nasty stuff I wish I could unsee. Animals come in all banged up, get patched up by us then sent straight back to the bastards who did it to them."

There, in that instant, I realized I'd be killing two birds

with one stone by going to the shelter. Injustices were closer to home than I thought.

When it came down to it, vengeance freelancing was pretty much the same as any co-op assignment, procedure-wise. The difference lay in the very first step, which is the procurement of the job itself. In a co-op program, students relied on their mentors to select their targets for them. A freelancer created his or her own jobs by seeking out kinks within the Concord, resolving the injustice stuck in the entanglement, and releasing the pent-up negative energies from the victims in the process. Those dispensed energies, stemming from helpless anger and frustration, were the vengeance markers that the training manual was talking about.

I needed ten of them to get back in the game.

The Council probably thought I wouldn't be sensitive enough to the Concord to detect its entanglements. If so, they'd underestimated me. While I might be lacking in full vengeance instincts, I planned to make up for it with resourcefulness and relentless hard work, plus a healthy lack of disdain for the mortal's own sense of right and wrong. They weren't all selfish and cruel. The very existence of the shelter proved that.

Why bother hunting for clogs in a system when I could go straight to the sources? If humans had set up a shelter for these animals, surely they also kept records of cases where justice hadn't been served. Every abused animal had an abuser, and every abuser deserved someone like me.

The abuser would get his or her comeuppance, the animals would get to be free of them, and I would get my vengeance markers. Everybody would win. Well, not the abusers, but who cared about them? And oh, did I mention there was a monetary reward to freelancing, just like the co-op assignments but at a better rate? That meant rent money. *Cha-ching!*

Plus, the sooner I got out of suspension, the sooner I could figure out who was trying to hurt me in the Shadow World. And if this was a true case of mistaken identity, then who was the intended target? There might be some way to do investigating on that front, but I'd have to enlist my half-brothers' help...

Stick with the rent payments, Megan. Focus on that for now.

When we arrived at the shelter, I was assigned to the understaffed and overcrowded grooming room. Once there, I was handed a brush, a trimming kit, five cats, four dogs, and a rabbit.

Three hours later, I was blow-drying a black Scottish terrier when a shadow came over me.

"I heard you've got quite the magic touch with the animals," Jordan mused.

I snorted, and then sneezed at the flying fur. Magic touch indeed. Even the meanest and barkiest stayed perfectly still while I clipped and brushed them. No wonder. Unlike humans, those little buggers had the instincts to know exactly what I was. "It's nothing."

"Is there anything you need?"

"I could go for a cup of coffee. In your office."

I added compulsion behind my words. Through the groom-room chitchat in the last few hours, I'd learned that Jordan kept records of all the new arrivals in his office. Sounded like a good place to start.

"Sure," Jordan said woodenly. I got up and followed him

as he led me through a few corridors, then opened the door to a tiny office with paperwork covering every inch of space. There was a small desk, a chair, four large file cabinets, plus boxes with files crammed to the top.

Now where should I start? I doubted there was any sort of filing logic to the mess. I looked into Jordan's eyes and remembered the Sherlock Holmes story of how he tricked Irene Adler, *The Woman*, into revealing the location of her most prized possession. "Alright, where are your files on the animal abusers?"

Jordan went to the upper drawer of the second file cabinet and took out two envelopes, both label-less.

"Leave," I instructed. "And forget that you took me here." With him gone, I sat on the chair and spilled the contents of the first envelope on the table.

There were pencil sketches of various animals, plants, and landscapes. Must be a hobby of Jordan's. And to be honest, they were pretty good, though useless for my purpose. I was just about to put them away when I caught sight of a portrait.

Of Rosemary. In her apron, holding a tray of dog biscuits with a smile on her face.

Huh, could Jordan have a crush on my roommate? Something to think about. Later.

I opened the second, much thicker, envelope. The first items to fall out were a couple of lottery tickets. Another false lead? But the rest of the envelope proved a lot more promising. Looked like Jordan kept the names of every asshole who'd ever sent an injured animal his way, from mild negligence to the really nasty stuff. There were pictures of the worst of the beaten animals, case notes, and best of all, a printout of an excel spreadsheet summarizing the cases, with the addresses of the offenders to boot.

Then the last item, a sheet of lyrics for a song called "If I Had a Million Dollars."

Lottery tickets, a spreadsheet of bad deeds, now these lyrics...could it be that Jordan had vengeance fantasies of his own? The If-I-Had-the-Money-to-Hire-Someone-These-Were-the-Assholes-Who'd-Get-It fantasies?

Deep down, I'd always hoped that living amongst humans would help my control issues. Since humans had no magic whatsoever, I figured it wouldn't even cross their minds to be tempted by it. Looked like I was wrong. In a sense, the lottery was the human way of seeking quick and easy solutions, wasn't it? The ability for magic might not be there, but the desire for it turned out to be pretty universal.

So was the desire for justice.

I took out my cell phone and snapped pictures of the spreadsheet.

From that afternoon on, I picked names off the list at random and with each abuser punished, made the human world a slightly better place. I'd first considered ranking the spreadsheet rows by order of the severity of the abuses but had decided that reading the entire list in one sitting would be far too depressing.

When I came across straightforward ones that wouldn't earn me much in terms of markers anyway, I sent them to Serafina so she could have some practice off the books. She needed it. The work they gave her was far too complex. It was like asking a beginner pianist to play Chopin.

Within three months, I had performed four vengeances in a wide range of technical difficulties, from sticking a careless owner who left her puppy in a sweltering car with a large parking ticket, to arranging for a dog poisoner to be mauled by coyotes.

I even filtered the spreadsheet with a new column, courtesy of a vengeance spell called the Six Degrees of Separation. It told me if any of the names on the list could be tied back to Dan Pillar, and lo and behold, it found one connection. The woman who got the parking ticket due to the overheated puppy? She was the mistress of Dan's lawyer. The parking ticket might seem like a small thing, but the car was paid for by the lawyer. One thing led to another and eventually the wife found out about the affair. She did a Lorena Bobbitt on her husband, and last I heard he was still recovering from his reattachment surgery. It'd be a while before he handled Dan's business again.

I might not be able to touch Dan, but there was no rule preventing me from getting at those who flanked him. Sounded like fair game to me.

The four vengeances tallied up to around three markers in total. I wish it was a simple 'one vengeance equals one marker' system, but it wasn't. Oh well.

A balanced range of successes in my freelance venture, big and small, made Enid at first very surprised, then very pleased. She didn't ask where I got my ideas, and I didn't tell. Things had gotten so good, I even started thinking about improving my efficiency by mishmashing various vengeances together, animal-related or otherwise, and getting more bang for the same buck. For example, causing a drunk driver to smash into a dog fighting ring owner, and the pile-up in turn prevented a bank embezzler from crossing the border in time. It'd take some precise calculation, but with my newfound confidence I felt like I could do anything.

These vengeance combos brought my number up to nine markers. Only one more to go.

Everything was looking up, thanks to one little spreadsheet. With the monetary rewards of credits well earned, I'd more than enough converted human dollars to cover the rent payments for the rest of the co-op term, and then some.

Little did I know, it was my final case that would prove to be a nightmare.

TEN

FOR MY FINAL FREELANCING CASE, I didn't choose it randomly. I picked a low-medium skill level job on the spreadsheet. My goal was to be unsuspended as fast as I could, and as long as the last assignment topped up to ten markers, that was all I needed. I wanted to save my energy for the other forms of trouble that might come my way in the future.

The assignment had led me to a puppy miller with a track record of providing pet stores with sick and malnourished animals. Unsuspecting pet owners purchased these animals and ended up with huge vet bills in hopes of getting them healthy again, or worse, had to watch their new pet die soon after welcoming it into their homes and hearts. The puppy mill was just small-time enough to avoid scrutiny, but through the years, it'd sent dozens of distressed pet owners to the shelter seeking medical and legal advice. Jordan was able to direct them to the right professionals for the former, but the latter often became a sad lesson in buyer beware.

The puppy mill wasn't in some old, abandoned farmhouse in the middle of nowhere like one would expect. It was in a busy building at the heart of the Annex, a vibrant Toronto neighborhood with a healthy mix of musicians, artists, and students.

I sat casually on the stone ridge lining the flowerbed in front of the rental building. I didn't bother to glamour up my age with faery dust, because my real one suited the purpose of this mission just fine. Also, I was cheap.

A thin man with a baseball cap and greyish skin rounded the corner, carrying the leashes to—let's count it—seven Chihuahuas, five bearded collies and two Shih Tzus. Though they all seemed puppyish, there was a particularly randy one that couldn't seem to help but try to mount every single thing in sight. It was funny but kinda disturbing.

In stark contrast to the very adorable furry animals was their not-so-nice handler. There was a mean look to this guy I didn't like, though I got the feeling he was perfectly capable of being charming when he wanted something from somebody.

Like supplying puppies to legitimate-looking pet stores.

"Oh, how cuuuute!" I crooned, bending down on one knee and letting myself become surrounded by a sea of fur balls. There was yapping and licking galore. And, oh no, was that randy one trying to hump my leg? I made a mental note to throw the jeans I was wearing into the washer and continued to sound bright and cheerful. "They're gorgeous! Are they all yours?"

Thin Man looked me up and down speculatively as I paid special attention to one of the bearded collies. My guess was he was judging if I had the desire and the means to buy pedigreed dogs, yet was not socially conscious enough to care where they came from. I'd dressed myself in Rosemary's best clothes. Her mother was a fashion designer who never let go of her hope of converting Rosemary, and Rosemary never stopped being content with just the plain white chef's uniform. She offered me access to her wardrobe, which was sweet on so many levels. It was almost as if we were sisters, if I could have a non-demonic, human sister who could bake like an angel.

I was wearing a top that had outrageous patterns and holes in at least five different awkward areas. It was guaranteed to be hip for only one season. Add a pair of four-hundred-dollar jeans, and I looked like I could be a rich little girl with money to blow on purebred babies. The fact that the said jeans were made using child labor suggested I was the type who wouldn't mind buying from a puppy miller, either.

The guy's next words confirmed he'd made just that assumption. "You like that collie there, sweetheart? You can have it for four hundred bucks."

My eyes widened in interest. "Really? That's a lot cheaper than the pet stores."

"Yep, in a store they're going for anywhere from eight to twelve hundred." Thin Man thumped his own chest, not caring that his motion yanked the poor dogs clear off the ground. I repressed the urge to hiss. "You get it from me, you cut out the middle man."

I pouted. "I love the dog, but I don't have the money *on* me."

Thin Man smiled the smile of someone who'd just hooked a fish. He tilted his head towards the lobby of the building. "I'm at three-twelve. Come when you get the cash, hon."

"What's your name?"

"You can call me Curt."

"Alright, see you later, Curt."

He allowed me one more moment with the bearded

collie before pulling at the leashes and taking all the puppies with him, including Mr. Humpy.

Apartment three-twelve it was.

I returned that evening with a teaspoon of faery dust and a dozen poop bags. The faery dust, custom formulated to induce a severe, lifelong allergy to furs, was for Curt, the puppy mill runner. The poop bags were for the dogs as I ushered them to safety.

Apartment three-twelve was at the far end of the building, at an angle away from the constantly occupied elevator area. Perfect.

I picked at the front door lock. Damn, it was much harder than the way they showed it in those human YouTube videos. I dared not use magic, as I wasn't what one would call full in the tank. The freelance gig was paying, but with rent, food, mobile phone expenses and all, I had to watch my magical spending. The faery dust had been bought on credit as it was. Mr. Sparrow, the owner of Unnaturally Yours, a local alchemy shop, had been friends with my father for decades and knew I was good for it. But still, magic saved was magic earned.

On the fifth try, I got it.

"Uh-ah, you're not getting this one." A voice said from behind me.

I turned, and there was Madeleine Abrianna Lex, her arms folded over her chest.

"Hello, Maddie."

"Don't call me that." She snarled, "So the rumors are true. The little half-breed is trying to earn freelance markers."

"Not *trying*, already *got* most of them under my belt." I grinned.

"Then you wouldn't mind if I take this one." She elbowed me out of the way. "I could do with some extra allowance. Why should you get all the credits? I became a laughingstock after the ball, thanks to you."

"Hey, back off." I rubbed my ribs. "I harvested this work fair and square. I have the right to this vengeance."

"And who's going to be your witness? Are they going to trust a daughter of Lex or a trickster?"

Madeleine grabbed onto the doorknob, turned it, and was suddenly flung against the opposite wall of the hallway. She winked out of this plane before she even slid to the floor.

Wow, I guess the *other* rumors were true, there were indeed invisible faeries who regulated vengeance rights. There really was a faery for everything.

Quiet as a mouse, I opened the door and found Curt sprawled on the sofa in front of the still-on television. He was sound asleep, six empty beer bottles scattered around the living room floor, waiting to trip anyone not paying attention to where he or she was going.

To be on the safe side, I chanted a temporary Multiplier spell to raise the intensity of his inebriation as if he'd taken in eighteen beers instead of six. In other words, he was dead to the world.

I did mention I'd packed ropes with me, right? Thanks to some rather bizarre online videos on full-body Japanese rope art, I managed to tie Curt up nice and neat. His chest seemed less secured than it should be, according to the video, as the ropes couldn't exactly crisscross over a cleavage he didn't have. But overall, I thought I did a pretty good job.

With the potential threat secured, I went searching for the puppies.

And found them sleeping in crowded, filthy crates stacked up against the balcony side wall. There were two metal crates in each row and four in each column, which meant a total of eight cases of young puppies exposed in the open without even a single blanket in sight. My upper lip pulled back from my teeth, and I almost couldn't stop myself from snarling. Poor animals, it did get windy and chilly at night, even in the summer.

Then at the bottom of the stack I found a crate that broke my demonic heart.

A mother dog was nursing five puppies, her eyes vacant of hope. But when she saw me, she lifted her head and growled at me. The warning was clear—touch her pups, and I'd get it. I had to respect that kind of grit, even though I was the bad guy in her eyes.

And could I really blame her hostility? How did it feel, to be forced to become pregnant over and over again? To have one litter after another, bond with them, only to see them taken away every single time? That must suck.

I gave the mother dog what I hoped was a reassuring look, then I opened one of the top crates and took down a large bowl of murky water with a thick layer of dog hair on it.

I went into the living room and dumped the water over Curt's head. He woke with a start, the effect of the Multiplier spell long gone.

"Curt, or whatever the hell your real name is, it is time to pay for your sins. Please note that the vengeance to be exacted tonight is specific to your role in this puppy mill operation. It does not absolve your guilt in other acts you might've committed, towards animals and otherwise. May you endure your Vengeance with grace and contemplation."

"What the f—" Curt struggled against the ropes in vain. They always struggled during this part. Nobody liked to take their punishment lying down, no matter how much they knew they deserved it deep down.

"Oh, and I'm taking the dogs with me." I added, dropping my formal tone.

"I'm going to kill you, you little bitch!"

"Oh, I'm so scared."

I gave Curt his Belinda rights, then with great care sprinkled him with the faery dust. Almost immediately his eyes started watering and he sneezed. Hello, severe allergy to cat, dogs, and every other furry animal in the world. Safe to say his career in the puppy mill business was over.

I jumped out of the trajectory of his very gooey sneeze. "What vengeance I do tonight, I do out of my own free will and as a nominally charged service to the human community on this plane, paid for by the Concord Council."

With the punishment properly dished out, all the animals' suffering and pet owners' heartbreak caused by the puppy mill through the years, which Curt had been carrying around in his soul, were ready to let him go. See, vengeance was in a way as good for the punisher as it was for the punishee. That was why every now and then a vengeance demon would come across a target who had enough conscience and self-awareness to recognize his or her own guilt, and wanted the vengeance done and over with.

I took out a small flask and directed the negative

energies into it. It was just enough to fill up the single marker bottle. I closed the flask, slid it into my front pocket and patted it. That'd pretty much wrap up the vengeance.

I went up to Curt's back and loosened the rope so he could climb his way out of the complicated knots. Eventually. There would be plenty of time for me to get the dogs and be on my way.

"Those dogs were going to get me a good price. Screw you to hell!" Curt spat.

You know the kind of target I mentioned earlier, who felt bad about what he or she had done? Curt wasn't one of them. Not by far.

Then I saw the empty beer bottles on the floor, took another look at Curt's swollen-shut eyes, and got an idea. With the tip of my toe I pushed the bottles into a rolling position, directly in his path.

I wouldn't call that a display of my trickery side. Just being a little creative with my vengeance, that was all.

Something was wrong. I felt it the minute I stepped onto the balcony.

I approached the crates with caution. At least the dogs inside were all accounted for. But they looked at me through the little metal doors quietly, their ears perked up in alarm, as if they too could sense that something was amiss.

I looked around me. Streetlamps bathed the small rectangular space in a dark shade of yellow. The sound of city traffic was at an ambient level this time of night. A car honked, followed by someone's curses. Inside the dark apartment, rope rustled as a sneezing Curt struggled to pull free. Nothing *seemed* off, but the hair on the back of my neck stood at attention.

I closed my eyes and sent my senses out. There was an almost negligible energy signature here. *Almost negligible* because it was at a consistent but low level, much like the city traffic noise being dismissed by the conscious mind. But now that I'd honed in on it, I could tell that it was expertly masking something a lot stronger.

The essence of a full-fledged vengeance demon.

Was it Enid, observing my progress? Or someone a lot less cordial, maybe Madeleine finding another way into the apartment or sending Cousin Fred in her place? Spying on a demon during vengeance was considered a major social faux pas, but such rules wouldn't apply to Enid. Fred and Madeleine wouldn't care about that in their bids to get back at me.

Humming in pretended casualness, I proceeded to take care of the post-vengeance cleanup. Professional vengeance practitioners like my dad could call in a cleanup team, but such were not available for a student, not to mention a suspended one.

So it was a very natural move when I conjured a broomstick and started sweeping the area of any trace of supernatural vibes.

Except that as I started sweeping, I silently activated a Revealing spell on the broomstick. This handy little spell had been a must-have growing up with my trickster half-brothers. Each time the broomstick hit the ground, the signature of the vengeance demon grew stronger and stronger. The moment I pinpointed the location of my invisible visitor by the entrance back to the living room, I pointed my broomstick in that direction and yelled, "Show yourself!"

A tall figure was leaning against the entrance in a relaxed posture. Upon my calling, it straightened and came towards me, moving into the streetlamp light, revealing itself to be a guy in his mid-twenties.

A *really hot* guy. Chiseled cheekbones, long untamed brown hair, and broad shoulders. He was dressed all in black, as prepared for a vengeance night out as I was. Power radiated from him, infusing the room with a steady heat like an ember, yet leaving no question that it was ready to leap up and turn into a ferocious inferno at a moment's notice. He had the deliberate movements and lean physical build of someone from the older families. Bold in nature too, if his uncamouflaged, wide-spanned, midnight blue wings were anything to go by. My breath caught at the raw male beauty of this stranger.

Stop drooling, I chastised myself. The guy's very presence here was downright suspicious.

I'd never seen this vengeance demon before, but a vengeance demon he most definitely was. There was no mistaking that bitter Earl Grey aftertaste that was in his power signature. I took a deep breath and rolled it around on my tongue. Underneath the over-steeped tea, there was an undertone of sandalwood and sage. Another indication of an old bloodline. Respectable and proud.

Yet there was a hard edge to this man's jaw and a defiant look in his eyes that made him different from anybody I'd met. There was something ragged and refined about him all at the same time. I had a feeling he wasn't quite as old as he appeared. He might even be my age.

The mysterious guy didn't seem upset at being found out by me. Instead, he gave me a lazy grin, softening the edge of his jaw but not quite erasing the menace it promised. My heart beat faster of its own accord. The damn traitor. "Took you long enough to figure it out."

"Who the hell are you?" I demanded. Unadulterated lust notwithstanding, I had a job to do and he was in my way.

"I'm Pete." He gave me a mocking bow, the type so perfectly executed that, had it been done without the attitude, it would have been perfect for greeting a Council member at a high society ball.

"Pete..." I let the name become a question.

"Just Pete. At your service, m'lady." His courteous words so contradicted his sarcastic tone that I couldn't help but give a snort. It was unladylike, but it was alright. He was far from a gentleman. A civilized gentleman would conceal his wings on a first meeting with strangers, female or otherwise. It was basic etiquette.

"Pete." I repeated, and raised my eyebrow pointedly at his healthy, glossy blue-hued wings. This vengeance demon was no more a *Pete* than my Sassy was a common household tabby. Odd—vengeance demons in general took great pride in introducing themselves in their full ancestral glory. Why would this guy tricksterize his own name?

I shrugged. Whatever his deal was, it wasn't my business. The fact that he was in my business was. Gotta chop-chop. Curt would make his way out of his bondage soon. "Alright, *Pete*. What the hell are you doing here?" On *my* vengeance territory.

Pete seemed to get the unspoken part loud and clear. It was there in his eyes. "Being nice, of course."

"Nice?" I blinked. That wasn't the answer I'd been expecting.

"Yeah, nice. Considering I have the right to this

vengeance. But here I am, letting you have all the fun." He curled his thick and sensual lips into a smile, but there was no real humor in it.

"What the hell are you talking about?"

"Not just *a* right, I have the *first* right. My client sent me."

"Your...oh."

Suddenly, his hiding in the shadow, his single-syllable fake name, his very ability to be here, it all made sense.

Mercenary.

I knew I'd been going around acting like working for the Concord Council was the only way of life, but the truth was, for a small segment of the population, it wasn't.

Most vengeance demons went to college, or not. Graduated from college, or not. But one way or the other, they all served the Council in some capacity, from the highest-ranking arch demons to the poor saps who scrubbed up after them, or processed their travel expenses, or deducted their payroll taxes. There was, however, a type of vengeance demon nobody ever talked about. The ones who went rogue, who hired their talents out for profit, without caring whether or not the target truly deserved it. Stories of their ghastly exploits had been whispered about since the beginning of commerce, which was almost right after the beginning of time.

Mercenary was a shameful profession, a last resort. How had a guy from an older family sunk this low?

"What do you want?" I tried to keep my voice calm. I'd never dealt with mercenaries before. In fact, they didn't teach us much about them in school except to tell us not to join them. But if I was to guess, by virtue of being for profit, it meant they had to have a business side to them. I had to speak to that side because the murdering nutjob side might be a little harder to get through to. Judging by the pure and strong energy this guy exuded, I wasn't one hundred percent confident in besting him in a fight.

Okay, make that not confident at all.

The guy gestured to the flask in my front pocket that had captured the essence of the injustice addressed. "You can keep that."

I nodded cautiously. It made sense. It wasn't like he cared about the kinks in the Concord, nor would the said kinks fetch him a good price if the Council was the only customer willing to pay for it. "Alright. So what do *you* get?"

He threw back his head and laughed. "You're practical. I like that. Most Rullies I speak to would still be in the outrageously protesting stage."

"Like you said, I'm practical." I gritted my teeth. "You can read my signature as much as I can read yours."

What he didn't know was that I'd been observing every weakness he might have, looking for every opportunity to come out on top.

But something he said made me stop, and I couldn't help but ask, "Rullies?"

"You know, sticklers for rules." He swept his gaze over me in disdain and mimicked. "*May you endure your Vengeance with grace and contemplation.* Yeah, like anyone's going to feel very gracious about getting theirs. Now back to my share. I'll let you keep your precious little bottle, and you get the official marker, but I'm taking one of the puppies. A female."

"A puppy? What do you want it for? And why a female?" No way was I going to let him take one of the animals. A low growl from the mother dog confirmed she felt the same way. "And you're not *letting* me keep anything. I did all the work myself."

"That's not how it works, hon. My client had prior claim to Curt, and she and I have a contract."

I understood now. "So you're taking the puppy as proof that you've done your job, and you collect your fee. Except it isn't your job. It's mine."

It was his turn to shrug. "As the humans say, tomayto, tomahto."

"Even if you promise to give the puppy back after showing it to your client, it won't do. Why would I trust you? You're a mercenary, hel-*lo*?"

"I don't intend to give it back." Pete admitted.

"Oh." That was honest in a too creepy way.

I had to call for help. But how did I reach for my cell without looking too suspicious? How did I distract someone who had the street sense to suspect I might be trying to distract him?

I was just weighing my options—stalling, charming, dirty fighting, and a combination of all of the above—when an overweight woman in a shapeless, yellow polka dot dress barged into the apartment through the unlocked door. She looked around frantically, spotted Pete, and ran towards him with the surprising speed of a quarterback in offense mode.

"Pete!" she yelled.

I almost thought she wasn't going to stop on time. That she'd go over the balcony, taking my current pain in the butt with her. I should've known I wouldn't be so lucky.

She stopped dead in her tracks, merely inches from Pete's face and struggled to catch her breath. "Is...it...done? Did you...do...it?"

"Sandra." Pete had his arms out to steady the woman who I suspected was his client, though as a sign of comfort or self-preservation, I didn't know which. "We talked about you waiting in the car."

"But...I *was* in the car." Sandra wiped large beads of sweats from her forehead, and I was happy to see that some of the droplets landed on Pete's pristine black top. He winced. "Then I felt this...peace. Like I was letting all this anger and hurt go. So I figured you must've done your job."

I cleared my throat. "Er, ma'am. That would be *my* job."

But Sandra wasn't paying me any attention at all. Her gaze fell onto the mother dog and her eyes filled. She cried, "Honey Bun-bun!"

The mother dog responded with a joyful bark and jumped in its effort to greet the human female. It would've succeeded if not for the crate.

"Honey Bun-bun?" I shook my head as Sandra crouched down on her knees to the level of the bottom crate and took a dog treat out of her pocket.

"When the mother dog was a pup, it was Sandra's," Pete explained. "Before Curt, her ex, stole it. He took off and opened a puppy mill. This lady had first right of vengeance, since she was the puppy mill's first true victim."

"That's why you wanted to take one of the puppies. An eye for an eye..."

"And a pup for a pup. It's only fair."

I looked at Sandra, who cried as she tenderly stroked the chin of the mother dog, cooing sweet nothings. It was plain that to her, it hadn't been about revenge. It had always been about getting her baby back.

I had two choices. I could try to fight my way out of this. But I wasn't sure if I could win, and the animals would definitely lose. Pete could always grab a pup and run off, and newborns needed their mom to survive. Even if by some miracle I could call Enid or Esme to the rescue, the ensuing legal limbo would tie up everything in the vengeance court for years to come. Years on top of what Sandra had already lost.

That took me to choice number two.

I couldn't believe I was actually going to do this. I sat down, crossed my legs next to Sandra, and touched her shoulder. "If I grant you guardianship of this dog, will you promise to take care of it?" I heard Pete snort, turned to him, and snapped. "Yes, *I'm* granting the guardianship, because *I'm* the legal vengeance demon in this case, first right or no first right."

His mouth twisted. "Touché."

I turned back to Sandra. "Well?"

She sniffed. "Yes."

"And will you do the same for the puppies?"

"Of course. I'll take care of them." Sandra bobbed her head up and down in earnest.

I got up slowly, my eyes never leaving Pete's. There were a few things I wanted to make clear. "This changes nothing about how I feel about your amoral operation."

"Of course." He had the sense not to smirk in the face of victory.

"The next time we meet, I won't be so nice."

And it was the truth. Sandra might've provided an easy and elegant solution for the problem at hand, but had she been obnoxious and cruel, I would've fought Pete to keep the animals away from her, destined to lose or not. Besides, there was a chance that I could win, as I had a few tricks up my sleeve that might just surprise him.

He must've read my intentions on my face. Instead of platitudes, he said in a soft voice, his expression serious, "I have no doubt."

It would've been easier if his attitude had been outright mockery. But no, he sounded...alright. And long after he left with Sandra and the animals, I could still hear his words. He was nowhere near my ear when he whispered them, but I swore I felt his lips brush against my earlobe. It made me blush and want to curl my toes. Or punch something. It was a trick, surely. And if so, then he was more of a trickster than me.

Asshole.

ELEVEN

WITH MY LAST FREELANCING CASE in the bag—and the fate of the animals purposefully left unmentioned on the official records—I turned my attention back to the whole figuring-out-who-was-trying-to-hurt-me-in-the-Shadow-World business. The Council had yet to pass a verdict about my suspension, and until that happened, I couldn't touch Dan Pillar. But since his weapon of choice seemed to be connected to the second trio of monks, investigation into the latter might be a roundabout way of getting to him anyway. First I'd weakened his support system in the form of his injured lawyer, now I got ready to dive into the mystery of his borrowed power. I knew that if I just kept chipping away at this Dan project, I would crack it one of these days.

Yet how did I investigate when I had almost nothing to go on? Sure, I knew that the second trio of monks, the one threatening me for real, had the ability to infiltrate Grandma's ball, cross into the Shadow World, and use some sort of magical web my dad seemed very weirded out about. But I wasn't even exactly sure if I was their intended victim, and I was reluctant to approach either Grandma or Dad unless I absolutely had to. The mention of my near brush with death would remind my dad to hide me in the family cellar until I turned ninety, and Grandma didn't believe my story anyway.

Since the night of the ball, I'd been careful. Well, as careful as one could be without knowing what to be careful about. I'd put safeguards on when I crossed dimensions to anchor me through my passage, I tried not to go anywhere alone unless it was on vengeance business, and I packed dad's Hellhound-grade pepper spray wherever I went. While I slept, Sassy stood guard. Getting past a shade was unheard of, so I wasn't worried.

The morning after I wrapped up all the paperwork on the puppy mill case, I was sitting at the breakfast table, pondering how to go about my investigation when Rosemary gave me an idea.

"...but the taste is just not the same." Rosemary shook her head as she slid a perfectly made sunny side up egg onto my plate.

I got out of my own head and held up my hand. "What was the thing you said before this?"

"Oh, about cleaning the cast iron pan?"

"No, after that."

"What, the knock-offs? I was saying how there are a lot of frying pans out there claiming to be one-hundred-percent cast iron, but it's not, and food just doesn't taste the same... Where are you going, Megan?"

I skidded to a stop by the kitchen door, ran back, and sucked down the egg in one swallow. "I just remembered I have to be somewhere. Gotta go."

The knock-offs. Why didn't I think of it sooner? I did have a bit more to go on with the first trio of monks, and they might know more about the guys I was looking for. Remembering the sorry prop of a plastic talon-like hand

and the silly bickering amongst its owners, I'd bet that the incompetent goofballs were a lot louder than the ones with real power. They'd be showier and a lot less careful about keeping their mouths shut.

In other words, a lot easier to find. I knew just the guy who had his finger on the pulse.

I called Mom and Dad's house. Fir answered on the second ring.

"Hi, how can I trick you today?" He offered the standard trickster greeting, which meant he hadn't looked at the call display before picking up the phone.

"Fir," I began.

"Hey, Megan," he said warily.

Since that fateful night at the ball, my half-brothers had been sending me gifts and calling to apologize. I ignored their calls, though I did accept the gifts. Their remorse at getting me into trouble was genuine, though given the chance, they'd do it all over again. In a way, I understood why they did what they did. To tell a trickster to miss a grand opportunity to misbehave would be like asking a scorpion not to sting. Part of me was even happy for them. Their notoriety at the ball was the ultimate game-changer, and even now the public's enthusiasm towards them hadn't cooled. They were interviewed on TV just last night. There were even talks of a reality show, but Dad shut it down from whatever backwater plane he was working.

Maybe the rest of the supernatural population simply enjoyed the hell out of seeing the arrogant vengeance demons being brought down a peg or two. I'd leave it to the scholars to debate the implications of that sentiment. For now, I needed Fir for a matter of a different nature. "Hey, do you know a tacky trio of supernaturals, maybe some sort of elves, medium height, with not a lot of direct magic in them? One of them can resist compulsion and open portals without spells, though."

There was a pause, then Fir said, "Huh?"

I repeated the list of criteria. "They're whiny, not too smart, and oh, the leader has a pointy chin and goes by the name of Bonaventure the Third. One sidekick is called Wistari."

Fir snorted, relaxed now that it seemed I wasn't going to make his ears ring for days with lectures on why he shouldn't try to kill my career to launch his. I might do it later, but not now. "You should've begun with those names, little sister."

"Well? Do you know these guys?" I demanded.

"It so happens I do." Fir was sounding smug now. Never a good thing in a trickster. Time to deflate his sense of strengthening position a bit before it got out of hand.

"Ahem, Fir, I heard about that little film option talk you're having behind Dad's back." That was the advantage of having a total of four trickster siblings. I could always count on at least one of them to be unable to keep his mouth shut.

"Damn."

According to Fir, the guys I sought could be found right on the human plane, in a trendy downtown Toronto nightclub called the Bureaucracy. It was apparently a mixed hot spot for both human college students and supernaturals on shore leave. Why anyone would name a nightclub Bureaucracy was beyond me. Maybe what sounded utterly boring had bounced right back to being super cool. Or something like that.

I was going to go there in my full combat gear with a dark, skin-tight bodysuit and an entire arsenal of faery dust and spell-breaking daggers hidden flat against my body. Turned out there was no need, as tonight was Paint Party night, which meant a lot of black light and glow-in-the-dark body paints, or in some supernatural creatures' cases, taking off the glamour that camouflaged their natural coloring. In a sea of glow sticks, neon shirts, painted body parts, and strawberry poison frog dryads, dressing in black from head to toe would make me stick out like a sore thumb.

So once again I raided Rosemary's wardrobe and picked out the most outrageously colorful outfit her fashion-obsessed mother had left behind: a halter top the color of turquoise, like a tropical bird in a postcard. While my back was exposed, the front was sewn with multiple layers of fabric that gave the illusion of being loosely draped all over my body, perfect for hiding all my weapons. I also taped a spell-countering charm right over my chest. I would've put it in my bra, except my outfit didn't allow for one.

And that was how I found myself at eleven forty-five in the evening, wearing something that was ironically both revealing and concealing at the same time, in front of an establishment with a huge lineup of patrons that would, to a human, appear more like a gathering of sci-fi convention enthusiasts. There was a group of Gothic Lolitas who were genuine Westside Witches, an Incredible Hulk who was a dwarf giant, and a couple of Klingons who were really the off-duty henchmen of Ares, the god of war. Hey, even the stuff of nightmares needed a party break and to get splashed with water-based paint every now and then. Who was I to judge? The humans who frequented the club, according to my half-brother, would've been beguiled by a perception filter not to notice the fact that they were surrounded by the creatures all the bedtime stories had warned them about.

I did a quick mental count of the lineup. There were over two dozen people along the sidewalk. Three if you counted the pack of pixies making up the meat-suit of a tall man in a trench coat. I had to get in before midnight; otherwise I'd have to pay an entrance fee.

As I approached the bouncers, a couple of buxom brunettes—succubus if I wasn't mistaken—cut into my vision from the left side and got there before me. They did that super mini-skirts, five-inch heels, and flirty giggle thing, and the bouncers smiled and let them in straight away. Holding the imagery of those girls in my head, I spun a Mirage spell over myself and followed suit. The bouncers let me in without batting an eye.

The Mirage was a trickery spell and went against my self-imposed mandate of keeping things vengeance unless I was in a grave situation. But it wasn't like I was on assignment, and I was here because I *had been* in a grave situation and could be again.

The nightclub was in a three-story complex, with a large dance floor on the main level that was open to the floors above. There was a sea of bodies rubbing against each other, with people on the higher floors leaning over the railing to check them out and squirt them with paint and who knew what else. The floor was sticky with semi-dried paint. People's faces were identified by the smudges on them rather than actual eyes and noses. Overhead, a giant neon-bright demon-butterfly soared to a higher railing, no doubt seen by the humans in attendance as nothing but a mechanical novelty. They probably thought the same of the mermaids in a tank on each side.

I moved my body to the rhythm of some kind of dance remix of Katy Perry, Rihanna, and Anthemusa, the reigning queen of the siren plane. My moves were average enough to be forgettable, and I stayed in obscurity at the edge of the dance floor, marking all the exits and back doors as I shook my head to the sides in supposed abandonment. I tried to stay away from the paint splashes, though often not successfully.

I danced for about ten minutes, making my way to the bar in the least conspicuous manner possible.

"Hey, can I get a Blue Unicorn?" I shouted over the heavy down beats to the bartender, a centaur with his lower body hidden behind the raised bar.

"Sure." He poured me the drink. I tried not to wince when he told me the price and drank up my purchase.

"So." I waited until he was free again a few minutes later, and leaned over casually. "I'm looking for Bonaventure the Third."

He stopped wiping the empty glasses and narrowed his eyes. "Who's asking?"

Crap. According to Fir, this place was a front for yin-to-yang energy laundering and counterfeit ritual artifacts. Who did I know who wasn't entirely on the up and up? Well, I *could* give the names of everyone on the trickster side of my extended family, but until I knew what I was heading into, it was best to leave them out of it.

The bartender looked at me expectantly; his eyebrow rose.

"Pete, of vengeance," I blurted out. I had no idea why the

mercenary's name came to my mind. It must be because he was a rogue vengeance demon and the closest thing I had to a shady character. It couldn't be because I'd been thinking about that arrogant ass at all. Nope, not me, I hadn't been fantasizing about stroking those broad shoulders, or his lips tracing patterns on my earlobe... Definitely not. I already had loads of problems keeping my inner trickster in check. I didn't need someone to bring out the naughtiness in me.

"You know Pete? You work for him?" The bartender sounded disbelieving, though a little impressed. I guess Pete was the mercenary's professional name, after all. Or maybe there was another supernatural around whose name was Pete, a bingo-loving trickster for all I knew. The former seemed like the type the bartender would offer some intel to. The latter didn't.

Time to do some more bluffing. Remembering Pete's bold and un-camouflaged wings, I stretched and arched my back, allowing my wings to unfold. It wasn't much, just an embarrassing grey winkled mess. But with a little help from the Blue Unicorn and a Fake It 'Til You Make It spell, it had the width of almost the entire bar in the bartender's eyes.

"Wow." He jumped back, awe in his voice. "I thought Pete'd gone solo a while back."

I filed that tidbit of information away for future use. "He owes me a favor." And it was true, when it came down to it. The bastard owed me the use of his name for getting those dogs to his client. "Now, about finding Mr. Bonaventure the Third."

I concentrated on the task at hand, refusing to give another moment's thought to Pete, or whatever his real name was. The attraction to him was potent, but all physical attraction could be controlled and managed with a little vengeance zen-ness. And if I found out this was the doing of some crackpot lust fairy, I'd crush her tiny yellow wings myself.

I looked up from the dance floor. For every floor, there was only one staircase to move upward. I hoped there were more staircases going down or the whole place would be a death trap in a fire. Each staircase was guarded by a set of bouncers, each pair more menacing than the last. According to the bartender, the boys I was looking for were on the top floor.

I danced again, this time taking note of who was going up the stairs. There seemed to be two very distinct types: the beautiful and the shady. It made sense. The beautiful were for the dancers on the main floor to aspire to. The shady were the ones whose business the nightclub really made profit from.

I approached the first staircase, and with the help of another Fake It 'Til You Make It spell, got through. Then repeated it to get to the third floor.

With magic, courtesy of the nightclub's management, the loud music was brought down to a fraction of the real volume on the third floor landing. While the entire second floor was one single space full of party animals, this level was subdivided into various sections by drywall, leaving just a small open area by the railing. The dancers on this floor were merely window dressing. The real draw was what was behind the walls.

I opened the door to the first room on the left and was greeted with the ruckus of bargaining, gambling, and wrestling. Each business, if it could be called that, was set up on a small table, except for the wrestling matches, which had tents at all four corners of the room. Some caterpillar spirits must be selling Wonderland-strength hookah, as a thick ring of smoke hung overhead, making me cough and my eyes water. The large room was lit by yellow fluorescent light bulbs, a sharp contrast to the glow-in-the-dark circus downstairs. I rolled the taste of the room around on my tongue, trusting that over anything I saw with my eyes. I detected everything from the earthy scent of woodland nymphs, to the metallic taste of the weapon-forging goblins, and everything in between. They seemed vibrant and happy, respectability be damned.

In the center of the room, surrounded by a bunch of eager-looking minor supernaturals, was the trio of "monks" I was looking for. Gone were the dark robes they'd donned in the Shadow World. Medium height, rugged-looking with hearty bellies, their clothes were colorful and trimmed with gold threads. In fact, they seemed to have put gold on their body at every opportunity. Gold earrings, gold necklaces, gold watches, gold rings...though it looked like most of it was fake.

I stood by my earlier assessment that they were some kind of elves. But I'd asked Fir about one of the sidekick's ability to resist compulsion and open portals through sheer will, and he had no idea what species that could be.

As the trio made their way through their bustling little kingdom, I stalked toward them. But my path was blocked by someone I'd never expected to find here.

"Madeleine Abrianna Lex." I breathed.

For the first time ever, Madeleine looked like she wished I'd tricksterized her name. She looked around furtively, squeezing the brown paper bag she held tight against her body. That, of course, only made me yank it out of her hands all the harder.

"Give it back!" She hissed.

For a split second before I opened the paper bag, I wondered if I was making a mistake. What if she'd purchased some weird cross-species porno I'd never be able to un-see? They always say the most respectable types are into the craziest things.

There was nothing in the bag but dozens of leeches, clawing over each other and yawning with their tooth-filled mouths. I almost dropped the bag.

Then I realized the particular type of leeches I was looking at.

Monk Leeches, the nicotine patch of choice for sex addicts. It absorbed a person's sexual energy to keep their libido under control.

I advanced toward Madeleine, clutching the bag, and at the same time tracking the three losers' progress through the crowd with my peripheral vision. The boys were still making their rounds, shaking hands and exchanging pleasantries with those around them. They weren't going anywhere for a while. I turned my attention back to Madeleine.

"What do you need a nympho detox for? Are you that slutty?" People in general tend to buy stuff that would enhance their sexual prowess and attractiveness. These Monk Leeches would banish lust more effectively than any cold shower. They were extremely dangerous to handle. If they were on a person for too long, his or her thirst for life itself would be gone, let alone their desire for the horizontal tango. Strange. Madeleine didn't strike me as the sort who needed it. She'd always seemed as cold and as uptight as any other vengeance demon I knew.

"I said, give it back." She stepped on my toes with her heel, and took the brown paper bag back while I was distracted by the pain.

But not distracted enough not to feel the pulsing of the leeches as they took in a tiny fraction of her power, then settled down, content. That was strange. While the Monk Leeches could take sexual energies from just about every kind of supernatural, there was a little ritual that had to take place before the exchange could happen. Unless it was a transfer between brethren. Then it could happen in close proximity even without physical contact.

Monk Leeches were a distant cousin of nymphs.

My, my, Miss I-Look-Down-On-Half-Breeds got a bit of nymph blood in her. That was never in any Lex family history I'd ever heard of. So she stayed cold and uptight *because* she'd been getting help clearing up her nympho magic.

"Don't say a word," she begged. "I'll do anything. Help with your school work, help you get popular—"

"What are we in, an off-Broadway production of *Wicked*? What's *Wicked*, your blank face asks. Never mind. Listen, get outta here. I'll think about what else I need and get back to you."

She beat feet out of there, the paper bag crumpled under her white knuckles. Good, I didn't want her here when I approached my three targets.

They were clearly respected, or at the very least, feared. That was evidenced by the way people either moved out of their way, tried to shake their hands, or in some bold females' cases, brushed against them with their breasts.

The three seemed very much in their element, and much more confident than when I'd last seen them. I started toward them, but was once again delayed, this time by an impromptu rally.

"Hail the seers!" one of their followers shouted.

"Hail!" everyone cheered. Even the wrestlers took the time to pump their fists in the air before pounding on each other again.

"Hail the foretold chaos at the vengeance ball!"

"Hail!"

"Hail the bet winnings!"

"Hail!"

Foretold, my butt. Chances were these three guys came across my half-brothers while trying to sneak into Grandma's ball themselves, and then told their followers before the news broke. I'd heard of supernaturals who'd make book on the failure of social events such as Grandma's ball. It must've been a nice little payout for everyone who'd received the tip.

"Thank you, my friends." Bonaventure the Third put his arms around the waist of a succubus, who was at least seven inches taller than him, which he didn't mind as he rubbed his cheek against her green-skinned shoulder. "We're honored by your continuous patronage here at the Monster Market. Prediction of the Week will begin shortly. Meanwhile, please make yourself at home, and eat, shop, and be merry with our many wonderful vendors. You know what they say, come for the Sight, stay for the goods!"

"Don't forget about the wrestling. A new match every ten minutes!" Wistari, formerly known as Sidekick Number One, put both thumbs up.

"And the best love potions on this plane and the next!"

Sidekick Number Two tried to lean into the succubus, and she hissed at him, causing everyone to laugh.

As people got down to the business of browsing, women in sexy retro cigarette girl costumes showed up, offering to sell drinks, faery dust, and one kind of counterfeit goods or another. There were even some stolen items, if a hex bag I saw with an anti-theft ink tag attached was any indication.

Time to make my presence known.

"Ahem." I pushed past the herd of supernaturals and stopped a few feet before the so-called seers, a hand on my hip.

The three losers' smug faces turned ashen when they saw me, their eyes as wide as saucers. While they froze in shock, I projected the mental image of the fake hand their way, daring them to remember me. Some supernaturals were better at picking up actual images than others. Based on the way the three guys jumped collectively, I'd say that they were just that type.

They exchanged panicked glances with each other. Bonaventure the Third gestured towards my direction with a "go get her" command to his sidekicks, while they spread their hands in front of them in the universal body language of "don't look at me." They knew I could take them in a fair fight. It was there in their eyes as they darted around for the closest exit, their chests, puffed-up just moments ago, deflated.

The people around noticed the change and looked at the three questioningly. The leader recovered first. He said in a loud voice, "Oh, there's our private appointment."

I nodded. If they were willing to chat with me in private, then so be it. Less eavesdropping was always better.

"This way, sweetie."

I allowed the endearment to stand as they gestured me to follow them to one of the backrooms. I even allowed Wistari to grip my elbow, hurrying me away from their entourage and earning me dirty looks from their female fans along the way. There would be plenty of time to make them pay later. They owe me a lot of answers.

As we were almost at the door, I said conversationally, "So, you guys are the seers. I know there's a line of elves with oracle skill, but I wouldn't take you for that type."

Wistari hissed. "Of course we have the Sight. We're not frauds."

Then Sidekick Number Two ruined it by saying, "we're way better than that elephant that predicts the human World Cup."

"You know that's not saying much, right?"

Bonaventure the Third walked into the backroom. I followed, with his sidekicks bringing up the rear. I looked around the room cautiously. It resembled any small office in the human world, or any other world. A small IKEA-inspired desk, a chair, a laptop, and a black file cabinet. There was nothing that spelled trap here, nothing that felt enchanted, yet the hairs on the back of my neck rose.

Bonaventure the Third gestured for me to sit on the single chair available, and I shook my head. He shrugged.

"Enough with the polite-yet-seedy-underworld-boss crap." I held up a hand. "Who are you?"

"We're the Off-Blacks." In unison, like in a bad human movie, they all bowed deeply and smoothed out their robes with a dramatic flair. They stared at me expectantly, as if waiting for me to recognize that name, to be shocked and impressed.

"The who?" I'd never heard of them, in or out of school.

Whatever their little group was, it couldn't be that important if their weak magical signatures were any indication. And yet, I couldn't seem to shake my sense of unease. "Listen, you tell me about those other monks in the Shadow World, or I swear I'm going to hang your feet over the Lake of Sulfur."

"Who wants to know, and why?" Bonaventure the Third demanded.

"It's a long story. Just answer the damn question."

"Not until you answer mine."

This is so B-rated movie. I took a deep breath. "Alright. I tracked you down because I need to find the other monks. I'm looking for the other monks because number one, they tried to kill me, or hurt me. I'm not sure which. Number two, they did so with weapons similar to the one *someone else* used when he tried to kill me in his senior residence earlier on the same day. No doubt about the murderous intent on that occasion. So I need you guys to play nice and tell me everything you know about the other monks, because I'm starting to lose track of whom I'm going after and why."

As I ranted the boys backed away from me. I stepped forward, gearing up my power.

"So, *spill.*" I stopped moving when they hit the wall. But something wasn't right, because their expression turned from terrified to triumphant the moment I paused in front of them. I sent out my senses to ferret out any traps. Still nothing.

Bonaventure the Third smirked at me. "Darling, you're thinking like a supernatural. But above all we're businessmen, in a business that creates a lot of unhappy customers. We know how to get rid of them."

Before I could ask him to clarify that statement, the square of floor I was standing on gave way, and I fell through.

And fell. And fell. I tumbled down a metal slide with sharp curves at every turn. I frantically tried to claw at anything that would stop the downward motion, but the surface was too smooth for any traction. I screamed, the sound snatched away by the air rushing over my face before it could reach my ears. After what felt like an eternity, the slide leveled out, and I rolled out of the side of the Bureaucracy building.

And face-first onto the grimy concrete of the alleyway.

"Owww," I moaned; my entire body felt like it was on fire with all the bruises starting to form on it. With shaking hands, I pulled out a small tube of healing faery dust I'd saved for emergencies and carefully sprinkled them over my most banged-up body parts. The rest would have to heal on their own.

I'd been on the lookout for supernatural sneakiness from those boys. Who would've thought I'd be foiled by a mechanical trapdoor instead?

As I picked myself up and started making my way to the front of the nightclub, I realized that the ride down the building might not have been as non-magical as I thought.

I couldn't get back to the club.

Oh, I could leave the alleyway, alright. I could step onto the main street. I could hear the heavy beat of the nightclub's music. I could feel the pulse of so many sentient minds crowded into a finite amount of space. And yet the nightclub wasn't on the street. Nor was the telltale long lineup of people eager to get in. It just...wasn't there anymore. Not for me anyway. There was number 264

Richmond Street West, and there was number 268 Richmond Street West, but the Bureaucracy, which should've been sandwiched between them, simply wasn't there anymore.

After going 'round and 'round the block for the eighth time, and attracting suspicious looks from a mounted police officer on standby, I was finally forced to accept the fact that the nightclub was now magically concealed from me. I could wander around there 'til dawn, and it wouldn't have made a difference. The bouncers, as I remembered, took turns getting a smoke on the edge of the pavement. But as they were part of the establishment I couldn't even follow my nose to the source of the second-hand smoke, though smell it I did.

Hell and damnation. There went my only lead.

I went back there the next night. And the night after. And the night after that. The concealment held. I even brought Fir and Serafina along with me, and all it did was get them as blindsided as I was through their association with me. The "seers" must have some really nasty and unhappy customers if the magic to bar them was that strong. To my best guess, the concealment either worked by placing the entire club in a blockee's blind spot, or having the knowledge forgotten as soon as it was acquired. The bottom line was, I couldn't find the nightclub again and had no choice but to seek another way to investigate.

Or I could always go straight for my real target.

While I couldn't touch Dan Pillar until the Council passed a verdict about my suspension, they didn't say I couldn't do a little research on him.

I stood invisible near the front of an auction room, the main feature of tonight about to be presented. From the brochure in my hand, I knew it was some kind of modern sculpture that was as hideous as it was pretentious.

According to my sources—alright, *Fir's* sources—Dan Pillar was going to be here tonight, He was still in town, and quite active in his various charities or whatever else people with a sordid past did to look good. This charity auction was his baby.

The old man must've thought I was long dead and no one else was going to come after him, despite my threat about my handler knowing where I was and all. Maybe he wasn't kidding when he implied he had supernatural friends in high places. And who was to say he didn't? He got his borrowed dark magic from somewhere.

Speak of the devil, there was Dan entering the room with his entourage. He looked healthy and distinguished, his steel grey hair slicked back, his suit tailored to perfection. One of his assistants carried a large box that held the feature auction item. He placed it at the front table, touched a mechanism on the box and all its sides fell flattened against the tablecloth.

As soon as the object was unveiled, I realized it was no modern sculpture.

Well, it was glamoured to look like a modern sculpture, but the brochure couldn't have communicated that rush of raw dark power that was permeating from the seemingly innocent object. The humans in the room couldn't sense it, but I could.

Yet now that I thought about it, were they really

humans? Most of those in the room had human essence that felt just a touch heavy-handed, like air freshener masking the smell of unwashed socks. I took a whiff into my lungs and identified a wendigo, three ghouls and even a kelpie.

I came here to collect facts. Now I understood. This was no art auction. This was a front for dark artifact laundering, catering to fringe supernaturals. This was it, the connection between the mundane and the supernatural in the world of Dan Pillar. The human might've stopped scamming women in nineteen ninety-six, but he sure stepped up his game in other areas. This must be how he'd made his supernatural friends.

"And this is as far as you go." Enid said. When she had appeared beside me, I didn't know. All I knew was that with her next breath, we were back in my room.

"What do you mean, my suspension isn't over yet? I earned those ten freelance markers fair and square!" I groaned.

Enid coughed. "Not quite ten yet, actually. Only nine point eight three. The Council decided to deduct a few minor points."

"For what?" I asked incredulously.

Enid's expression was neutral. "For two typos on your final report."

"Seriously? They're going to hold me back on some technicality? Can't they round the score up?"

"It's not ten until it's ten, Megan."

I rolled my eyes. "Alright. How do you propose I earn that zero point one something of a marker? Do another full assignment? The next semester is starting soon."

My would-be co-op term of four months was almost over. The summer was almost over. I wanted nothing more than to get back to school and get on with my life.

"You don't have to do another full." Enid looked like she was glad to have happy news to share. For once. "I have something here that would just fill the gap."

TWELVE

THAT SOMETHING, AS IT TURNED out, was a bit of minor vengeance volunteering.

Vengeance volunteering was essentially a poor man's version of freelancing. It was small. It was tedious. It earned a stingy number of points. But for my purpose, it was perfect. An investment of one single evening, and I'd be done.

I might still have nightmares about the whole somebody-could-be-out-to-hurt-me thing, but that didn't mean I couldn't be a nightmare to somebody else.

"No, please stop singing, I beg you. I'll do anything!" Ms. Wilson, the temp agency owner begged me, clutching a blue-colored marker as if she was tempted to shove the tube into her own ears.

"The sooner you finish writing, the sooner I stop." I continued with the *Show Boat* tune, with a little variation of my own:

"After the ball is over,
After the break of morn,
After the tricksters' leaving,
After the monks are gone,
My own career is sinkin',

If you could read it all..."

What could I say, my mama was a sucker for cheesy old human musicals. The song was shrill to begin with, but combine that with my off-key, banshee-style singing, and it wasn't a bad torture device. It was perfect if one was trying to save on magic. My trickster half-siblings might believe frugality was a disease of the vengeance demons, but I was the one with money left over in the bank at the end of the day, so who was really laughing?

"There. I'm done. See?" Ms. Wilson pointed frantically at the white board in her office. Her foot was tied to the solid antique table on the side with a cable. Every inch of the board was covered with the sentences "I will never again post a job opening when there are no jobs available in my agency." The dense scribble reminded me of Bart's handwriting in *The Simpsons* opening.

When I first got this assignment from Enid, I thought to myself that there was small time, and then there was *small time*. What was the big deal about a little fake job posting? Then I learned that some recruitment agencies, in an effort to brag to their potential clients that they had a wealth of candidates at their disposal, would put out fake postings on job boards to fish for resumes on a regular basis. The result? Job hunters wasting thousands and thousands of man-hours applying for jobs that never existed, when they could be using the time to go after the real ones that could actually help pay the bills. A pretty low thing to do to people who were already broke and desperate, but not at all illegal in the human world. Turned out with the economy the way it was, more of these postings were popping up. Such small injustices were getting stuck in the Concord, and they were relying on volunteers to sweep the magical chimney.

"Alright, that'll do." I nodded. "And remember, don't do it again, or there'll be more singing coming your way." I bent over to release Ms. Wilson from her bond.

"You should use a thinner cable," a voice said behind me. "'The use of force and restraint must be kept to a minimum,' Article 10.5, section C."

I twirled around. It was Esme. Well, a worse-for-wear version of her, anyway. The messiness of her normally impeccable hair suggested that she'd been in a hurry when she'd teleported here, and there were dark circles under her eyes that bespoke more than one sleepless night. Her face was even more pale than usual. Her previously black skin tight bodysuit had faded with too many wash cycles. And don't get me started on her nails. She had the appearance of someone who hadn't been taking care of herself. The flavor of her power signature tasted different, too. Less calm. More volatile. Even her stickler-for-rules comment seemed off, as if it was more a force of habit than a critical assessment.

Vengeance demons took great pride in their appearances and tranquil mental states, not to mention in their ability to cite regulations. What the heck was going on with Esme? Despite my recent annoyance with her, my chest still tightened a little at how terrible she looked.

Why had I been annoyed with her? Well, she'd sorta disappeared on me. I hadn't heard from her since that night at the ball. She'd ignored my emails, voicemails, texts, even a fairy-a-gram with singing and tap-dancing. With Dad being away on remote assignments all the time, courtesy of that fiasco at the ball, and Mom going with him, there weren't even any family gatherings for me to attend in hopes of running into her organically.

At first I'd been confused and concerned, then worry had become anger when I'd hacked into the Demon U student bulletin board—they froze out my account—and found out that Esme had been named Student of the Year by the Council soon after the ball. Remember the ball, that unfortunate event which Esme did *not* get into trouble for? Then I'd started suspecting she was avoiding me because as the new poster child of vengeance, she was embarrassed to be related to a suspended hybrid. Guilt by association, one might say. It made a sick sort of sense. I mean, why else would she all of a sudden go incommunicado?

After that, I'd stopped trying to reach out to her.

But now, taking one look at her drawn face, I realized I might've assumed the worst of her. Something was troubling her, and I'd let hurt, pride and jealousy get in the way of finding out what had caused her radio silence. Then I remembered her generosity, how she charged me up and brought me back from the edge after Dan Pillar's attack. That made me feel even more ashamed. Our bond was there, an almost physical pull of shared power and affection, taunting me with its strength and my lack of faith in it.

It wasn't her fault that they favored her, that she didn't get blamed for what happened at the ball—though technically she was involved, if we were going by the same definition of how the Council deemed me involved.

I unbound Ms. Wilson from the cable knot that tied her to the solid antique table. Once free, she ran out of the office screaming. Esme waved her hand, and the screaming became mute to all within this floor.

"Thanks," I muttered. I was stingy about wasting even

that much juice. Juice that I'd bet my full-blooded vengeance half-sister would have no issue expending. There I was, being bitter again. I mentally kicked myself and gave Esme a small awkward smile. "Hey."

"Hey." She was biting her lips in unconcealed nervousness, and her eyes betrayed an uncertainty that was completely foreign on her face.

I leaned closer. "Are you alright?"

"I'm sorry," she whispered. "I'm so sorry for being out of touch. I don't know what was wrong with me. Since the ball, I haven't been able to sleep. I haven't been able to eat. I couldn't even bring myself to go out to the Student of the Year photo-op. I thought I was going crazy. Oh, Megan, I'm so sorry."

"What's wrong?" I pushed Esme into the closest chair and crouched down beside her. All my previous annoyance with her went out the window. "Are you ill?"

Vengeance demons were immune to most stuff. But with all the inter-species marrying, there was a new supernatural superbug being born every day.

A thought occurred to me. "It's not goblin-brownie-mono, is it? Give me the list of your last ten targets. Fir knows this crone who's like a wizard with the home remedies. She's bat crazy, but what do you expect from a cr–"

"Megan." Esme caught my hands. "I already checked it out with Grandma's physician. He didn't find anything."

"Oh." Grandma's physician was the best of the best. If he had no clue what was going on...

"But I think I know what is wrong. And I need your help." Esme's tone was so solemn I was sure the doctor had found something. "I haven't been the best sibling lately, so I understand if you say no."

"Just spit it out. I'm dying of suspense here."

Esme took a deep breath. "I met my *solus iungere*."

"What? No way!"

For vengeance demons, a *solus iungere* was essentially a soul mate. Despite being rather effective bringers of pain and justice, or maybe because of it, vengeance demons preferred to mate for life. Not that divorces didn't happen, my father and Esme's mother being the case in point, but most of the vengeance population had this romanticized notion of finding The One. Which was pretty ironic for a race that prided itself in relentless logic, come to think of it.

When vengeance demons fell in love, they basically turned into lovesick human teenagers. You know, all irrational, impulsive, poetry writing, and balcony climbing. But the process was no laughing matter. When a bond was established, being separated could create real physical discomfort, and in worse cases, side effects could include depression, sleep deprivation, and even chronic fatigue. And if that had been happening since the ball—wait, that guy I saw her with by the French windows. Esme, under the influence of Blue Unicorn, had been kissing a guy I'd thought was a little off. That was right before everything went to hell.

Why didn't I think of this earlier? Because everything *did* go to hell afterward. The events that came before the tricksters' chaos and the Shadow World had a dreamlike, surreal quality to them. I hadn't even spared the scandalous scene a single thought in the past months, not even while I cursed my half-sister's apparent distancing of herself from me. What type of sibling did that make me?

"Are you sure he's your *solus iungere*?"

Esme nodded. "Positive. I'd never felt that way before, but I just knew it. Megan, I need your help. He asked me out formally today. Can you help me prepare for our first date?"

He'd just asked her out? But the ball was months ago. If he was really the one, he would've felt the same way about her. Why didn't he speak out sooner?

Looking into Esme's expectant face, so full of excitement and nervousness, I knew that now was not the time to ask that question. Preparation for the first date was traditionally a mother-daughter bonding thing, but Esme's career-minded mother had been disappearing for months or years on end. I knew that at a time like this, Esme would miss her mom. Right now she needed assurance and support, not doubts and misgiving.

"Alright, let's get started then."

A date.

Not a date with destiny, which was what vengeance felt like from a target's perspective. No, it was a *date* date.

Esme was one of the most gorgeous girls I'd ever seen, and she always looked great in her usual wardrobe of black leather pants and sleek jackets. But in vengeance demons' courtship, females were expected to dress in bright colors.

This mating dance was one of the rare occasions in their lives to be caught dead in the rainbow colors they normally despised. It was like those *Star Trek* Vulcans, so darn logical at all times, then going crazy during Pon Farr.

The comparison was just a little on the gross side. But

there was no denying the importance of a first date between vengeance demons, as the mating dance was deliberate and ritual-based, with both sides being super cautious and selective.

We were in *Vengeful Vixens*, one of the most exclusive boutiques on the vengeance plane. So exclusive, in fact, you needed an appointment to even enter its doors. Thanks to a little phone call to Miss Madeleine-Nympho-is-My-Real-Middle-Name-Lex, getting in wasn't a problem at all.

I must say I liked the position of being a blackmailer. It was like that Schrödinger's cat experiment. There existed two possibilities. I could tell on Madeleine, or not. But until it was certain one way or another, I got to enjoy the perks— such as finding Esme the most awesome outfit for her date, all on Madeleine's store account.

Esme was in a fitting room. Serafina and I waited on the benches outside. When I called Serafina to join us, I thought it was going to be a short and fun venture. Now it was our third hour on that bench, and my thighs were getting numb from all the sitting around.

"What do you think?" Esme asked enthusiastically as she stepped out of the fitting room in a neon green number with an 80's sequin bodice.

"No," I said immediately. Serafina shook her head, managing to look horrified at the ensemble and embarrassed about her own negative assessment at the same time. How she retained that level of civility at this point in the shopping process, I had no idea.

So far, Esme had channeled Björk the Oscar swan, Lady Gaga's "Poker Face," Heath Ledger's Joker, and the hooker standing on my street corner. Ouch, who would've thought Esme would be such a fashion disaster once the color black was taken out of the equation?

Her crestfallen look tugged at my heartstrings. I couldn't let her down. There had to be a way.

An idea struck me.

"Come on, let's go back to my place." I turned to Serafina. "You game?"

Serafina took a step back. "I...I...have tutoring to go to. My uncle said it'll help my grades. I have to go."

Ha, not so patient after all. Good, I liked not-too-perfect friends. Hades knew I had my own dark side to combat.

I dragged Esme to the duplex that was now my home. After kicking away three layers of day-old shirts and socks, I opened a dusty trunk under the bed. A large assortment of shimmering sun dresses in cheerful patterns nearly popped out of the trunk on their own.

Esme breathed, fingering the delicate material. "They're so beautiful."

"They're awesome, aren't they?" And they'll fit, too. They're enchanted to conform to whatever body shape the wearer has.

"Where did you get these?"

"They're from my mom." I smiled. "Top-quality trickster-spun material, with a built-in beauty glamour—not that you need it. Do you remember me telling you how my old roommates at the dorm kept trying to set my closet on fire?"

"Yeah."

"That's what they were going after. They thought having these dresses gave me an unfair advantage with the boys."

"Does it?"

"Of course." Not that I'd ever pressed that advantage. Why would I want snobbish boys who denounced me in front of their friends while wooing me in private? "Come on, put one on."

In high school, I used to enjoy the game of teasing boys in all my trickster fineries every now and then, but since starting at Demon U, I didn't even do that anymore. I'd spent so much time wanting to fit into the vengeance world that I'd convinced myself the riot of spring colors wasn't my style at all. But it was.

And it could be Esme's. If she looked like a classic demon in black, then she was a woodland goddess in that pink floral dress she just put on. Her red hair, freed from her usual bun, appeared lighter by several shades, and her pale skin was as delicate as ivory.

Who needed to look badass and deadly when one could look sweet and deadly?

"Megan." Rosemary knocked on my door, a funny tone in her voice. "Your dad is downstairs. He said he happened to be in the neighborhood."

My poor roommate probably still remembered the very first night I moved in, when an imposing man came charging in and, without a word, started sealing all the cracks in the wall, lest any supernaturals-in-disguise might sneak into his little girl's new home.

Esme blanched and made a universal *I'm not here* hand gesture. Not hard to guess why. Best to leave Dad out of the whole first-date business.

Dad might've been possessive of Esme to a much lesser degree, seeing how her mother was a vengeance demon who catered to scorned women and had trained her on a whole arsenal of male-focused torturing tactics, but having your father getting involved in your love life was never cool, no matter what species you were or what plane you were on.

"Tell him I'll be right down," I called out.

"Sure, I'll be in the basement. Today is canning day. I got strawberries on sale."

With a nod to Esme, I ran downstairs. There was Dad, alone in the kitchen, holding a brown paper package and beaming at me. He always seemed so...*relieved* to see me being well. It was kinda sweet but slightly annoying at the same time. I guess to him I'd always be sixteen. Or six.

I felt a pang of guilt. I'd been a bad daughter. Ever since the suspension, I'd been so engrossed in the whole vengeance freelancing business that I hadn't really been giving my father's own punishment much thought. But it was because of me that he'd been getting these crappy assignments.

Speaking of which. "Dad, when did you get back? Where's Mom? I thought you were on this case in the middle of nowhere."

"I still am, but I managed to steal ten minutes of temporal dilation to visit you. Your mother sends her love. Here." He thrust the paper package into my hands. "I got you a Hellhound-grade pepper spray."

"You already gave me two, remember?" I couldn't help but roll my eyes. I had a triple of every weapon Dad could think of. Maybe I should make some credits by having a demonic garage sale.

"Oh, I did? Well, doesn't hurt to have another one around. This one is made with pure organic pepper. Anyway, off I go. Don't let the suspension get to yoouu..." Dad phased out of my dimension with a slight time delay that was characteristic of temporal dilation. It made his body appear to be twisting and melting, like a distorted image in a broken television set.

I heard a loud series of crashes behind me, and turned toward the source of the noises. Rosemary had dropped three or four large glass jars onto the floor. Her face was stark white. "I...I thought I saw..."

Great, she must've caught sight of the last of Dad's exit.

I got Rosemary seated on the kitchen chair and started scooping up the pieces of broken glass. "Are you alright?"

"I must be daydreaming." Rosemary fanned herself with a recipe card she'd grabbed from the counter. "I thought I saw... Never mind, it's silly. Just the other day I could've sworn I saw a transparent cat stalking across the hallway. If I believe everything my eyes tell me, I'll go crazy."

Rosemary laughed at herself, and I silently breathed a sigh of relief. So Sassy had allowed Rosemary to see her. It showed that my roommate must be growing on my cat, but it wasn't necessarily a healthy thing for the human if it made her think she was going insane. I quickly changed the topic. "So, um, how are things with Jordan?"

A sweet smile came over Rosemary's face. "It's going great. Hitting our second month anniversary next Monday."

See, after finding the pencil sketches Jordan had drawn of Rosemary in his office, I'd casually maneuvered the two to go on a shopping trip to the local farmer's market. That seemed to be just the nudge they needed, and things just sorta took off without further intervention from me. I mentally patted myself on the shoulder.

I gestured at the trashcan full of broken glass. "Hey, that's a lot of jars you've got there. The last time I was in the basement, I counted at least four dozen. Even with these write-offs, there are still a lot left. Won't we get sick eating the same strawberry jam over and over again?"

"Some of them are not for making jam." Rosemary gave the pocket of her apron a pat, and for the first time I noticed the purple flowering plants she kept in there. "These are lavender. I've been growing them in pots. I'm going to make a batch of strawberry lavender hair mask. My mother owns a chain of spa salons and she agreed to sell my products there. She's already getting rave reviews for my seaweed facial."

"Wait a minute." A light bulb turned on in my head. "Your mama runs a spa? So you're good at hair and makeup, right?"

Esme could really use her help. Though a swallow of Blue Unicorn could've gotten the beauty job done, it was considered rude to show up on a vengeance demon date with foreign substances in one's blood. It messed with the demonic pheromones and made it nearly impossible to determine compatibility. Esme had to be dolled up the old-fashioned way, and I sure as hell didn't know what to do. Heck, I couldn't trust myself *not* to turn her into Dead Hooker Number Two from *CSI*. Rosemary couldn't have come in at a better time.

"Of course. My mom is also a fashion designer, remember? I've been helping her with her runway projects since I was seven."

"Look, I have a favor to ask. Esme's going on a date, and I don't know anything about this whole beauty business."

"I'll do it." Rosemary smiled. "You're my lucky charm. Since you moved in, I haven't been robbed once, and now I have a boyfriend!"

Lucky charm. Ha, if only she knew.

"Would you like the smoldering-kitten or the girl-next-door look?" We were all in Rosemary's bedroom, and she showed off her makeup suitcase with a wide rainbow of color palettes.

Esme glanced at me questioningly. She probably had no idea what the meaning of "girl next door" was. In our world, there was nothing innocent and harmless about a demon next door, girl or otherwise.

"The girl next door would be fine," I replied. The sweeter look matched the sundress, and besides, vengeance demon first dates were all about being proper and respectful.

"Sure, one fresh and dewy, coming right up." Rosemary started laying out her tools. Brushes, tweezers, a torture instrument that pulled on one's poor eyelashes until they got longer, then mascara to slap on the said wounded lashes. It was a suitcase of horror that would make a vengeance demon proud.

Maybe I'd buy one for myself as a graduation gift. It would be like a mechanic getting his first toolbox.

"You have a very nice selection of eye shadows." Esme smiled shyly at Rosemary. My roommate beamed. Ah, the magic of compliments. Esme was getting the hang of that aspect of human interaction. They couldn't sense impressions like us, let alone read minds, so any positive opinions should be expressed verbally.

"So, are you going to tell me more about him?" I asked as Rosemary applied a subtle brush of color to Esme's eyelids. I'd been biding my time for hours, resisting the urge to grill her. This was a big deal for her. I mean, the girl had come to me with even more hollow cheekbones than usual, and that was saying a lot. I wondered what it would be like when it was my turn one day. Who knew what romance awaited a hybrid of a race known for its promiscuity and another known for exclusivity?

An image of Pete the mercenary came to mind, and I repressed the hell out of it. I squished the raw fantasy of pressing my palms against his chest into a corner so far in the back of my mind, it would need a GPS to get back out again. I so did not need a bad boy in my life, no matter how glossy and large his wings were, and you know what they said about guys with a large wingspan...

Oh, shut up.

Mercifully, Esme decided to cooperate and distract me from my own traitorous thoughts.

"His name is Guillermo Cristobal Canus." Esme peeked at her freshly painted toes sticking out from the hairdresser gown. Rosemary had decided to throw in the pedicure at the last minute, once she'd caught sight of Esme's feet, which had never made friends with a pumice stone before. "I met him at the—"

"Party." I finished the sentence for her with a pointed glance at Rosemary. The average human tends not to go to balls very often. Well, the average supernaturals were the same, for that matter. But anyway, no need to have one more thing about me sticking out like a sore thumb in my roommate's mind.

"Party. Right. But after that night I didn't hear from him for months. I thought...I thought he'd forgotten all about me."

Esme pressed her lips together and her jaw quivered slightly. A wave of unexpected protectiveness filled my heart. I felt like throttling this Canus fellow just for making her feel so insecure about herself.

His leaving had made my strong, professionally cruel half-sibling sulk for months. Sulk and long for a guy who'd kissed her, bonded with her and then disappeared.

Asshole.

But as much as I'd like to hate him, he wasn't the only one who'd disappointed Esme. She'd been hurting while I'd been stewing and assuming the worst of her. I hadn't been very good family.

I reached over and placed my hand on Esme's shoulder. She brightened upon my touch and continued, "Anyway, he contacted me today and explained that he'd been called home until now. He said he missed me and wanted to ask me out."

"Couldn't he have reached out earlier?" Rosemary asked the exact question I was thinking.

It was Esme's turn to glance at Rosemary, measuring her next words. "His home is a faraway place with not a lot of access to long-distance communication. He's from an old family that, er, immigrated away from here a long time ago."

I realized what Esme was trying not to say out loud. Canus's blood kin was settled in one of those remote planes that were popular safe havens during historical times of political instabilities. Vengeance demons had gone through their share of political upheavals through the ages, often in dispute over our role as a superior species over the other supernaturals in the Concord. The past was a pixie-taxing, goblin-dispossessing, tricksters-imprisoning mess. Believe it or not, the current power-that-be I'd been complaining about were considered rather moderate, in the grand scheme of things.

So the guy was from an old family and as I recalled, he had on a tailored suit that looked overly expensive and formal even by vengeance demon standards... for all we knew, he might even be some long-dethroned member of royalty. A prince or a duke of something. That type was notorious when it came to arrogance and conservatism. The Council would look like naked hippies compared to them.

That combined with the fact that he didn't sound as destroyed by the whole separation anxiety thing as Esme suggested an imbalance of power in the relationship, and I was liking this date less and less. No way was I buying that I've-got-no-way-to-contact-you crap. If he'd liked her, he would've found a way to say hi before now.

But seeing the way Esme's eyes shone when she said his name, I decided to keep my mouth shut and let her come to her own conclusions, trusting that she could shrink his balls if something went wrong. It was hard, as the vengeance demon in me demanded self-control in the situation, while the trickster side craved to interfere.

And I wouldn't mention the kiss I'd witnessed, either. No need to embarrass her unnecessarily.

See, I could be tactful if I wanted to be. Even when I felt like ripping the guy's freaking head off for making Esme miserable.

"You said his family immigrated *from* here? But this is the land of immigrants." Rosemary frowned. "Immigrated from here to where? Antarctica?"

"Something like that," Esme said vaguely.

"Okay, you're done, girl." Rosemary removed the hairdresser's gown with a flourish. Esme looked absolutely lovely in her flowing dress and understated makeup. Her dark red hair was teased with large curls in a feminine and flirty way. "I present to you, Princess Esme."

Rosemary had no idea just how right she might turn out to be, empty title with a steep price tag and all.

Esme got in front of a full-length mirror in the corner and spun around in delight. Wow, did I just hear a giggle? Esme seemed to notice it too, so she collected herself and said to Rosemary formally, "Thank you."

"Don't worry about it." Rosemary waved her off as she started packing up her makeup suitcase. "Have fun tonight."

Then with her eyes moist with tears, Esme did something unexpected. She ran to me, hugged me, and whispered, "Thanks, sis. My own mother wouldn't have done better."

Right, her absentee mom, the male genitalia specialist. We never talked about her, so I wasn't even sure how to respond. Instead, I said, "Go get him, gorgeous."

THIRTEEN

AFTER SEEING ESME OFF, I joined Rosemary at the shelter. It was cat-grooming day, and the hours went by about as fast as the fur was flying.

All the trimming and nail clipping, though it had to be precise and done with care, wasn't very mentally challenging, as all of my subjects were smart enough not to struggle. While my hands got down to business, my mind wandered over my now fulfilled freelance markers. Getting the full ten turned out to be harder than getting a complete set of collectables from McDonalds happy meals, but the Council was just about out of excuses not to reinstate my student status. With any luck, I might even get a small window between the lift of the suspension and the start of the semester. Maybe I would be allowed to spend some quality time with Dan. I'd managed to get to his lawyer. I'd tried to find those monks that were connected to him. I'd uncovered his supernatural dealings. It was finally time to use the direct approach. The thought cheered me up.

"I'm done with the last kitten," I announced in between coughing out fur balls and opening the door to the animal shelter's kitchen. Ick. There was enough fur on the flat brush I was holding to create three large cats from scratch, given the correct incantation. "Do you need any help with the baking?"

Upon hearing my voice, Rosemary hastily pushed the baking tray she was holding into the oven, shut its door and leaned against it like a mama bear protecting her cubs. The smile she threw my way had a panicky look to it. "Too bad, I'm just finished with the last batch of dog biscuits."

My shoulders sagged. "You're all done? No other baking I could help out with?"

Rosemary said just a little too quickly, "That's alright, I'm all good."

I squinted my eyes and noticed that my roommate's face had gone pale. Poor girl, she must be feeling a little lightheaded after being on her feet for hours. But wait, why was I picking up the images of soggy dough and chocolate powder in her mind? She wasn't still worried about my baking skills, was she?

Alright, so there was also this little incident last week when my overdose of baking soda had collapsed an entire batch of banana bread. But I blamed the bananas. They were faulty.

"You can help me with the clean-up," Rosemary offered.

I grumped. "Sure, garbage duty for the girl who can't cook. Remind me why I'm here again?"

"Let me see, why are you here?" Rosemary started counting off her fingers. "Reason one, Esme is off on her date, and you're feeling just a little bit jealous. Don't deny it. We all want a little validation now and then. Reason two, you owe me because she looks fab, thanks to me."

Actually, there was a third reason. I was here in gratitude for the freelance leads that Rosemary, through

Jordan, had unwittingly provided. I would like to be someone who remembered her debts.

I went about picking up all the used spatulas and sniffed the air around me. With biscuits that good, I wouldn't mind being a dog. I got called a bitch in my line of work often enough as it was. Why not get a treat for it?

Seemingly reading my mind, Rosemary took a fresh tray out of the oven and placed it on the cooling rack. "You can have some if you want. All my products are human-grade. That means it's suitable for human consumption."

And I bet it was good enough for demon consumption, too. I took a handful from the tray and wolfed them down. They were hot, but my supernatural enamel could handle it.

Greedy much? a small voice inside me mocked.

Oh, shut up. My trickster blood might've given me a bit of an addictive personality when it came to food, but it was a hundred percent under control. Totally, utterly under control, just like my other trickery tendencies.

"More?" Rosemary held out a large tin of dog biscuits containing a previous batch cooled enough to be stored.

"Please." I grabbed a dozen extra and put them in my back pants pocket for later. What? I wasn't greedy. The biscuits were kinda tiny, that was all. And they were human-grade, so I couldn't go wrong having some around, now could I?

I heard the door to the kitchen swing open, and Rosemary greeted her newcomer with a smile in her voice. "Oh, hi there, Bo. Coming in for another kitten? You have your friends with you. Megan, you remember Bo. I told you all about him."

With my body twisted back, eyes and hands focused on smoothing out the new bulge at my back pocket, I repressed a shudder and took a moment before facing the newcomer. I remembered, alright. Though I'd never met the man, his reputation at the shelter preceded him. Bo was one of those wealthy, crazy, cat dudes who had like fifty cats. He was a frequent flyer at the shelter's feline adoption program and one of its biggest financial supporters. He was also a dog person and a long-time loyal customer of Rosemary's awesome gourmet dog biscuits.

I looked up, expecting to see someone with wild eyes, shapeless clothing and a cat clinging around his neck. Instead, I saw sunglasses, stylish hip-hop jeans, and a large money-sign necklace.

And Bonaventure the Third with his cronies.

Those three seemed to realize the jig was up the same moment I did. One of the sidekicks dropped a black metal tube onto the floor, and I only had a second to close my eyes before a blinding eruption of lights, noises, and magic surrounded me.

It wasn't an actual explosion, I realized as I dropped to the floor on my hands and knees, keeping my eyes tightly shut. The lights had no heat in them, the bang had no shockwave, and the magic was weaker than a baby brownie's scratches.

It was nothing but a supernatural version of a flash grenade, meant to be deployed before making an escape.

Escape.

I sent my senses out. Those three elves were gone. Likely ran from the kitchen the moment the flash grenade had been dropped. Rosemary was unconscious, but otherwise seemed fine. With my eyes still closed, I clawed out of the kitchen, resisting the instinctive urge to hide under the nearest cupboard. That was the knee-jerk reaction the flash grenade was intended to evoke.

Refusing to hold my breath against smoke that wasn't really there, I soldiered on.

"Hey guys, miss me?"

Even before I'd gotten out of the shelter's kitchen, I could sense that the Scooby Gang was no longer on the premises. But their trail had still been fresh, and I'd used a trickery spell called Trick You Later to track them.

With a legitimate P.O.T.O.—Point of Teleport Origin— as my guide, I'd bypassed the safeguard surrounding the Bureaucracy and had landed straight in the office of the club. I'd sealed the entrance to the backroom after I'd jumped there through a temporary portal.

Bonaventure the Third and his sidekicks stopped what they were doing and gawked at me. I walked past them, steering clear of the floor in front of the wall, which I'd fallen through the last time, and hopped onto the small IKEA desk. That was the surface in the whole room least likely to have traps on it. Except if you counted the very fine act of bookkeeping.

I dangled my feet off the ground, all casual like. "Well?"

"Well, what?" Bonaventure the Third asked woodenly. He was in shock, but not overrun by fear, which was exactly what I wanted. Their own little office was becoming a boxed-in prison, and I didn't want them desperate. Like my dad always said, if you back a hellhound into a corner, it's gonna bite.

"Did my absence make your poor hearts ache with longing or relief? Wait, first things first."

I cast the Blackout Dates spell, which ensured that they couldn't open portals and escape at the drop of a hat, just like how humans couldn't buy airline tickets on certain days with their mileage points. No more surprises.

They responded by charging at me. I expected that. They had to at least try before they would listen to me.

They came at me with staplers, rulers, and even a full package of paper. The three elves might not have much magic in them, but they were strong as oxen. Instinctively, my limbs started moving to block the hits that came my way. I gave a silent thanks to the basic combat challenge I'd had to pass as a part of my SAAT—Standard Assault Aptitude Test—for college.

I jumped over their heads and landed where one of the sidekicks was seconds ago. Another good bet of a trap-free spot was where the enemy had just been. I grabbed onto Wistari's boot and twisted his ankle, causing him to fall. Then I used his leg to trip Sidekick Number Two as the latter approached. Rolling myself into a ball, I landed on top of Wistari's round belly, planting my feet hard on it. When he sucked in air again, I used the momentum to launch myself in the air. Like a graceful human gymnast, I did a cartwheel midair then kicked out my left foot to make contact with the jawbone of Bonaventure the Third.

By the time I landed my feet on the ground, none of the three losers were left standing. They didn't stay down for long, though. The boys scrambled to their feet and gave each other the "let's get her" hand signal.

The rather chaotic nature of my opponents made this situation ripe for some fantastic trickery magic. And I would use it, not just for myself, but also for all the animals that had passed from the shelter to these bastards' hands.

Who knew what had happened to them? Most valuable patrons, my butt.

What I had in mind was called the Slapstick Merry Go Round, a confusion spell that worked best in tight spaces with multiple players. As Wistari clamped down on my shoulder with his enormous hand, I transferred the hold to Bonaventure the Third, so when that grip tightened, it was the latter who was screaming in pain. When he shot out his foot in reflex, my spell made him find aim on Sidekick Number Two's shin.

All in all, everyone got a little bruising, while thinking that the attack came from me. It made me look way stronger than I really was.

The real fun began when they panicked and started using magic in their effort to subdue me. What they lacked in power, they made up for with enchanted brass knuckles and good old-fashioned blood-curdling war cries. Showers of punches, doubled in strength and at reality-bending velocity, rained down all around me. But none were able to touch me. The raw energy my attackers packed behind their pounding fed into my trickery spell, making the perception even more distorted. A little diversion here, a little switch of position there, and to their eyes, I was blocking and moving and throwing punches like a Buddha with a thousand hands. And I wasn't even breaking a sweat.

It wasn't long before all three of them were moaning and wincing and pressing their hands against various sore spots on their bodies. Dammit, they'd stopped the attack. I couldn't hurt them unless they hurt themselves.

But they don't know that, the trickster voice in me encouraged.

Right. I lowered my stance and stretched out the span of

my wings, the classic posture of a vengeance demon just before making a fatal blow. Fooled by my bluff, they were certain I was ready to smite them once and for all. Bonaventure the Third put up his hands in the age-old sign of surrender. "Stop. Alright, alright."

He was leaning heavily against the wall he'd banged into when he'd become the unwitting victim of his sidekicks' double one-two punches. He looked like he was about to pee himself. Slowly, the sidekicks put their hands above their heads as well. They huddled together and their eyes kept darting around the room. Sensing their intention to flee, I remembered the trapdoor on the floor and had no doubt they knew quite a few ways to trigger it. I took off an enchanted bracelet from my wrist, one of the many gifts of apology from Fir for what had happened at the ball. Not that I'd officially forgiven him yet, but I'd kept the bracelet because it was so darn useful.

I threw the bracelet towards the three guys, who'd so conveniently grouped themselves together for a single, easy catch. The bracelet expanded to become a large, thick rope. It looped around their middle and tightened like a cowboy rope around a horse's neck.

"Better." I slapped my hands together. "Boy, do I have a few bones to pick with you. Why don't we start with what you've done to those cats you 'adopted'? Did you eat them? Was the shelter just a food bank to you, or are you using the cats as currency in poker games?"

Bonaventure the Third looked genuinely horrified. "We did no such things. We would *never* do that."

"Alright, next question. Why did you attack me in the Shadow World?"

Three voices replied, overlapping each other.

"We weren't attacking you."

"We were trying to attack *her*."

"But you're not her."

You're not her. They'd said those exact words to me before. What did it even mean? I closed my eyes and wished I could've prayed for the patience of Job, had I not been a demon. "Yeah, yeah, so who the heck is *she*?"

"The girl our competition wants." It was as far as Sidekick Number Two got before earning an elbow in the stomach by Wistari.

"Your competition?" My eyebrow rose. "I assume you meant the other set of monks, right? You know, the ones with the real firepower to hurt me?"

Bonaventure the Third drew himself to his full height. It would've been intimidating if he wasn't all tied up. "We have just as much firepower as the Greys."

His sidekicks nodded grimly. But it was the kind of nod that carried more pride than true conviction.

"Try flinging me across the room and then we'll talk." At least I'd gotten a name for the other team now. The first break in a long while. Then his words sank in. "Wait a minute, you called yourself the Off-Blacks and they're the Greys? What are we, in a laundry detergent commercial?"

"We don't have to explain ourselves to you." Bonaventure the Third stiffened.

"Well, too bad. I'm a vengeance demon and you're in my jurisdiction."

"On what grounds?"

"On the grounds of whatever animal abuses you've committed." And that was the reason I'd use if that was what it took to hold the Off-Blacks. Not to mention, I was indeed pissed about the missing-and-assumed-dead cats.

An image of Pete helping his client transport her dogs home popped into my mind, and I kicked it back to where the sun didn't shine.

"We already told you we did no such thing."

"Oh yeah, let's see if you'll change your tune after a bath in boiling oil." I made a gesture as if I was conjuring a large crockpot that was almost as tall as me.

"Wait!" all three of them screamed, covering their faces with their arms.

"So tell me about the girl you supposedly thought I was."

"Look." Bonaventure the Third was talking fast. "We just heard that the Greys were going after that Aequitas girl, and we didn't want to be left out, that's all. But since you looked nothing like her, it was just a misunderstanding. Can't we just walk away and pretend it never happened?"

With a sinking heart, I pulled out my cell phone and showed them a picture of Esme from my album. "Is this the girl?"

"Yeah, that's her." For a moment there, Bonaventure the Third looked as if he thought I ought to be cheered by the case of mistaken identity, until he realized the implication of Esme's picture being in my album.

He might not have targeted me. But he'd targeted one of mine.

The three guys swallowed as a whole, but before I could incite more terror in them, a tweet from Esme popped up:

Enjoying #perpetualsunset at #purgatory

She'd tweeted a picture of her and Guillermo smiling against the backdrop of the Land of the Undecided. Their bodies were outlined in the never-ending sunset, with a few lost souls serving as background extras. Guillermo had folded his hands in front of him, keeping a respectable distance away from Esme as was traditionally expected at this stage of the courtship. Despite the lack of physical contact, the couple looked as happy as two peas in a pod. Only a pair of vengeance demons would consider purgatory a romantic place for a first date. Esme looked positively radiant in the pink floral number she'd chosen from my trunk.

Somehow I got an odd feeling that everything I needed to know was already in that grainy picture. So I squinted at it and did a double take.

No way.

I magnified Guillermo's right hand. Sitting on one of his fingers was a giant ruby ring, with the exact same knotting design as the one Dan Pillar had used on me.

Shit! Shit! Shit!

I typed a private direct message to Esme, my fingers flying over the keypad:

DANGER get away from your date NOW!!!

While I got busy typing, the badass wannabes started edging away from me. Being bound together, they couldn't exactly go very far. But that didn't stop them from trying. From the edge of my vision I could see them trying to hop away in unsynchronized motion, like some mutated three-headed bunny.

With no time to waste and even less patience to spare, I took out a secret weapon from a back pocket with my spare hand. I pointed it at the boys and pressed down on the button, my eyes never leaving the cell phone screen.

In less than a second, the three losers were howling and twitching on the ground, courtesy of my dad's Hellhound-grade pepper spray.

Esme didn't answer my direct message. In fact, she pretty much went off the reservation around the same time I sent out my warning, which made me very nervous.

I tried calling her cell, but it was shut off. I tried turning it back on remotely but couldn't. So much for the supernatural GPS. Esme wasn't missing long enough for me to call the demonic police, but I knew in my guts that she was in trouble.

The gatekeeper at purgatory swore up and down he never saw the couple go in, let alone leave. Crossing planes with a full-blooded vengeance demon against her will would be as inconceivable as keeping her in purgatory, as the prolonged presence of a living being could wreak havoc on that plane. So where was she then?

Dammit, I knew I jinxed it when I thought she could handle herself. While Esme might be powerful, on a certain level she was incredibly trusting. All that abrasiveness, her play-by-the-rulebook mentality and her murderous vengeance track record was just business, a product of her race. Underneath that was a sweet girl who could've turned her nose up at her hybrid half-sibling, but didn't. She could be especially vulnerable if she let her guard down in the company of a fellow justice handler. I could just see him subduing her using sneaky means. Most likely some kind of magical roofie. Man, if he dared touch a single hair on her head... My blood boiled just thinking about that.

I needed to find her, pronto.

I checked all of Dan Pillar's usual hangouts. The local seniors chess competition, the taping of the demonic version of *Antiques Roadshow*, the ribbon-cutting ceremony for the latest faery-powered stairlifts...he was gone. No one had seen him since around the same time Esme had dropped off the radar. Well, at least I'd gotten myself a few suspects to torture some information out of.

"Please, I can't stand it anymore. Oh, anything but that!" Bonaventure the Third begged.

We were in my parent's basement. Mom and Dad were still away for that crap assignment the Council had ordered Dad to do. Clef, Boone, and Ty were all out, dutifully being up to no good. Fir, however, was home and more than happy to help me, though it was as much about making it up to me as it was about having a little fun for himself.

I didn't care. My priority was finding Esme. Even if that meant milking Fir's ability for all it was worth. On a normal day I'd be uncomfortable going all trickster-style, but today was anything but normal.

"Please...I...can't...breathe. It's...too...much," Bonaventure the Third said, his face turning an alarming shade of crimson. His two friends weren't doing so swell, either.

Fir looked to me and I nodded. He waved his hands, and countless mini-feathers the size of paperclips stopped tickling the three silly-asses' bare feet.

It was a new trickery spell invented by my half-brothers. They ran a little side business of designing unique spells. They were like the Weasley twins in *Harry Potter* that way. This death-by-a-million-feathers spell, called The Itch, turned out to be a rather wonderful interrogation tool.

"Now, tell me where Esme is or I swear, I'll turn the spell right back on," I told the boys.

"We don't know," Wistari said not for the first time in the last hour, rubbing his feet together ruefully.

Fir put his hand on my arm. "Megan, you're going about this the wrong way."

"What do you mean?" I frowned.

"Now, I hung out with elves a bit. You have to ask your questions in a way that makes sense to them."

A light bulb went on in my head. "They are sneaky about the small stuff, but linear thinkers when it comes to the big picture."

"In other words, Evil Lite." Fir grinned.

"Hey." Sidekick Number Two, whose name I now knew was Naracion, protested.

"Especially that one there with the giant blood." Fir pointed a finger at Naracion and continued, "So start your questions from the beginning. The very beginning."

I wanted to kick something. I didn't have time for this. Esme's life might be on the line here. Yet I couldn't afford to *not* be patient. I tried to focus on the five W's they'd taught us back in *Target Recon 101*—the who, what, when, where, and why. I took a deep breath and addressed Bonaventure the Third. "Who are you, as a group?"

"I told you, we're the Off-Blacks." He rolled his eyes.

"Yeah, but what *is* the Off-Blacks?"

"We're the followers of the Blacks," Wistari said with maddening reasoning. "But we're not as black as our masters yet, so we call ourselves the Off-Blacks until we're as black as they are."

"Huh?"

"Megan," Fir whispered in my ears, "I think by the

Blacks, they mean Evil."

"Evil, as in *evil*-Evil?"

We exchanged a look. Now we knew for sure the Off-Blacks were delusional. Absolute Evil hadn't been heard from since almost the Beginning, just like Absolute Good. It was about as real to us as Big Foot was to humans, stories to scare little demon kids into listening to their mommies and daddies.

"Alright, what are the Greys then?" I turned back to Bonaventure the Third and crossed my arms.

"We're sworn enemies."

I laughed sarcastically. "That implies being equals."

"We *are* equals."

I snorted. "Yeah, right. The whole relationship looked to me more like rock stars and groupies, or serial killers and copycats."

"That's not true." Naracion was indignant. "We're *way* more evil than them. We're the *Off*-Blacks. It's still many shades darker than the Greys."

I sighed. I understood the whole insecure thing. I really did. Growing up the way I did, I knew what it was like to want to be more than what everybody thought you'd ever be. In normal circumstances, I might even feel sorry for these guys, but I had a family member to rescue and didn't have all day. "Wait, are you saying you guys are vying for the attention of the same master?" Those losers following a force that didn't exist, I got. But the Greys? I suppose there was no accounting for fanaticism. And the power only made them more dangerous.

"Of course."

"Look, just tell me what you know about them. Don't make me make you beg." At this rate, I might be the one who ends up begging. If the three musketeers had had the smarts, I'd say they'd dragged this out on purpose.

"So as I said." Bonaventure the Third took pity on me. "We and the Greys have a long history. We spy on them whenever we can. It takes work, because they have money and know people."

"Yeah, just because they got all those things, they think they're better than everyone else," Naracion grumped. It made sense that the Greys were well-connected. It would take the greasing of some major wheels to pull off the kidnapping of a vengeance demon.

Bonaventure the Third continued. "A few months ago we heard that one of their agents just bought a fake invitation to the ball on the black market, under the name of Prince Guillermo Cristobal Canus, Duke of Naukra, Earl of Florgato."

"Let me guess, the name was so grandiose and fake it made you suspicious?"

"Er, no." Bonaventure the Third paused, then muttered, "Although, that should've been a red flag. But no, we got suspicious because we know the *real* Guillermo Cristobal Canus, and he's a small-time incubus stripper with a fancy stage name. Anyway, one thing led to another and we uncovered the plan to snatch the Aequitas girl and take her to the Shadow World. So we decided to intercept the package and see what all the fuss was about."

I remembered the kiss Esme had had with Mr. I'm-Sharing-A-Name-With-A-Stripper. The chaos my half-brothers created must've messed up the Greys' plan, whatever it was, and I'd ended up in the Shadow World instead.

"Any idea where they might've taken her? Is she still in

purgatory?"

"No idea." Bonaventure the Third and his sidekicks shook their heads.

I was ninety-five percent sure these guys were telling me the truth, but I decided to put them through one more round of torment just to be sure. I turned to Fir. "Give me the In His Shoes."

Fir nodded. "One In His Shoes, coming right up."

I looked at the three idiots. "By this spell, may you suffer the same fate you put every animal you ever adopted through."

"No!" they howled in unison.

I expected starvation, skinning, and mutilation. What happened next was far, far worse.

The three stooges changed into the prospective costumes of jailbird, tooth fairy, and panda. Invisible hands repeatedly stuffed their mouths with gourmet tuna bites, silencing their screams of terror. Other invisible hands cuddled and squeezed and brushed them to within an inch of their lives right before my very eyes.

It was beyond pathetic.

"I think it's fair to say this is a dead end," Fir said dryly. "So hey, are we even?"

I snorted. "The sooner I say yes, the sooner you get me into trouble again. Hold these knock-off monks for now while I go after the real thing, will ya?" I asked as I walked up the stairs leading out of the basement.

"With the spell on or off?"

"If I tell you to turn it off, would you do it?"

"No. This is way too much fun to watch."

"Figured."

FOURTEEN

WHOM COULD I ASK FOR help? Because if Esme's douchebag of a date was working with the Greys, then I was going up against some serious magic. The tone in my dad's voice right after my attack in the Shadow World, when he'd mentioned the silver web—whatever that was—had said it all.

My magic wasn't all that strong even on the best of days, and now was definitely not it. I was going to need some help.

Dad's covert mission was on an undisclosed plane, very rugged from the sound of it, and Mom was with him. I didn't have the faintest idea how to find Esme's mother. Last I'd heard, she'd branched out into the digital world, pouring her essence into the Internet for weeks on end, triggering mass heart attacks for men who sought affairs from sites such as Ashley Madison. Enid was on vacation and had made it clear to the world she wouldn't be checking any of her communication devices before the new semester began.

There was Serafina, but I couldn't call her. Though her vengeance power was potent, it was also mostly untrained. That coupled with her shy nature, I knew that bringing her along in a dangerous situation would likely cause harm to both her and others.

There was Madeleine. But just because I had something over her head didn't mean she'd make a good ally. The very fact that I saw her at a club that was run by people who had a connection with Esme's kidnapper was making Madeleine rather suspect. And come to think of it, she was part of Esme's date preparation, however reluctant she seemed at the time. If that little witch was somehow involved...I'd get her later, after I got Esme back safe and sound.

Only the Council knew how to contact Dad. I'd have no choice but to go to them. They might not like me, but they liked Esme and would for sure want to help locate their star pupil.

I stood in front of Hart House at the University of Toronto in the early morning, Esme missing now for a whole night. I hadn't slept a wink. My heart was beating in that accelerated, yet steady rhythm. My throat was dry from breathing through my mouth in an effort to prevent hyperventilating. I was beyond tired, beyond worried, maybe even beyond vengeance. I just wanted to find Esme. *Then* I'd let them have it.

On the human side, the collegiate gothic building of Hart House served as a student centre. On the demonic side, it was the offices for the Board of Governors, University of Demonic Studies.

As I was suspended, I had to get into the demonic school ground through the human one. I did it without issue, thanks to a little cloaking spell Fir cooked up.

I landed on the demonic side just behind the thick oak front door. Luckily there weren't any students around. I walked forward, my footsteps echoing in the empty hallway.

The coats of arms of all the supernatural families who'd donated to the university were displayed in the enormous lobby. They bore the same last names as many currently sitting on the board and, by default, the Council. Still very much the old boys' club.

But maybe they'd be a bit nicer if I caught them in their offices and interacted with them on an individual basis. Well, maybe not High Judge Advocatus, but the others. It would get them away from the whole mob mentality. I hoped.

I briskly walked towards the Great Hall on the east wing of the House. The warm color of the Italian travertine floors and pastel glass windows did nothing to calm my nerves. I was quite sure the Greys weren't some embittered past target of Esme's. Promising as she was, my half-sister simply hadn't been around long enough to deal justice to many powerful supernaturals yet. So I had no idea what the bad guys wanted with her, and that only made me even more anxious.

I was so lost in my own thoughts that I turned a corner and almost ran into someone. That someone caught me by the shoulder.

"Megan! How did you get in here?" Enid asked incredulously. She was in a classic navy Chanel suit and held a clipboard. She looked like she'd just come out of a meeting.

"Enid! I thought you were on vacation." Man, was I happy to see her. Maybe she could talk to the Council on my behalf. They'd listen to her a lot more than they would to me.

"The board had an emergency meeting about a

temporary staff placement, and I was called in." She smoothed down her skirt, removing a piece of lint. "I'm going back to Cancun now. There is an advantage to being a supernatural. Sunny destinations are always just a finger snap away."

"So the board members are still close by?" I looked around. The hallway was as empty as before. "I need to talk to you. And to the board. It's urgent," I said.

"Sure." She took in my disheveled state and seemed to understand right away that something was wrong. Her expression turned serious as she gestured towards one of the many reading rooms lining the hallway. "Let's go in here for some privacy."

I went into the room, and Enid shut the door behind us. I quickly explained the whole situation, everything from seeing the so-called *prince* at the ball to connecting him to the Greys, to Esme's disappearance.

After a long moment, Enid said, "Your father is too deep under cover. No one can reach him. Not in time, anyway."

"What about the Council? There must be something they could do. They pretty much have an army of vengeance demons at their disposal." I wrung my hands and wished I could wrap them around somebody's neck, preferably someone associated with the Greys. I hated this helplessness I was feeling.

"Megan, you know how they are. They're not going to spring into action without any proof. Why don't we wait for at least another twenty-four hours to make sure Esme is really missing?"

That was not the answer I needed. I might hate the fact that Esme was skinnier and smarter and prettier, but at the end of the day, she was still of my blood, and I loved her.

There was no way in hell, and I meant that literally, I would just let them take her.

"You're supposed to mentor me, not tell me to drop it and hope for the best. You've said many times that I should trust my instincts. I'm telling you now—they're on full red alert."

"Megan—"

"Forget it. I'll go after her myself." I started for the door.

Enid sighed. "So they were last seen in purgatory."

I halted. A tiny hope rose within me. "Yes."

"And you're going to go after her?"

"Yes."

"Even if it means running on limited power, risking your life, and offsetting the feeble balance between your competing natures?" A rueful smile touched Enid's lips.

"Yes, yes, and yes!" I screamed. "What's going on here? I thought you liked Esme."

"I like her. I do. But you can't just go after her. They are using her as bait."

"Bait?" I asked in utter confusion. I never thought of that before. "Really?"

"Yes. Can't you see? They took her so you'd go after her."

"What makes you think that? What would they want from me? Do you know something I don't?"

Enid didn't seem very interested in answering my questions. "But you won't go after her now, will you? You're not going to fall for their trap." She gave me the look of a teacher expecting her student to give her the desired answer.

She must not have checked my grades recently.

My tiny hope died, replaced by sheer anger. "And why won't I? Because I oughta be smarter than to take the bait? I oughta have a better plan?"

"No."

"No, what?"

"No. You won't go after her." Enid shook her head. "You won't go to the High Monks of Greys because you're *my* prize to bag, not theirs."

"Wha—"

Quick as lightening Enid pulled out a long, silvery whip and started cracking it my way. The whip struck with intense electricity, chipping chunks off the hardwood floor with each hit and singeing the air with blistering menace.

I jumped back, avoiding getting a new hole in my shoe by half a centimeter. I darted behind the room's various furniture. Lucky for me, the old-fashioned reading room consisted of many heavy upholstered chairs, bookshelves and coffee tables. I managed to stay just a little ahead of Enid's progressively faster cracks. Barely.

"Wait, you're a bad guy?" I cried. "Come on, you let me pass the last semester. You let me into the co-op. I thought I meant something to you."

She didn't answer. Not that I expected her to. I was nowhere near being her match, so my best bet was evasive action while looking for a way to escape. My priority in life for the next minute, which felt like an hour, narrowed down to avoiding the next whip, the one after that, and then the one after that.

I didn't scream, just concentrated on being as agile as a cat, leaping, rolling, and cartwheeling between objects that could serve as shields. That wasn't because I was brave. Oh, no. I would have loved to have taken the time to be hysterical, but I knew it would be pointless. I could sense that the immediate area was cloaked in a mute spell. Enid must've activated it the moment she'd closed the door behind me. Maybe my combat training was kicking in, but more likely after a night of worrying, I was too drained and shocked to freak out. My heart was already galloping, and my mouth had gone completely dry, whatever moisture left in it when I entered the building now gone. I couldn't swallow. I couldn't breathe through my nose.

And I couldn't stop my hands from trembling. I almost twisted my wrist on the last cartwheel as my shaking proved too great for a stable landing.

"Are you too scared to confront me?" Enid was homing in on my location, as most of the furniture was now charred, cracked, or had outright disintegrated. "Fight back, you sorry excuse for a half-breed! You'll never be rid of the stink of your mother's blood."

How dare she insult my mama.

I thought I was calm. I thought I was too cool to get mad. But the ice in my veins thawed without warning, and in its place was wild fire. A burning so fierce it was as if there were a thousand army ants biting the tips of my fingers and toes. I dug my nails into my palms and curled my toes in pain. I could feel the moment I snapped and tapped into my emotional side.

My trickery side.

I'd always tried to control it, hide it. But it was always there. And now, I let it rip.

Nobody insulted my mama.

Above my hiding place behind a grand piano, Enid's face appeared. She raised her whip for a final blow just as I weaved a spell of entanglement around her. I wrapped her up good, like a silkworm in a cocoon.

Problem was, she was my mentor and knew my fighting

style way too well, trickery magic or not. She blasted out of the cocoon and directed the whip my way again. This time she threw the whole thing at me, and in midair it warped and transformed into a silver web, catching me from my left side and pressing me against the reading room's oak-paneled wall.

For the second time in a matter of months, I was caught in a silver web. From my last experience, I already knew that struggling was futile, so I glared at Enid instead. Well, it was more of a semi-glare, as I couldn't actually see her that well from my cheek-squashed-against-the-wall angle.

"Come now, Megan. You're telling me you can't even break this little web? Well, you'll just have to sit tight while I kill you—"

There was a thud, and Enid went down. Hard. I tried my hardest to turn my face towards her to take a look, and almost cranked my neck when the silver web was suddenly dissolved.

"Ouch." I dropped to the ground and looked up, a word of thanks to my rescuer on the tip of my tongue.

Grandma Aequitas held her signature bejeweled staff over Enid's cracked-open skull. For all the matriarch's fantastic magic, she got the job done with a simple quick whack of her favorite walking stick.

For the first time in my life, I saw something other than perfect composure on her face. It was dismay with a hint of smugness. "Oh dear, I might've hit her a little harder than I intended."

As if in a dream, I let Grandma pull me to my feet and push me towards the window of the reading room. My brain was having a hard time processing what I'd just witnessed. My formerly beloved mentor, dead. All that blood and goo spilling from her skull, some of which was sticking to my top; there was no coming back from that. Not even for a mature supernatural.

The demonic campus ground, a mix of grass carpet and gothic structures basking in the morning summer sun, spread out before me. I felt no warmth. Just numbness.

Then Grandma pushed me out of the window.

"Ahhh!" I barely had time to let out a scream, let alone close my eyes as the pavement rushed up towards my face.

I found myself landing on an ottoman, bouncing off it, and sprawling on the dark carpet underneath. It was thick and smelled like lemon-scented cleaner.

I turned my body and stared at the ceiling of a dimly lit bedroom. I wasn't at the university anymore.

Grandma jumped off the ottoman and landed on the carpet with the sleek grace of an ageless jungle cat. "We should be safe here. I constructed this portal in secret ahead of time so it wouldn't create a ripple of power in the Concord for others to detect. It's one of the many I installed..."

"Hold on. Hold on." I held up a hand. "Go back a little bit. What's going on? How come Enid went psycho on me? How did you know where we'd be? And, *hello*—a little warning before pushing me out the window!"

I was probably a little less respectful than I ought to be, but someone had just attacked me. Again. And my half-sister was missing. I think I was entitled to a little hysteria.

Grandma ignored me and pressed a button on the wall. "Aidan, we're back. We'll stay in my bedroom for now."

I looked around in surprise. This was Grandma's

bedroom? A contemporary black-and-white design with utilitarian blinds and a streamlined bed. I was expecting, I don't know, the Marie-Antoinette-style, overdone luxury fluff or something like that.

Grandma continued as if installing unlicensed portals all over the campus and jumping through one after icing a long-time colleague was an everyday occurrence. "Before I jumped, I put a heavy glamour over Enid's dead body, so we've got a bit of time before they find her. Now—"

"Hey, slow down—"

"—the purgatory trail has already gone cold, but there's another way to find Esme."

That pulled me to a full stop. "Whoa. You know about her?"

"I do," Grandma said carefully, rearranging her suit dress as she sat down on the carpet and gestured for me to do the same. If I didn't know better, I'd say the old woman was a little nervous.

"Oh, right, then." I didn't know what else to say.

"Don't you want to know how I found out about Esme?" There was now a hint of challenge in her eyes.

"It doesn't matter. Let's go. We have to get to her *now*." Why the hell was she getting all comfy and settled, for Hade's sake? I couldn't afford to get comfortable. I could feel Enid's blood and brain stuff starting to dry against my flesh, and it was creepy and gross and I just wanted to keep moving so I had no time to freak out and hide in a hole for a week. *Then* what would happen to Esme?

"But in order to do so, you have to understand how I found out about her kidnapping," Grandma said with maddening calmness.

"Why?"

"Sit down and I'll explain. I was able to get a glimpse of her in the scrying stone. She's trapped somewhere. Unconscious but unharmed at the moment. It could change quickly, of course."

"Then let's—"

"If you're going to have a snowball's chance in hell of rescuing her, young lady, you have to hear me out."

"Alright." At least Esme was okay. For now. I sat down just a little too hard on my bum, but I didn't give Grandma the satisfaction of a wince.

"I wouldn't have gotten any satisfaction from that," she muttered.

"What the—" I tried to jump to my feet, but Grandma's hand grabbed hold of my arm and pulled me back down. Then, before I could yank my limb back, Grandmother did something she'd never done before.

She leaned over and tugged a piece of hair behind my ear.

As if to prove that she indeed could read minds, she whispered, "I've touched your hair before, don't you remember? And no, not reading *minds*, as in plural form. With everyone else I only sense impressions, but with you I can read your mind. Even from some distance away. That's how I knew you were in trouble in that reading room."

She looked me in the eyes and muttered a chant under her breath.

A veil lifted from my conscious mind, and I was six months old again. Cuddled by a younger and happier Grandma as if I was the most precious thing in the world. She sang a long-forgotten nursery tune while stroking my newborn peachy fuzz. Then the memories sped up, and I was a little older, just moved from my crib to a little princess bed.

And trapped there, by an equally tiny silver web. My chubby legs tried to kick out but failed. Dazed, I wondered if that was why I had faint memories of sleep paralysis episodes from my childhood. My adult mind might've translated my infant experience into something that it could comprehend.

Mom's scream of terror filled the room, and Dad was struggling with someone in the background.

A hooded someone.

More images flew by, and Grandma was alone with Dad in my bedroom, with me dozing off in the little princess bed. I was drooling all over a teddy bear with a red heart embroidered on its chest. The silver web was absent, but there was the word *Impure* written on the wall in lime green ink.

"She's going to be okay," Grandma said. "See, not even a scratch on her body."

"The bastard used a silver web." Dad's voice shook.

"Are you sure?" Grandma frowned.

"I'm dead sure. The web was made from silk only the uni-spiders from the Grimmian Forest could produce. This is a signature ensnarement of the Greys. I read about it when I did my minor in vengeance history."

"Why would the Greys want anything to do with our little Maggie?"

"Their mandate is to bring back Absolute Evil and to keep the vengeance bloodline pure. You saw what they wrote on the wall. They think my child is an abomination. A freak of nature not deserving of a place in society." Dad's knuckles whitened. Alright, that kinda explained his lifelong overprotectiveness towards me.

"This is worrisome, considering the other trend I've been seeing." Grandma started pacing the room.

Dad's head lifted sharply. "What other trend?"

Grandma sighed. "Nick, you've been out of the loop because of this boycott of your marriage. There've been whispers of an old, dark power rising. The members are made up exclusively of vengeance demons. They've been doing some quiet recruiting on every level of our society. And they're gaining ground."

Dad palmed his forehead. "You think this old, dark power is the Greys."

"After what happened tonight, yes, that's what I fear. And they're elusive. Even with my connections, I know close to nothing about them except what's in the history books." Grandma's face was one of deep frustration.

"How are we going to fight it if we don't know who to trust? How are we going to protect my daughter?"

Grandma straightened herself. "To begin, we cancel her Rite of Acknowledgment."

"How's that going to help anything? Without the Rite, she won't even get a proper vengeance middle name. It would be like announcing to all the planes that you consider my child no better than a bastard."

"That's the point. *Think*, Nick. If I recognize her officially, that'd only fuel whatever animosity is coming her way. Legitimacy in this old family means being in the society paper. A seat on the Council when she grows up. How would that sit with the fanatics? As an outcast, she's got a shot at being left alone. There are always rumors whirling around saying we're fighting because of your new wife. Well, let them believe it. It's a good thing the Acknowledgment hasn't been announced yet."

"You know what kids will say about her in school one day."

"Better that than to be targeted," Grandma said fiercely.

My bedroom dissolved, and a montage of my childhood experiences of bullying and isolation formed in my head. But now those memories were re-synced with that of Grandma's to show a blind spot I'd been enchanted not to notice. Amazingly, it even provided me with her inner thoughts that were associated with the memories.

Grandma, cloaked from view, looking pained when no one joined me at the grade school lunch table.

Grandma, who conjured the wind to land a nice, fat lump of bird poop on ten-year-old Cousin Fred's blond locks, after he called me "Fatty Maggie."

Grandma, who'd pretended to favor Esme in order to keep tabs on me.

Grandma, who tried to stop me from attending Demon U in order to keep me away from danger.

Grandma, who showed up at my Becoming, the vengeance demon Bat Mitzvah. Staying invisible, she stood proudly behind my dad as I read from a dusty old demonic text, a tear falling from her eyes.

Grandma reached over and wiped a tear off the present-day me. She stared at the single teardrop and smiled. "I put my tear from the Becoming into your pearl pendant."

"Oh." Not as store-bought as I thought, after all. Demon tears were potent magic. They could make a dagger's aim true and a shield impenetrable.

Grandma laughed. "No, not so store-bought, after all. But it looked cheap and tacky enough to make people *think* it was. The truth is that I got the pendant sculpted by the high priestess of the Baltic mermaid-witches herself. Add that to my own tear, and the pendant is worth ten times more magic than the standard pearl earrings I gave to all my other grandchildren."

"If it's so powerful, how come I nearly got killed by Dan Pillar?"

"You got out of that situation, didn't you? The pendant helped you on a subconscious level by encouraging you to lean on your trickster side. But to tap into its power directly, you have to activate it. And I'm going to show you how."

"So I had the power all along." It was such a foreign concept, yet somehow familiar.

Grandma swallowed. "Just like you've had my love all along. I've always been...partial to you over my other grandchildren, even though I'm not supposed to have favorites."

I wasn't unwanted.

Deep down, part of me always knew that my gran loved me, always remembered what I was meant to forget. All the hurt I'd felt over her rejections through the years stemmed from that very knowledge.

One last memory came to me. Grandma looked up from the ballroom floor, amongst the chaos caused by my half-brothers, and saw me being attacked in the Shadow World. She summoned Dad, skewing his teleporting route so he'd inadvertently come to my rescue. She knew the whole blame game would bring the Council's scrutiny on me, but she didn't care because it was better than losing me.

Yep, she loved me, alright.

I tried to imagine what it must have been like from Grandma's perspective. To love me, to have to be mean to me, and to be able to read my mind and know that my resentment for her grew day after day, year after year.

"It was necessary," Grandma said. Sadness touched her eyes, though her words were meant to be reassuring. "Being uncaring to you took the attention away from you, and my closed-minded stance made our enemies complacent, made them easier to flush out." Her eyes grew hard. "And as you can see, Enid paid for that mistake with her life."

Enid, who'd gotten her start in the vengeance business by being Grandma's protégé. Enid, who'd been my champion ever since I'd set foot at the university. Even after seeing her true nature firsthand, I still couldn't believe it. A part of me inched to reach for the phone and ask for her council.

I shook my head. "Good old loyal Enid. Who would've thought, huh?"

Grandma sighed. "I wish I could say she was an exception, but I simply don't know how many traitors are among us. I even fed people like your Cousin Fred the occasional gossip just to track how it would go around in the grapevine."

"So *is* he a traitor?" I rather liked the idea of him being in league with the Greys. It would give me a reason to pummel him next time we met.

"The boy sure talks, but does that mean he's a traitor?"

It couldn't be easy trying to flush out the real bad guys. You never knew if someone was truly extreme or just talking big to hide their own insecurity. Case in point, Madeleine the nymph descendant and her I-Hate-Impure-Blood stance.

"The Greys are so savvy and slippery," Grandma continued. "They even infiltrated my own charity ball and got their hooks into one of mine. I'm afraid Enid was right. Esme is the bait and you're the target."

Something was bothering me about that. "Why go through all that trouble just to kill me if I'm a hideous abomination to them?"

"Exactly. That's why I don't think the point is to kill you. I think they want something from you."

"What is it?"

"You've heard of the legends of Fleur, of course."

Every trickster in existence had. I remembered the bedtime stories my mama used to tell me. They were fun tales of mischief and pranks in a prehistoric world. Tipping the tyrannosaurus. Tricking an Australopithecus chef into pulling out his own fur. That kind of thing. "Fleur, the First Trickster, right?"

"Yes. While she's well known in all the planes for being the first mistress of trickery, what most supernaturals don't realize is that she was the one who trapped Absolute Evil."

"Absolute Evil? Like, evil in its purest form? I thought it wasn't real." Or as real as the Loch Ness monster was to humans.

"It's the original, purest, and the most absolute kind of evil. And it's definitely real. The story goes that Fleur secretly passed down a harp to her female descendants, one that could free Absolute Evil from its prison."

"Alright, but I still don't see what any of this has to do with me, or Esme."

"Your mother is the last known female descendant of Fleur. Well, second to last." Grandma looked at me pointedly.

"What?" Mom had never told me that. My first reaction was, "That is *so* cool!" I could get into any trickster party with just the mention of my ancestor, if I wanted to. Heck, I could pull the prank of the century, calling to arms the most talented tricksters of our generation. Then it hit me. If word got out about my lineage, it would make me even less popular in the vengeance world.

"The Greys must think you have the harp and would be willing to trade it for Esme's life. The passing of the harp happens not at the death of the mother, but at the daughter's eighteenth birthday."

"Oh." This was all too much to take in. "Wait, does my mother actually have such a harp?"

"I already asked her all those years ago. At one point in history, her line was rumored to have it, but it has been lost. Even if you *do* have it, I don't think it would be wise to—"

"I know. I know. I can't just give it to them even if I've got it. Esme wouldn't want that anyway. Who knows what they're going to do with it?" Nothing good, I was sure. I closed my eyes. "It's too bad Enid turned out to be so easily killed. We could use some answers."

Grandma nodded. "We supernaturals sometimes get arrogant with our magical safeguards to the point of neglecting our physical weakness."

"But you mentioned there was another way to rescue Esme."

"Before Enid died, she revealed that Esme's captors are the High Monks of Greys, and the fact that there's some fighting going on within the group. We might be able to use that to our advantage. But first things first, we have to locate Esme."

"How?"

"You already know how. Think."

What did I learn today? I was connected to Grandma,

through a bond of love and forced amnesia established long ago. That was how she knew Esme was taken. That was how she knew I was being attacked by Enid.

Esme was connected to me, through her recharging of my power recently.

My trickster blood had always made me a great hider in the game of hide-and-seek. Grandma could flip that into a seeking ability using the hunting instincts of an advanced vengeance demon.

As an added bonus, Esme was wearing trickster-spun clothing, making the seeking just a bit easier.

"Hang in there, Esme. I'm on my way."

FIFTEEN

"A HUMAN OUIJA BOARD?" I looked at the opened department store-bought board game box and raised an eyebrow.

We were sitting cross-legged on the floor next to Grandma's bed, the black-and-white checkerboard design of the carpet contrasting sharply with the faux parchment appearance of the Ouija board.

"Don't underestimate the power of simplicity, my child. With all the necessary symbols and letters laid out, this board will do the locator job just fine. Now, give me your necklace."

I unclasped my pearl pendant necklace and handed it to Grandma. She smiled at the puzzlement on my face and took the pendant off the chain. She then placed it on the center of the Ouija board and put her finger on the planchette, gesturing for me to do the same. I shrugged and followed her lead.

"Now I'm going to show you how to tap into the power of your pearl. It's programmed to respond to voice commands only. To mine or yours."

Grandma took a deep breath and chanted a line repeatedly in a foreign language, Sumerian from the sound of it. The pearl grew bright and transparent. And I felt a corresponding rejuvenation in my wings. I twisted my upper body for a better look.

They'd never looked so good. What was previously dark grey and winkled, was now full-fledged, with the ridges defined in the gorgeous color of soft dove.

I mouthed a word of thanks to Grandma just as the pearl lifted itself out of the pendant's base and melted into the planchette.

"May this board, born from human superstition and fear, help this child of trickery seek her heart's sister." Grandma's voice rang loud and clear across the bedroom.

The planchette lifted its pointy end and gave itself a little full-body shake like a wet dog. Grandma and I struggled to keep our fingers on it. Losing contact now would mean redoing the whole setup.

I'd rather not. Grandma was wearing old lady perfume, and we were leaning pretty close to each other.

"I heard that," she said.

Damn, this mind-reading thing had its disadvantages.

"I heard the D-word too."

Dammit.

Wanting to get started as much as I wanted to avoid a lecture on swearing, I asked the Ouija board, "Where are they holding Esme?"

The planchette moved across the board to point at various letters. C-A-M-P-U-S.

"Campus? You mean at Demon U?"

The planchette pointed at the word "yes."

"No way." The Greys wouldn't dare to hold Esme at a place under Grandma's direct jurisdiction, would they? Wouldn't she know if that was the case? Geez, I was just there less than an hour ago. Could it be that I was drawn there because deep down I knew Esme was near?

"Perhaps. You might've sensed her despite the very strong magic they're no doubt using to hide her presence. Now, try to keep your words in the form of a question," Grandma cautioned. Right, no confusing the planchette, aka Shaky-Shake-Shake Fido.

"Okay, okay." Inspiration struck me. What if Esme was on campus, but not *really* there? "What plane are they keeping her on?"

The planchette spun 'round and 'round like a puppy chasing after its own tail.

"That thing is confused." I was going cross-eyed tracking its frantic movement.

"That's because it has nothing to anchor its detection," a new voice said.

I looked up and saw Serafina at the door. Her posture was tentative and, frankly, a bit scared. And who could blame her? She was looking into Grandma Aequitas' private chambers, and to the rest of the world, she was very much the Demon in Prada.

"Ah, come on in, Miss Advocatus." With her free hand, Grandma gestured Serafina to come into the room. "Have a seat here next to my granddaughter. I believe you've met."

I snorted. Grandma didn't just *believe* Serafina and I had met, she *knew* we were becoming fast friends. Some of the images that flew through my head when our memories had re-synced included me helping Serafina break free of Madeleine's tormenting with the drop of an iron dagger, her disguise at the ball, and even an impromptu double-dare of stepping foot into a sex shop that ended in red faces and giggles.

"Stalker," I muttered, the idea of Grandma having seen

me in front of such an establishment was a bit unsettling.

Grandma pretended she didn't hear me at all. "I already explained the situation to Miss Advocatus. I summoned her to help us in this matter because of her outstanding tracking ability, courtesy of her changeling adopted family."

"'Summoning' is hardly a comforting word to use. See how freaked out you're making her," I complained.

Grandma was unrepentant. I guess I was finally learning where I got my weird sense of humor. "To be honest, I already reached my daily quota for discretion when I called her kidnappers *family*."

Serafina sat down and looked like she wasn't sure what to do in the face of my mock bickering with Grandma, or like she couldn't decide whether or not it was indeed mock bickering at all. Couldn't blame her. Last she heard, I wasn't on very friendly terms with Grandma. I tried to convey the don't-worry-my-gran-won't-bite message to Serafina with my most reassuring smile.

"Now, back to Miss Advocatus' tracking ability. See, changelings as a race might at any point in time have thousands of children they've sent out into the world. These kids move around, go on vacations, get hurt in school sports and occasionally land themselves in situations where their true nature might be exposed. The changelings keep tabs on all of them so a damage-control team can swoop in at a moment's notice."

I never thought of it that way before. That would indeed make them experts in tracking. "So what were you saying about anchoring the detection again?" I asked Serafina.

Serafina bit her lips. "Huh, how do I explain it? Well, you know how a human smartphone has this GPS tracking app?"

"Yeah."

"The app has to be downloaded before the first use in order to establish a traceable link. A magical baseline is the same deal. The Ouija board can provide you with a location, up to a certain extent. But if it doesn't have a baseline to anchor the detection, that's the farthest it could go. If I touch something or someone Esme has touched, then I could locate her using my changeling magic. The stronger the connection, the better the chance."

"Well, this part is easy." I reached over to clasp Serafina's wrist. Her eyes widened when she felt some of Esme's life force flowing in me. It was a generous gift, and now it had proven to be a vital one.

Serafina blew her changeling magic onto the planchette, stilling the madly spinning piece of wood immediately. Then she put her own finger on it, careful not to loosen my grip on her wrist. "That will do nicely. Megan, ask your question again."

I cleared my throat and pressed harder on the planchette. *Let's hope this works.* "What plane are they keeping Esme on?"

The planchette moved along the board with a steadfast movement I found reassuring, spelling out the letters H-U-M-A-N.

Well hello, the University of Toronto campus.

"Wait, it's not as simple as that," Grandma pointed out.

"Why?"

"Because it hasn't stopped spelling."

The planchette spelled out BOOTLEG.

"Oh."

A bootlegged plane was a micro-world created by the planeswalker demons for the purpose of allowing individuals to enjoy a slice of the human life without all the pitfalls. It had everything the real human place would have and none of the unpleasantness—like hangovers and parking tickets—as everything in it wasn't real. Depending on the price paid to the said demons, the size, quality, and duration of that copied world varied greatly. There were permanent bootlegged planes out there that went on a continuous copying loop, updating that world with the latest pop music and gadgets, and replacing broken bar stools, accidentally run-over pedestrians and what not.

These planes were illegal, for the obvious risk of some serial killing supernaturals using it as a practice ground before moving on to the real thing.

How were we going to find out exactly which bootlegged plane Esme was hidden in, let alone how to get there?

I changed into fresh clothes in one of Grandma's spare bedrooms.

My eyes misted when I saw my old princess bed in the center of the room, with a worn teddy bear resting against the pillow, the embroidered silk heart on its chest as vibrantly red as I'd remembered it. I guess I really did always have a place in Grandma's heart.

I opened the closet and found an assortment of clothes in my size. I picked my outfit and headed for the ballroom.

I studied myself in the mirror opposite the landing on the top of the stairs leading down to Grandma's ballroom. It held the reflections of a girl in a fresh, body-hugging, blood-and-gore-free T-shirt. Along with my own leather jacket, pants, and boots, I was covered head to toe in black.

I might not know how to get to the party yet, but I was dressed and ready to rumble.

On the surface, I looked like any average wannabe-cool university girl with not enough sense to *not* dress in black, long sleeves, and leather on a hot summer day. It was the best I could do to conceal as many weapons as I could while moving in the bootlegged world. Best not to alarm the humans there. We might know that they are fake, but *they* don't. There was a secret compartment on each side of my jacket, one holding an extendible knife and another a dagger. I wore an arrow-shooting ring on my finger, and a snap-together shield was hidden in the base of my sneakers. And did I mention my belt, which could shapeshift into an ax? Also, my dark hairband was made of trickster-spun material, which could induce illusion and interfere with my targets' senses with hyper arousal.

"I think it's best if we leave hyper arousal out of the equation, dear." Grandma coughed from behind me.

"Oh, alright."

Awkward silence.

"Aren't you going to question, say, the merits of following rules when our enemy is playing dirty?"

That would be what I'd have asked even a day ago. But now the last thing I wanted was to get into a fight with Grandma. I'd been fighting with her all my life as it was. I felt like I was walking on eggshells, unsure of how to move forward. A part of me wanted to hug her and ask for a pony like a five-year-old, and the other part was clinging to a lifelong habit of having someone to be mad at. It was weird and strange and off balancing.

Grandma chuckled. "If it helps, it's jarring for me too, and I knew my own intentions all along. And no, I don't mean that I have any moral issues about your choice of weaponry. It's just that...well, I have the answer we're looking for, but you're not going to like it."

She gestured to the downstairs hallway that led to her drawing room, and out walked a vengeance demon I'd never expected to see in a place that was the very definition of vengeance pride and respectability.

I'd recognize those chiseled cheekbones and broad shoulders anywhere. I'd dreamed about them since that night at the puppy miller's. Pete's black suit was utterly starched, so much so that it passed the point of refinement and came out the other side of mockery. He was as lithe as a jungle cat; every step up the stairs was calculated, resonating with a robust energy that bespoke a way of life far less gentlemanly than the average guest in this very ballroom.

As he approached the landing, the harsh lines at the corners of his mouth twisted with the beginning of a lazy grin. Upon his arrival, the ripple of his energy signature caused a few strands of my hair to blow away from my face and tickle my ears in a sensuous way, making me remember the final moments from the last time I'd seen him.

Grandma's eyes narrowed.

I blushed. And hated myself for it. So Grandma didn't

mean leaving hyper arousal out of the equation because it wasn't a fair fight. She meant she knew what I was thinking when I thought about Pete, because she could read my mind and...

My grandmother was able to read my lustful thoughts for this boy. Ick. I repeat, *ick*.

"This man here is a freelancer." Grandma kept a straight face, as if she had no idea Pete and I had met before or what was going on in my mind just now. Yeah, right. "We've done business in the past."

Grandma Aequitas, honorary and lifetime member of the Council, had done business with a shady mercenary before?

Her eyes sparkled. "I've got to keep my ear to the ground somehow. His name is—"

"Pete," I supplied.

"It's Gregory, as a matter of fact." Grandma coughed. "He's a—"

"Bastard," Gregory offered with a smile. I could feel his eyes on me, as if trying to see if he'd shocked a reaction out of me.

And surprised I was. That would explain the odd combination of his obviously highborn power signature and lowly occupation. The vengeance society was still very traditional in a lot of ways. Lots of doors would be closed to someone like him, which I bet contributed to his present career choice.

Gregory was still looking at me. Being a pariah all my life myself, I knew the last thing he wanted was pity. I shrugged. "Hello, bastard. Meet freak of nature."

He threw back his head and laughed. "I like her, Lady Aequitas."

Grandma huffed. "Just do what you're paid to do. You rascal."

"Which is?" I asked.

"A safe passage to the bootlegged plane. Gregory is...friendly with the planeswalker demons."

"You mean he beat the crap out of one of them, found out which plane Esme is on, and got the portal code out of him?"

"Please." Gregory rolled his eyes. "I only resort to violence *after* diplomacy fails."

"And did it fail?"

"Of course."

"So what's the deal? Can we get going now? I'm ready." I eyed Grandma's elegant dress suit. "But I'll wait for Gran to change."

Gregory shook his head. "I can only carry one of you. This being an illegal space, it has a narrow entrance on purpose. Two is a tight squeeze. Three is impossible."

"You should be the one to go." Grandma covered my hand with hers. "Your bond with Esme is stronger than mine, and that will guide you to her. I'll try to track down both Dan and Enid's associates before they get away. Maybe they'll know something of use. Now, Gregory, I need a moment with my granddaughter."

Gregory bowed—again, more mockery than true manners—and retreated downstairs. Grandma waited until he closed the door of the drawing room behind him.

"You're not going to warn me about him, are you? 'Cause that's going to be embarrassing for the both of us." I didn't know if I could take an impromptu talk about bad boys and consequences.

"No."

Awkward silence again.

"Oh, okay."

"I just want to tell you that Serafina is staying to help me. And though she doesn't know it yet, I intend to give her a token of my appreciation when this is all over."

I groaned. "What are you going to do, appoint her Student of the Year? That would isolate her even more, not less."

Grandma seemed a bit offended. "It might be hard for you to imagine, but I was young once, too. I did no such thing to Miss Advocatus."

"Then what?"

"I failed her this semester."

"What! After all the help she's given us, this is how you repay her?" I jumped.

"Megan, that girl was returned to us barely a year ago. Her parents should never have pushed her to go to university this soon, and without the Advocatus name, it wouldn't have happened. It's time she does things at her own pace. You can't succeed if you aren't allowed to fail first."

Alright, I allowed, that was kinda wise.

"Here, let me give you back the pendant." As Grandma put the necklace back on my neck, I thought about the years that could've been. I heard a small sigh next to my ear. But when I turned back to see her face, there was only fierce pride on it, not wistfulness. "There, all good."

"Thank you." I didn't know what else to say, but she seemed to understand.

"I do. But hurry now, I can feel Esme waking up. She's terrified. I don't need a scrying stone to know that."

"When you said *carry*, you meant it literally?"

"As I said, it's going to be a tight squeeze."

We were in Grandma's drawing room, standing by a large potted plant with a five-foot-tall trunk and a manicured ball of leaves and flowers at the top. Gregory waved his hand over the thick trunk, and it doubled in width, stretching out to reveal a break in the fabric of reality.

He crouched low on the floor, offering me his back. "You coming or not?"

"I am not piggy-riding on your back." It wasn't so much as a yuck thing as an I-don't-want-to-be-caught-sniffing-his-shirt thing. A girl had to preserve her dignity.

"Correct as you may be about my lifestyle, this isn't about me trying to cop a feel." Gregory let out an exasperated sound. "Even with the right code, the entrance has an erosive, magic-robbing barrier I have to plow through. The closer you are to me, the more likely my protection is going to hold."

"Fine."

I'd already said goodbye to Grandma in the hallway. All my gear was checked and double-checked. I had to get to Esme. So onto his back I climbed, resisting the urge to pull on his midnight blue wings for support.

Even through his suit, I could still feel the heat of his body and the hardness of his muscles as I squeezed my legs against his middle. Everywhere my body pressed against his was toned and well-defined. If he'd gotten that body through faery dust steroids, then he hadn't skimped. But I had a feeling he'd worked out the old-fashioned way, as a mental image of him fighting a planeswalker demon came to mind.

When he placed his hands on the back of my ankles and pulled me higher onto his back, I couldn't help but draw in a breath of surprise. He might have a gentleman's genes, but his hands were large and callused. A workingman's hands. The feel of them on me, the closeness of him and his scent, a mix of sweet sandalwood and bitter oak bark, was wreaking havoc on my already frayed nerves. Add a little disgust at my own reaction into the mix, and it made me want to kick something.

Save the shame for later. Esme needs you right now.

Before I could collect myself, Gregory put his left leg into the trunk of the potted plant, then his right. My skin tingled when I entered the threshold, then the pins and needles ballooned into an intense burning sensation, engulfing every inch of my flesh. I cried out in pain.

"Hang on, we're almost through." Gregory tightened his hold on me when I started sliding off him. "Come on, tough girl, just a few seconds more."

Then the heat was gone, and cool air hit me like a splash of water. Instead of being refreshing, the effect was like rubbing salt on a fresh wound.

Gregory gently laid me on the floor. "Hey, you alright?"

"It...hurts..."

"It'll pass in a moment."

And it did. The pain came fast, but also left fast. I braced my body on my elbows, blinked, and found myself facing a box full of miniature figures. Warriors with badass swords and scantily clad women with as much boobs as menace.

"Looks like we've come to the right place," Gregory said dryly.

I struggled to my feet, brushing off a smear of paint on my shoulder from a still-wet figure left drying on the floor. "I think you're right."

Our landing spot on this plane was supposed to be the backroom of a games and hobby shop just a little off campus. Judging from the impressive collection of comic books, board games, and trading cards, we were on the right track.

"And this is where I leave you." Gregory gave me another one of those mocking bows. "I'd say it's because you need to go on this journey on your own, blah, blah, blah. But the truth is, here is as far as I'm willing to go. This is the tipping point in what is called acceptable risk in my business."

"But..." I hated the faint note of pleading in my voice, but I couldn't help it. I was scared. On my own in a strange plane. "Sure, you taught me how to get back. But what about that erosive barrier? How am I supposed to get through that on my way out?"

"There's no barrier in leaving, just going in. Think about it, would they place bouncers at a club's exit?"

"Fine!" I bit out, heading towards the door.

"Alright. This one is on the house," Gregory said as I passed him. "Male."

"What?"

"Your glamour." He shook his long brown hair, as if he couldn't believe he was saying what he was saying. "Set it to male for the next minute."

"Why?"

"This plane is occasionally patrolled by succubus. They don't come out much, but any ripple of excitement would be like blood to a shark."

"Oh." I was in a nerd store. A girl in a form-fitting outfit.

Talk about not attracting any attention to myself. I transformed myself into a dude who would look right at home in a place like this.

So that was the last mental image I'd left with Gregory. A baseball hat on my head, baggy Spiderman tee, my curves turned into man boobs, and a hairy bum sticking out from a pair of unwashed jeans.

I prayed that he'd feel at least a fraction of an attraction towards me. A fraction would be enough to totally gross him out.

Ha.

I made my way out of the games and hobby shop, past a D&D session in full swing, and not a single soul batted an eye.

Not that these cardboard humans had actual souls. But still.

Midway to the campus boundary, I hid in an alley between two school buildings and changed my appearance from Mr. Comic Book Guy to that of Enid. It took a lot more magic to imitate a real person than a fictitious one, especially in the presence of those I sought to fool, as the essence and energy signature had to be bang on. I relied on a little trickery charm called the Lookalike. I'd perfected it in grade school, pretending to be a teacher and scaring the crap out of my bullies.

It'd gotten even more fun after they'd figured out the ruse. Once, a tormentor of mine kicked a real teacher, thinking she was me. Oops.

As I passed by a convenience store catering to resident students, I stopped and took in my new reflection in its glass windows. I now looked a hundred percent like Enid, from her tight hair bun to her classic navy Chanel suit.

Now that I was on campus, where should I go from here?

I closed my eyes and muttered the most powerful weapon I had, handed directly to me from Enid herself during our final confrontation.

The name of Esme's captors.

There was great power in knowing a name. It was a fair trade, considering she'd been busy killing me at the time.

"High Monks of Greys, High Monks of Greys," I said repeatedly, allowing the name to seep into my very being and letting it guide me.

Hart House. Second floor.

Hart House. Figured. There were plenty of elegant rooms there that would be perfect for a secret society to conduct business in. I went to the building, ran upstairs, and tried to check out the East Common Room, an alcove space with candle wall sconces and refined coffered ceilings. I opened its double doors.

And walked into a wedding.

Lucky for me, all eyes were on the incoming bride, and I slipped out without causing a stir. I should be glad it wasn't a chapel. No, thank you. Just in case there was a chance that I'd burst into flame like in one of those bedtime stories every demon child had heard since infancy.

The Debates Room.

The bootleg version of the school was a true to reality copy. With the human summer holidays in full swing, there weren't a lot of students milling around in the hallway. Good, less potential for attracting excitement.

There were voices on the other side of the Debates Room, and I recognized them as belonging to those I was looking for.

I opened the door to yet another majestic room with coffered ceiling. Seriously, after this ordeal, I would stare at exposed concrete walls and IKEA furniture for a year.

Three figures at the center of the room turned abruptly upon my arrival, their hoods not drawn up like they'd been at our last meeting. I noted the fine cashmere their robes were made of, the platinum collar links. The Off-Blacks were right. These were not the simple-living kind of monks.

Beside the three in attendance was Dan Pillar, his clothing no less expensive than that of his supernatural masters.

"Greetings, Damarion, Taurean, and Kameron." The names just came out of my mouth. Sometimes the Lookalike charm offered bonus points if the pretender had a personal connection to the person he or she was pretending to be. Guess nothing bonded like a would-be murder. *My* would-be murder. The shock on the monks' faces almost made Enid's attack, which made the knowledge of their names possible, worthwhile. Almost.

I ignored Dan like any egoistic species-intolerant bigot would.

"What do you want, Enid?" Damarion demanded. Underneath the anger, there was a trace of fear in his voice. This was the same guy with the talon-like hands I'd mistaken as fake props the last time. I was happy to see some self-doubt in him. He'd seemed just too indomitable in my nightmares since the Shadow World encounter.

I just hoped he wouldn't try to fling me again.

"I've got the harp," I said with the cold triumph of a cobra, a tone the real Enid would employ. Inside, I felt like there was a squadron of army ants biting through my stomach lining, but I couldn't allow it to show. I kept my heart rate as normal as I could, my shoulders relaxed.

"No," Taurean breathed.

Sensing all was not well, Dan took a step back without trying to look like he was on retreat.

"That's right." I covered the quivering of my lip by twisting it into a sneer. "That stupid Megan girl thinks she's working with me. She trusts me. So the harp is currently in my possession, and your witless kidnapping scheme won't lure her out. Now, to keep my unsuspecting little pet happy for our big plan, you have to let Esme Aequitas go."

"Are you making a claim for leadership? Is that why you're here? I thought we agreed we're all equals in the serving of our master," Kameron said bitterly. This harp thing must be very important. The three monks looked like they'd want nothing more than to fry me on the spot, but nobody made a move. I started to think that I might just make it out of here alive.

I decided to plow my way through the questions. Luck was on my side; I could feel it. "Don't be a fool. There's a hierarchy in every plane and every level of society. Hand me the girl. The sooner we do that, the sooner we can bring back Absolute Evil."

I realized something was wrong a second after the words left my mouth, because the High Monks went deadly silent. Then they weren't so defeated-looking anymore. They straightened and started crowding me, surrounding me at every angle. Even Dan, who, like me, wasn't exactly clear on what my mistake might have been, leaned closer.

"Say it again," Damarion asked, real quiet-like. He flexed his long fingers. I did mention he was the guy with the talon-like hands, right?

"What do you mean?" I tried to sound as arrogant and

authoritative as possible. "You heard me the first time."

"Say it again." Damarion gave me an awful smile, and my heart sank. "The sooner we hand you the girl, the what?"

"The sooner we can bring back Absolute Evil," I couldn't help but answer. They'd already heard it once, after all. *Er, Lady Luck, are you still there?*

"Absolute Evil? Are you certain? The first sacred duty of the Greys is to bring back Absolute Good, not Absolute Evil. Enid and I might have many professional differences, but even *she* wouldn't get that wrong. So I guess I should say, 'Hello, Megan.'"

Dan's lips curved. "Ah, we meet again. Was the last time not enough?"

Dammit! How could it be that not only the Off-Blacks, but the rest of the supernatural world, had gotten it wrong when it came to this blasted secret society?

The Greys thought they were on the side of the good guys. Heck, they thought they *were* the good guys. From the fanatic gleam in the eyes of the men in a tight formation around me, I could see that they genuinely believed in their own goodness, even while they were doing nasty things. That was inherently more dangerous than aspiring to be badasses while cuddling and playing dress-up with kittens.

What was my Plan B again?

Sixteen

"I DON'T HAVE THE HARP. You know that, right?" I'd reverted back to my own appearance, as there was no point in keeping up the pretense anymore.

I was tied to a disgusting wall covered with glowing slime in some basement dungeon. How clichéd was that? Oh right, I was in the company of a group of crazy, elitist vengeance demons.

"I never thought you did," Damarion nodded when Dan finished the final touches on my knots. "You're going to be part two of my double bait."

I cursed inwardly. I'd never considered that, and neither had Grandma. We'd totally played into their hand.

"Soon my master will reenter this world and burn away all its wickedness. No more impure scum. No more morally ambiguous Cosmic Balance." Damarion stroked his knuckles in fanatic excitement.

"C'mon, this ain't a bad world to live in. The system is in place for a reason."

"You're loyal to the Council, after all they've put you through?"

"'Loyal' is a strong word. It's a matter of relativity. The Council might be old-school and nepotistic, but I'd take them over crazy idealists any time."

"Well, we'll just have to agree to disagree, love."

"Right, as if you and your sneaky ways will have a place in this new, supposedly pristine world."

My little dart seemed to have found a chink in his armor, because Damarion huffed and turned towards the door. "I'll be back. Keep yourself entertained while I bully your family into giving up the harp. I might even be in the mood to trade two for the price of one."

Damarion crossed the threshold. Dan did the same and then closed the door behind him with a muffled thump.

Touché.

I had to get out of the dungeon and find Esme. But how? I looked around me. There were two guards outside the door. The room itself was devoid of any furniture, and, ick, were those mice in the corner? As a kid I'd gone through a human Disney phase, but even then, I hadn't been that big on Mickey Mouse. Mice in general creeped me out a bit.

They'd taken away every single one of my weapons, from the extendible knives, the arrow-shooting ring, all the way to the snap-together shield. They'd even confiscated my trickster-spun hairband. They'd left my pearl pendant necklace alone though, as a twisted sign of respect for a vengeance demon captive, however tainted they thought that blood was. But they'd made sure to rub anti-magic balm all over the pearl. My little amplifier would be out for at least a day, if not more.

I had to face the facts. I was guarded by radical vengeance demons who knew exactly who I was. To escape, I could safely rule out using any vengeance magic and even most of the common trickery magic.

That meant I had to think outside of the box, literally. Who do I know who has free access in and out of my jail?

I looked at the mice in the corner again and smiled. I remembered now a story I'd once read about Walt Disney during my aforementioned Disney phase. When he'd started out, he'd been so broke that he'd had to live in an infested apartment. When life had given him mice, he'd drawn mouse cartoons and made millions.

Maybe I didn't mind Mickey Mouse that much, after all.

But first I had to get the mice to come closer. If I couldn't do it the vengeance or the trickery way, what about the human way? What did magically impaired humans do to get what they wanted? They had to know something. They'd managed to build everything from the pyramids to the Internet, after all.

They lied and they bribed.

All of a sudden I remembered the dog biscuits I'd put in my pants pocket, given to me by Rosemary at the shelter, what felt like a lifetime ago. My life seemed to have divided into two Befores and Afters since then. There was before and after Esme's kidnapping, and before and after the rediscovery of Grandma's love.

I concentrated my will on one of the bigger mice, subtly enhancing the smell of Rosemary's awesome dog biscuits and lowering its fear towards the giant they belonged to—me.

It seemed I could still use some limited magic as long as it wasn't combat-related in a direct way.

The large mouse crawled towards me, its approach tentative. I did some weird yoga move to slip two fingers into my pants pocket and took out a dog biscuit.

"Hey there, little one, want a bite?" I crooned.

As soon as the mouse bit into my food, it was mine. I used a form of mind-control called The Drone. This was a little trick I knew for sure the High Monks wouldn't have safeguarded against, because it was newly invented by my half-brothers and hadn't reached the market yet. Fir planned to market it to teenagers who were under the gun to clean their room but didn't want to do the grunt work themselves.

My little drone mouse climbed into my pants pocket, grabbed more dog biscuits, and shared them with his friends. Soon I had a tiny army of four.

One mouse worked on unbinding my hands. Another one did the same to my feet. The other two took the remaining dog biscuits out and laid them in front of me.

I enchanted the biscuits with a Sleeping Beauty spell—another one of my half-brothers' inventions—and the pair of mice slipped out the dungeon door carrying them. Before my guards had a chance to cry foul, my little soldiers had stuffed a dog biscuit down each of their throats.

I heard two almost simultaneous *thuds* just as my limbs were freed from the ropes, and I knew that the coast was clear.

"Thank you, my little friends."

Emerging from the basement dungeon, I blinked like a baby owl in the waning sunlight. I would've bet it was evening already. Turned out it was still daytime, though it wouldn't be for much longer.

I was at the university just as before. On the bootleg or the real human plane, I didn't know. I stood in front of Hart House and simply sent out my senses.

Definitely bootleg. There was a lack of souls all around, despite the appearance of being at the heart of a bustling city.

They would've moved Esme after my little failed impersonation. Now, if I was a pretentious, deluded religious nut with an overdeveloped sense of self-righteousness and a cliché-ridden sense of style, where on campus would I be relocating my hostage?

I ran through a list of all the likely suspects in my head: student theaters, large-capacity lecture halls, student centers housed in Victorian mansions...problem was, there were simply too many possibilities.

"I know where they're holding her."

I spun around. There was Gregory, leaning against the wall of the front entrance with his arms crossed over his chest. He'd changed into a simple sweatshirt and jeans, as if he'd been chilling out at home before coming here.

"You know where she is?"

"Where she is and where she was before that."

"And you didn't bother telling me when we first got here?" I looked around for something handy and sharp to stab him with.

Gregory shook his head as if I was the most naïve girl in the world. Maybe I was—for not kicking him in the nuts the moment I met him. "I'm a businessman. I saw no need to offer that information. You had nothing to trade for it at the time."

Bastard. *Wait.* "And I do now?"

"I'll exchange what you need for a boon." The guy made the offer without batting an eye. He didn't use any power to sway my decision. Just good old-fashioned negotiation skills.

Too bad I was a bit too pissed to be just as cool-headed. Cold, hard business, my butt. I'd gotten my cover blown. I'd barely made it out of my dungeon of a prison. And this guy had known a better way all along? "A boon? What am I, the freaking Wall Street fairy?" Then I couldn't help asking, "What kind of a boon?"

"Your help in this new job I was just offered."

"What is it?"

"Can't say. Client-mercenary confidentiality."

"Well, that's vague."

He raised his eyebrow. "It's a good deal. You only have to do it if you survive this mess."

"Geeze thanks, asshole. I'm not promising you anything if I don't know what it is." He might want me to perform vengeance on an undeserving party or something. Or worse, to use my trickery powers to do the same. That would open a floodgate I might never be able to close again.

"Well, I'll give you a promise of my own then. The job is going to be legal for both vengeance and human laws. It doesn't involve trickery." Gregory counted off his fingers, proving that he knew of my heritage as much as my reluctance. He did his homework, I'd give him that. "It'll even have your grandmother's stamp of approval. Plus, you get to help a friend. Your changeling friend."

"What does Serafina have to do with all this?" I asked sharply, "Just what is it you're playing at?"

"Let's just say that she'll be very happy if you say yes to my offer, mark my words. So do we have a deal?"

"Alright." It wasn't like I had another choice. I couldn't suffer any more delays in getting to Esme. At least if I'd promised this guy something, it'd increase the likelihood that his information would be reliable.

"She's at the Rotman School of Management."

Rotman, the business school on campus where students

learned how to succeed in a capitalist world. It was a place I would never consciously associate with the High Monks, yet when I thought about it, it made sense as they were all about living the high life. Talk about hiding in plain sight.

I started in the direction of the school.

"Wait." Gregory blocked my way. "A little bonus to help you out."

"Why?" I asked suspiciously. When a guy who viewed the world as one giant freaking chess game wanted to do you one, you took notice. "Another one on the house?"

"Of course not. My reputation won't survive it." He shuddered.

"Then I ask again, why?"

"Because it's the little things that make the difference between someone returning the favor willingly, or out of obligation."

"Or being alive to return the favor at all," I shot back.

"Yeah, there's that," he conceded, then pointed at my necklace. "Give it to me. I could feel the bind on your pearl all the way from here. I can free it."

Reluctantly, I unclasped my necklace and handed it over. Powerless or not, it was my little security blanket, and I hated his hands on it.

Gregory placed the pendant at the center of his palm and chanted something in Sumerian. The pearl grew bright and transparent, just like it had at Grandma's place. But this time, instead of lifting itself up, it absorbed all the anti-magic balm on its surface and gave off a little burp, as if saying in defiance, "Is that all you've got?"

I laughed. The pearl sure had some attitude. My magic was now back in full swing.

"Remember this moment," Gregory advised as he

retreated. "When I come back for my boon."

I knew about the Rotman School of Management because I'd been there once when a third cousin twice removed, from the trickster side, had graduated from there.

I repeat, a trickster obtaining a business degree and getting a steady job. That would be like a reaper training to be a baby-delivering stork, or a human mobster aspiring to be a cop. A *clean* cop.

Once I got near the school's contemporary structure, I knew Gregory had delivered the goods. Connected to Esme as I was, I could feel the mental breadcrumbs she'd left behind for me to chase.

I made myself invisible and followed a student into the building via the automatic doors. The atrium was set up with rows of chairs for what appeared to be a guest lecture with the banner overhead that read, "Speaker Series: The Challenges in the Valuation of Derivatives."

Yep, definitely Rotman.

The library upstairs.

What was that? I could have sworn I just heard Esme whisper her whereabouts to me. That level of connection was almost unheard of. I rushed upstairs, walked towards the library, and passed through the anti-theft detection gates.

And got transported into the demonic dimension of the same room.

The *real* demonic plane. I was a hundred percent sure of it. I didn't think there was a difference while I was in the bootleg plane, but now that I was out of there, everything felt more solid and vivid, from the air I breathed to the carpet under my feet.

So much for getting angsty over my ability to leave the bootleg plane when the time came.

Somehow, I managed to remain invisible through the shock of the transition. Not wanting to lose that competitive edge, I dared not make a sound as I observed my surroundings.

Esme was sitting at a nearby cedar table among rows of bookshelves, playing chess with her date-turned-jailor. One of her ankles was chained to the leg of her heavy wooden chair, the metal links peeking through the edge of her pink floral sundress. The links were made of duralumin, from the look of it. At least the dress appeared clean and in one piece. Good, I didn't have to rip the asshole's heart out for messing with her. I'd just rip his heart out for the kidnapping part.

On the surface, Esme seemed rather relaxed, which kinda pissed me off. I thought she was supposed to be terrified. Here I was, risking my neck, and she looked like she was enjoying a grand old time with her man of the hour.

Until I heard her frantic mental call urging me to be cautious. She couldn't exactly read my mind like Grandma did, but connected as we were, she could feel my presence and tried to project warnings into my head.

As I got closer to her, I could feel her concern for me, her fear for both of us. Yet her face remained neutral and even almost pleasant. If the vengeance gig didn't work out, maybe acting would be a good fallback plan for her.

Prince Guillermo Cristobal Canus, or whatever his real name was, lifted the wineglass at the corner of the table and took a sip. "Now, this is not a bad way to kill time, is it?"

"Until when?" Esme asked, sounding casual and bored.

"Patience, my sweet." Guillermo shook his head. "You waited months for me. Surely you can wait a bit longer now."

"Months." Esme sighed and lowered her eyes so her captor couldn't read the murderous intent I could feel rolling from her in waves. "I was so stupid."

"Don't feel too bad, sweetheart. I laced my lips with powdered love potion when I kissed you at the ball, and it was some potent stuff. I know, because I swallowed a bit of it myself by accident." Guillermo winked at Esme and attempted a seductive smile. "Even aware of its effect, I found myself missing you just a little bit. You should be flattered."

Esme made a disgusted sound from her throat that was completely unladylike, but which I approved of. I was relieved, frankly. That whole mooning, lovesick thing had me worried there for a while. So it was nothing but a spell that had turned my level-headed sister a little crazy. I was afraid it was the start of a lifelong trend of choosing losers or something.

"I wanted to call you sooner, you know," the ever-gallant prince offered. "But my superiors said I had to set a few things in motion first. We couldn't afford to miscalculate again after that disaster of a ball."

Yeah, I bet. Cross-dimensional demon-napping was delicate work indeed. So he bewitched her, then he left her alone to deal with the withdrawal symptoms that came with the love spell. Jerk.

I made a mental note to talk to Grandma about her physician. He was either not that good, or he'd been paid off to act clueless when Esme went to see him. Either way, a little disturbing.

I concentrated on remaining invisible and swept the room for a makeshift weapon. That little footstool close to the end of the second row of bookshelves on the left was made of metal and seemed promising. I inched towards that slowly, careful not to leave any traces of energy for Guillermo to detect.

"What will happen to us when Megan gets here?" Esme asked as she moved another pawn.

Guillermo rubbed his chin thoughtfully. "Something painful and grisly, I'm sure."

In other words, he wasn't sure. It was beyond his pay grade to know.

Esme seemed to have come to the same conclusion. "You don't know yourself, do you?"

"'Course I do," he protested in the typical fashion of an underling with an overdeveloped sense of self-importance. "I heard them say at least one of you had to die."

Esme snorted. "I'd like to see you try."

Guillermo moved a bishop with a triumphant smile. "Checkmate, my sweet."

"Oh, no. That's the fourth one in a row," Esme whined and glared as if she'd just cracked a fingernail rather than lost a game of chess. She formed a perfect pout with her full lips that was guaranteed to make the males of any species think of her as less of a threat. Wow, that subtle shift of mood from defiance to dourness was a lightning-fast one. Such inconsistency was common among flighty human females, but rare for the self-controlled vengeance demons. But Esme pulled it off. Nothing motivated like survival instincts. "You must be cheating."

My half-sister was up to something. I knew it. I stopped

moving and focused on her, ready to act the moment she made her play.

Guillermo laughed, being put at ease by Esme's apparent sullenness. "I assure you, I won fair and square. I might've lied to you about many things, but I *am* from a prominent family and chess is second nature to me. I didn't have to cheat to win."

Old-school, huh? Yeah, he did seem the type who enjoyed dumber females. Esme was playing to his ego. Good girl.

Her eyes flared with challenge, bratty and sultry at the same time. "Prove it."

Guillermo folded his arms over his chest. "How do you propose I do that?"

Esme leaned closer to him, "Let me touch you."

He leered. "Oh, is that what this is all about?"

Esme blew out an exasperated sound and held out her hand. "I mean, let me touch your hand. Then I'll know if you're lying. Just one touch. You know full well I don't have the skills to take power from you. Not shackled with *these* anyway."

She made a point of shaking the duralumin links that were binding her ankles. As human technology progressed, vengeance demons had found to their dismay that some of the new manmade alloys, such as duralumin, had the unintended effect of disrupting vengeance magic. It was most annoying, as duralumin was being used in creating aircrafts, which meant no bringing someone to justice while he or she was enjoying the mile high club. That was why the Cayman Islands airport was always full of grumpy vengeance demons waiting for their took-the-money-and-ran charges to get off the plane before getting on with the vengeance.

If Esme's magic was affected, Guillermo's would be too, though to a much lesser degree.

Esme continued to hold out her hand. "Well?"

Vengeance demons generally tended not to hold hands with people they didn't trust, because there was much power and revelation in such a connection, just like that time when Esme had recharged me. I understood what she was trying to do now, so I got into position beside her, opposite Guillermo.

Overconfident with his success so far and given my half-sister's chained-up position, Guillermo gave a smug nod. "Alright. But I reserve the right to take power from *you*."

Gotta hand it to Esme, she didn't even flinch at his suggestive tone as she held still for his advancing touch.

The moment Guillermo got hold of Esme's left hand, I did the same with her right hand. With Esme in the middle, acting as a conduit, we girls started pushing our combined power into Guillermo, fraying his nerves, then ended the connection right before anything could backfire into us. Thanks to our connection, Esme and I had been able to coordinate our attack with precise timing.

Screaming, Guillermo landed hard on the ground, his body twitching in spasms. But I dared not celebrate, because I could tell that strong as he was, he'd recover from this little sensory overload in no time.

"Come on," Esme urged. "Make sure he stays down or he'll finish us."

I did a double take and turned to look at Esme. *Really* look at her. Was this actually my kind, rule-following, ladylike sister, who wouldn't hurt a fly as long as it wasn't on her work assignment list? "Whatever happened to

Article 10.5, section C about using minimum force?"

"Screw that," Esme spat. Wow, looked like captivity had unleashed my half-sister's inner bitch, and she was just a little scary.

Better stay on her good side, then. I took a leaf out of Grandma's book and whacked his highness over the head with the solid oak chess box conveniently located right on the table. He grunted then stilled. I checked his breathing.

"He'll live," I announced. Making myself visible again, I unchained Esme's ankle from the leg of her chair.

"Megan!" Esme hugged me as soon as I straightened up. "You came for me."

"Of course I did." I tried my best to play it cool. "Who's going to be my alibi when I prank Cousin Freddy at the next Annual Under-Thirty Demonic Picnic?"

Maybe we got cheery a little bit too early, because as soon as the words left my mouth I could no longer feel my tongue.

Nor could I move the rest of my body, for that matter. And was that a sting in my butt?

Oh.

The only thing worse than being hit in the butt with a tranquilizer like a dumb hippo in the zoo was to do so and then be transported like low-fare cargo while staying conscious the entire time.

"It's not a tranquilizer, in case you're wondering," Dan Pillar helpfully supplied as he supervised his henchmen moving Esme and me. "It's an anesthesia for human cosmetic surgeries. For demons, the drugs have the unexpected result of loss of mobility, but not consciousness."

Great, just like a *Nip/Tuck* episode from hell.

As soon as Esme and I lost our ability to move, Dan and his henchmen had swooped into the library like vultures converging on dying men in a desert. The henchmen wore black suits like in any B-rated human movie, and Dan was in a tailored Italian number that belonged more in an estate home than the hellhole we were travelling through.

I had no idea where they were taking us. All I knew was that we were in some underground tunnels with poor lighting, even worse ventilation, and lots of steps. On top of being transported as low-fare cargo, Esme and I were also packaged as such. We were each stuffed inside an oversized cardboard box, like the ones humans used to deliver fridges. A small balloon-sized cutout was made for us to breathe through and to see out of. The boxes were rather awkward shapes to be carrying, especially up and down narrow stairways. Judging from the faces of Dan's henchmen—mere humans from the looks of them—they weren't very happy about the situation, either. I just hoped they wouldn't drop us.

Now I knew what it felt like to be one of those adopted kittens at the animal shelter, ready to go to an uncertain future in a hand-basket, hoping it wouldn't be hell. Well, in my case, if only I was so lucky. My dad's best friend's cousin's girlfriend was in charge of security at the gates of hell. She'd cut me some slack if I ever landed there.

Since I couldn't have the blessing of oblivion during the trip to wherever, I might as well start a little conversation here with Dan Pillar.

"August the second, nineteen ninety-six," I said in a stage whisper.

Dan did a double take and turned to look at me. "What?"

"You heard me. That's your grandson's birthday, isn't it? I believe his name is Will."

"Is that a threat?" Dan tightened his fist.

"I'm not exactly in the position to threaten anyone at the moment." I swallowed. The guy cared about his grandchild. I was sure of it. He'd stopped scamming women in Will's honor, after all. Considering that he'd simply moved onto more serious crimes, that wasn't saying much. But I had nothing else on Dan, so I did what anyone who was running out of options would do. I grasped at straws. "I'm just trying to point out that what you're doing here, it affects him too."

A muscle on Dan's cheek twitched. "He'll never need to be part of this world."

"But oh, he is. You're playing with some nasty dark forces here. And who's to say it won't spill over? Now me, I was being fair. Believe me, if I'd wanted to punish you through him, it'd be done already. Remember that."

"She's right, you know," Esme added. "According to the vengeance rulebook, it's considered perfectly acceptable to hurt a target through someone they love."

Like the daughter of a man who made unsafe toys could get lead poisoning from the dolls herself. I could have conned Will Pillar out of his rent money like his grandfather had conned others. I hadn't done it, though. Being a victim of guilt by association all my life, I wasn't keen to do the same to another. But Dan didn't have to know that.

The elder Pillar didn't seem terribly impressed by my show of mercy. He ignored us and smoothed his cufflinks as if we were going to have an audience with the Queen of

England.

"You really think serving Damarion will end well for you? Hate to break it to you, but he's serving Absolute Good. *Good*, get it? Not evil. And he didn't even bother telling you that. You know, you're not exactly pure of heart." I snorted.

This remark did get a response from him. Dan adjusted his tie with steady, confident hands as he replied. "Even the pure need somebody to do their dirty work."

"Or somebody expendable to kick-start their devious plans," I countered.

"What do you mean?" Dan frowned.

"Think about it. This whole kidnapping mess was set in motion by me targeting you. I got my assignment through Enid, who was working with Damarion at the time. Your boss armed you, but sicced me on you. Whatever his end game, he risked your life. Remember *that*."

It seemed almost too wild a conspiracy theory, that everything from my failed assignment to Esme meeting Guillermo at the ball to me being suspended was all part of some big plan. But maybe not so wild if we were talking about a society shrouded in a millennia worth of secrecy.

I heard a gasp from Esme and could sense her horrified embarrassment rushing through my mind. It must've been hard for her, knowing that the months of mooning she'd suffered through made her nothing but a pawn in this sick, sick game.

Dan went back to ignoring me, walking ahead of the gang, and disappeared around a curve ahead. Well, I'd done the best I could at finding a crack in that armor and to be honest, I hadn't expected any success anyway.

After much lifting and grunting from the laboring henchmen, we arrived at what I could only describe as an underground throne room made of stones and enough lit candles to make the set designer from *The Phantom of the Opera* proud. And a throne room wouldn't be complete without thrones. There were three at the back of the long room, a large one covered in red velvet cushions flanked by two smaller ones. Damarion and his buddies looked mighty pleased with themselves sitting on them.

The henchmen left the boxes containing Esme and me on the thrones' left side. Dan and his men retreated respectfully to the right. To my frustration, I couldn't see Esme from my angle.

Damarion gave a hand signal, and over three dozen hooded monks in brown cloaks poured in from the doors at the back, filling the high-ceilinged chamber. Murmuring low, they were so clichéd I started wondering if they'd gotten their costumes from some theatric supplies shop. But close up, I could see that these were no rentals. The fabric was made of expensive cashmere, hand-woven and probably super soft. The monks came from money. Every single one of them. That made me wonder if there were any of Grandma's associates here. Perhaps some I'd already come across at the ball? Maybe even a few members of the Council.

That thought filled my stomach with dread. I was used to the in-your-face kind of bullying. But this time, the enemy was tangible yet faceless. It could be one of my professors, someone on the faculty who'd been kind to me, like Enid had been. Maybe even one of my dad's drinking buddies. It gave me chills, realizing just how clueless I was about what was really in people's hearts and minds.

"Glad you could join us, Megan." Damarion smiled that nasty smile of his. "This is a glorious day for Absolute

Good."

"What about Absolute Evil?" I retorted. "Doesn't the story go that the two were trapped together? If you let one out, the other will follow."

"I have every faith my master will defeat Absolute Evil. Now, most of the human plane might get destroyed, but we vengeance demons always survive."

"Bullshit. There's a little bit of good and evil in every single one of us. No one will survive."

Damarion turned his back to me, effectively cutting off our conversation. His voice rang out to address his followers. "Welcome to the time-honored tradition of hostage exchange."

With the sound of a gong, the main door opened. Damarion's followers parted in the middle like the Red Sea, revealing the lone figure coming to take part in the exchange.

Grandma Aequitas.

SEVENTEEN

I FELT ESME'S SURPRISE AND dismay beating at the wall of my mind, matching my own. Oh, crap. Grandma came here on her own. For us. She was powerful and all, but there were too many creepy monks around. I hoped she'd brought backup. Wait, that must be it. The backup was lying in wait somewhere, getting all the exits covered. Dad had to be among them and Mom too. He couldn't have kept her away even if he'd tried.

The monks had better like a good case of itchy fire ants. It was one of Mom's specialties.

Grandma walked up to Damarion, her steps regal. Her face was wiped of all emotions, betraying nothing. I held my breath and tried to act as natural as I could, given the circumstances, knowing that any time now, she could give the signal for all hell to break lose. I hated the fact that I couldn't help, and that my own failings had forced Grandma to bring in the big guns, but a part of me was fascinated by the scuffling to come. It was going to be one heck of a thing to watch. A coordinated attack from a group of trained vengeance demons was a mighty sight. The extended wings, the expertly cast spells, the utterly professional focus and indomitable will...

Which didn't appear.

After what felt like a lifetime, Grandma reached Damarion. But instead of bringing on a sneak attack, she simply held out her arms to him. They grasped the backs of each other's elbows in the age-old greeting of two upper-class vengeance demons of equal power.

"My dear lady, you've found us," Damarion said gallantly.

"You didn't make it easy, my friend," Grandma replied in kind. "You're aware that you could have just sent me an invitation."

"I was curious to see if you could figure us out."

"I did, thanks to Megan." Grandma nodded towards me with a thin smile.

It was a frosty smile she'd thrown my way many times in the past, and I couldn't help but tighten my guts. Was this all an act to get Damarion to lower his guard? If so, it was damn convincing. A part of me was telling myself to be patient, that I should have more faith in Grandma. Yet the other part of me was wondering if I was the one who'd lowered my guard and got screwed over for my trouble. I mean, sure, that whole re-syncing her memories with mine thing had felt wonderful and right at the time, but who was to say it wasn't a trick of the mind? After all, she'd been awful to me all these years, and history was a bitch. Also, it was someone she'd hired who'd come up with a reason why she should stay behind when I entered the bootleg plane. Rather convenient, come to think of it.

"Grandma, what are you doing?" Esme demanded.

"Hush, girl." Grandma used a harsh tone she'd never directed toward Esme before.

"Now that you're here, I trust you know what I seek?" Damarion seemed eager to get on with the negotiation.

"Indeed." She gestured towards the main door, and Serafina came in, her movements robotic. One look into her glassed over eyes and I knew that nobody was home. She was in a deep trance if there ever was one. In her hands was a harp.

It was the sight of Serafina and the harp that finally convinced me, beyond a doubt, that I'd been played. If Grandma were on the up and up, she would never have risked handing such an important artifact over to a lunatic. If she cared about me at all, she would never have endangered my friend by bringing her here against her will.

The harp was made of hammered gold, with unfamiliar ancient symbols and elaborate silver leaves adorning the handle. Its surface, worn by age, had been polished recently. It had the look of a well-preserved antique.

Grandma took the harp from Serafina. She bowed in a jerky motion and stepped back to the left, opposite Dan and his men.

Damarion looked like a cat who'd just swallowed a canary. He addressed the room. "Brethren, we're here today for an historical event, the gifting of the very instrument that will bring back our true master in all his righteous glory."

The monks cheered and clapped, temporarily abandoning their stoic personas.

"No, no!" Esme cried, her voice almost lost in the jeering. She struggled within her box, nearly tipping it over. As a full-blooded vengeance demon, her metabolism was super-fast and it looked like the anesthesia had already worn off.

I wish I could say the same about me. I thought I could feel a slight tingle in my left baby toe, but that was it.

"It's not a gift," Grandma said. Though her voice was soft, its authoritative tone quieted the celebratory sounds from the lot.

"So let us negotiate." Damarion swept his sleeve into a graceful arc.

"There's nothing to negotiate." Grandma tilted her head haughtily. "I've got the harp and you've got the girls. A simple exchange."

"About that. How *did* you manage to get the harp when so many have failed through the ages? I have to be sure of its authenticity, you understand?"

"Of course. I took it from that disgraceful daughter-in-law of mine a long time ago. That dimwit thought I didn't see through her lies when she claimed the harp was long lost. Once I figured out where she hid it, no amount of cheap tricks could keep me away from it."

That old battle-ax. How dare she call my mama a dimwit?

"I'll let one of them go," Damarion offered, making it sound like a jewel of a deal. "The other I'm keeping as insurance. So which girl will it be?"

Grandma's eyes narrowed. "How dare you make demands? I am Andromeda Philippa Aequitas, daughter of—"

"Now, my esteemed lady, you're not in a position to bargain. I made this room slightly out of phase from reality and every entry is pre-approved. So let's keep this civilized and allow me to ask again, which girl will it be? Don't worry, I'll return the other one as soon as my true master returns."

Without hesitation, she answered, "Esme."

"No, Grandma. I'm not going! Megan came here to save

me. I'm not leaving without her." Esme struggled more against her box.

I made a decision right there. Whatever happened to me, I wanted Esme to be safe. It wasn't her fault our grandmother turned out to be a total shit. I also wanted Serafina to get out of here, out of harm's way. None of that could happen if Esme continued to protest. "It's alright, Esme."

"Megan—"

I called on a trickster spell called the Believable Con, an enchantment that beguiled only if the victim was in a situation so helpless that deep down he or she *wanted* to be beguiled. I flooded Esme's mind with images of an army of vengeance demons lying in wait just outside the door, ready to storm this party once Esme got out of here. If only she'd be a good girl and get out of their way, everything would be alright.

Esme's box stopped moving. I could hear her breathing become even and deep as she fell into my mind trap. Her sense of relief and drowsiness was bittersweet to me.

"Esme it is." Seeing what I'd done, Damarion gestured for Dan and his henchmen to release Esme from her fridge box prison, knowing she wouldn't fight them now. Once free, Esme headed for the throne room's exit, dragging Serafina along with her, believing in her mind that she was helping the fight by getting out of the line of fire. My heart squeezed painfully as I watched them go, wondering if I'd live to see them again. I just hoped that the entry to this room was indeed pre-approved, and that the girls wouldn't be able to come back here once they realized what I'd done. Oh, they were going to be mad at me, but at least they'd be safe.

"Well played, my friend, well played." Grandma handed the harp over to Damarion, a trace of grudging admiration in her words.

They shook hands, all cordial and well-mannered. There was even a lift to the corner of Grandma's mouth in what could pass as a smile. Then she turned to leave.

That cold-hearted bitch.

"I heard that." Grandma turned around at the door and glared at me. "You don't get it, do you? You were useful when I needed you to track down Esme, but you can't really expect me to love a half-breed, now can you? I only said I wanted both of you girls back for Esme's benefit. Truth is, I couldn't care less if they let you go."

She waved her hand, and my necklace was yanked off my neck and flew into her open palm, effectively taking away my only means of defending myself. Then she left, and the heavy door closed with a note of finality. All the warmth in the room seemed to have vanished along with her, and I was cold to my very core, colder than I'd ever felt.

I was trapped, both in the box and in my own body, unable to escape whatever was ahead of me. I had no power. I couldn't even see what was going on, save for the cutout. I was so royally screwed.

Then little by little, the anesthesia-induced numbness in my body dissipated, burned off by the intense fury running through my veins. I clutched my fists so tightly all my knuckles popped with a resounding crack, tears threatened to blur my eyes, and I was almost too tired to blink them away.

I'd trusted her, loved her, and she'd betrayed me. Deep down, I'd always feared that I would never be good enough, normal enough to be accepted. But this still hurt like hell.

I would always be a freak, an afterthought.

Now that the little sideshow of love and treachery was over, the monks shuffled about, their focus turned to the harp in Damarion's hand. Their whispers grew louder by the minute.

"Alright, Megan, why don't I get your death over with so I can welcome Absolute Good home?" Damarion passed the harp to Taurean and laced his fingers together, all businesslike.

Dan leaned forward with an air of anticipation. Damarion covered my cardboard prison in a silver net and proceeded with the same chanting he'd done when he'd attacked me in the Shadow World.

But this time, he was joined by all his followers.

And this time, Dad wasn't going to come to my rescue, because Grandma wouldn't even let him know I was in danger. I didn't want to die. If I died here, even my body might never be found. I wanted my life to mean something, not to be wasted as some soon-to-be-forgotten sacrifice. I wanted to fight, to wail. Anything but to face how alone and helpless I was feeling. My parents, Esme and all my half-brothers were going to be devastated. And I wouldn't be alive to warn them about the apocalypse that was to come.

That thought pissed me off so much that I pushed the last of the anesthesia out of my system and flexed my wrists. These people dared to threaten me and all that I held dear. They wouldn't get away with this.

Then my thoughts circled back to Grandma, and I was filled with unadulterated rage. All the love I thought she had for me was fake. The warm and fuzzy alternate memories she'd filled my head with had been fake, every single last one of them. I guess if I'd never thought she loved me, it would've been easier. Now I was disappointed, embarrassed, and just plain mad. The anger mingled with my fear of death. It was a bitter taste in my mouth.

With my necklace gone, there wasn't an instrument to properly keep my emotions in check, let alone amplify the magic it triggered. My trickery magic was unchecked, raw and temperamental, and I was too mad to keep a grip on it, too mad to be logical.

I had always relied on my vengeance side to pull my trickery tendency back, to act as a sprinkler system to my fire. Now with my emotions running wild, I felt like a house with the ground floor engulfed in flame and the basement completely flooded.

My trickery magic, which was controlled by my emotions, said *screw it*.

My vengeance magic, which was controlled by my brain, said *screw it* as well.

My competing natures clashed inside me, threatening to disintegrate me atom by atom with their intensity. Blood roared in my ears, and my heart beat as wildly as the chaos within me.

Never mind Damarion and his friends, my own selves were doing a fine job of killing me without them.

I roared in pain. My two opposing magics rushed out of me and filled the room, like molten lava bursting out of a volcano.

Once they got away from me, I felt light and strangely elated. It was as if I was in a drug-induced high, and I thought I could do anything, get away with anything. I could invoke terrible vengeance on anybody with no regard to the rules, because *I* made the rules.

A faint humming started in my head, but I ignored it.

This girl was in too good a mood right now to care about a little annoying sound.

I called to the twin magical forces zooming around the room, and they responded to my command like a dream, even more so than when they were within my body. Chortling with delight, I directed my powers towards Damarion and made his robe catch on fire. He screamed and rolled on the ground. I proceeded to do the same with the other monks in the room. I felt no remorse, no hesitation. The roaring in my ears ceased, and my heartbeat was as steady as a rock. Dishing out vengeance had a way of making a person focus.

And boy, did I get more to focus on. Shadowy figures of those who'd been mean to me all through my life— Madeleine, Cousin Fred, and even my biased first grade history teacher— materialized before me, their bodies not entirely solid. I didn't care. I didn't question where they came from, why they didn't look right, or why they weren't saying a single word. They were here to harm me. They were here begging to be harmed. I pulled the power around me once more.

"No!" Esme screamed in my head. Esme? I thought she was long gone. What was she wailing on about when I already had that annoying buzzing sound to deal with? She'd better stop if she knew what was good for her.

The humming in my head wasn't unpleasant. It was almost like a long-forgotten friend I never knew I had. I wasn't having a migraine or anything like that, but my eyes seemed to be having trouble seeing properly.

You know how if a person crosses her eyes hard enough, her brain can perceive two images instead of one? It was somewhat like that for me, but not quite. I could see one single room in front of me. The wall and the furniture were exactly the same, yet two very different scenarios laid out before me.

On one hand, there was Damarion on the ground, frantically trying to put out the fire on his clothes along with the other monks, while various bullies from my life waited patiently for my torment. On the other, a small wind tunnel was opening up right in front of me, yawning wider as the humming continued. Somehow, I knew that the tunnel was there *because* of the humming. In the second scenario, Damarion stood right at the edge of my blind spot, looking very much untouched by fire and victorious.

There was something hanging on my neck.

I reached up and felt the familiar weight of the pearl pendant necklace. The pearl vibrated slightly under my touch. That was strange. When had I gotten it back from Grandma? Had I ever lost it to her? What was real and what wasn't? I couldn't tell anymore.

It was as if I was in the Shadow World again, living two overlapping realities, each of them feeling as genuine as the other. While in one I was the mighty avenger, in the other Damarion was calling the shots, and Esme was still trapped in enemy territory along with me.

And she was horrified by what I'd just created, which was some kind of weird inter-dimensional tunnel. Fuelled by my anger, it was amplified by my very-much-there pearl pendant necklace.

What the hell was happening?

They want something from you, Megan.

The first sacred duty of the Greys is to bring back Absolute Good...

Absolute Evil hadn't been heard from since almost the

Beginning, just like Absolute Good.

Fleur was the one who'd trapped Absolute Evil.

Then the room, the tunnel, Esme, Madeleine, Cousin Fred, Injured Damarion, Smug Damarion...they all faded away. The two competing realities dissolved, and all that was left was a pure white background and the silhouette of a woman I'd dreamed about all my life, but never remembered during consciousness.

As I approached her, more details of the woman revealed themselves. She had lustrous dark hair all the way to her waist and was dressed in a white top and a pair of jeans that looked oddly familiar. I squinted. It was one of *my* pairs of jeans. Last I checked, it was in the laundry pile waiting to be washed, not clean and on someone else's body.

"That's because I'm taking elements from your life to create this time out of time, so we can have a chat. Don't worry, you'll return to where you need to be with only seconds missing." The melodic voice of the woman rang around me. "I am Fleur, the First Trickster."

"Why did you—"

"Shh. Don't you remember this?"

I found myself crouching on the edge of a cliff beside her, overlooking a barren landscape of red rocks and volcanoes.

Before me was a scene that had unfolded a million times in my forgotten dreams. Dressed in a deep purple floral gown, another Fleur stood at the foot of a cliff lower than the one I was on. Her hair was blowing all over her determined face. Next to her was a long-haired vengeance demon, his green-scaled wings gleaming in the waning sunrays. They opened their minds, letting the two very distinctive resonances from their brains merge into one single pattern. The vibration opened a tunnel in midair, dragging two bright bulbs of energy that were Absolute Good and Evil to their prison.

The humming was similar to the one I'd unwittingly produced before entering this time out of time. So if Fleur and the vengeance demons' combined vibration was equivalent to "close sesame" to the tunnel, did that mean mine would open it?

"That's right," the jeans-wearing Fleur confirmed. Surrounded by an infinity of bright nothingness, her voice echoed as if she was from far away and everywhere, though by all appearances she was right next to me. "In the beginning, the world was a lot more black and white. Absolute Good was strait, and Absolute Evil was, well, evil. When Absolute Good wasn't busy fighting with Evil, it was hunting all creatures it deemed too impure to exist. Eventually I befriended a vengeance demon who was willing to stand up to them. After Absolute Good and Evil were gone, we created a justice system that would encompass creatures both naughty and nice. Not too straight-laced, yet not too loose. It was the birth of the—"

"Cosmic Balance." Most supernaturals assumed that the Cosmic Balance had always been there. We took it for granted. We moaned about its glitches and inefficiencies. But now that I thought about it, it almost always came through in the end.

"Justice arrives on a wooden leg. Slowly but surely," I repeated the age-old adage.

Fleur nodded. "Whenever injustices pile up, vengeance

demons make sure the wrongdoers get their comeuppance; whenever we become complacent with the status quo, tricksters throw in the randomness that's the spice of life, and by doing so, push forth creativity and innovation."

"I don't get it. That sounds like a good partnership. So what happened?"

"Somewhere along the line, the tricksters' role of recalibrating the Cosmic Balance was forgotten, and my kind's flamboyancy began to be seen as graceless and uncivilized. In time, prejudice became presumed wisdom, and the gap between the two races grew ever wider."

"Hence my crappy childhood."

"Because you are unique." Fleur placed her hand over mine for emphasis. "And more vital than you could ever imagine."

So I *was* the real target all along. Fleur's harp from the legend wasn't a physical thing—it was in the very blood passed down from my mother's line. Mix that with my dad's vengeance genes, and voilà, I was a damn get-out-of-jail free card for Absolute Good and Evil.

"That Grandma who betrayed me, she's not real, is she?" I came to realize.

Fleur tilted her head. "No. Neither was the Serafina who came along with her, or the Fred and the Madeleine afterwards. That entire reality was constructed for one purpose and one purpose only: to induce your loss of control and take advantage of your anger. That was the end game all along. That's why you managed to stay just a little ahead of Enid's whip, and why the heat bubble in the Shadow World didn't move too fast towards you."

A ridiculous sense of relief rose within me. It was a little shameful that in the face of pending cosmic disaster I should spare any thought to my own puny feelings, but I couldn't help it. I felt like a little kid who wanted to jump up and shout, "Yay, Gran does love me after all!"

The moment passed, and I turned my focus back to what I had to do. I had to go back. Because it wasn't just Mom, my trickster half-siblings, and countless other "imperfect" creatures who would be purged in the new order. Dad and Grandma wouldn't survive, either, given their support of me.

"Then go, love," Fleur said.

With those words, my ancestor and the bright surroundings around us started to juxtapose with, then slowly be replaced by, the cardboard prison that was my reality.

My *real* reality.

EIGHTEEN

A THRONE ROOM FULL OF monks? Check.

Esme trapped beside me in a fridge-sized cardboard box identical to mine? Check.

Damarion standing around with a shit-eating grin on his face while the humming grew louder and louder? Check.

Since it was the worst-case scenario, of course it had to be the real one.

The tunnel had expanded dramatically during my mental absence, though it was only a few seconds in actual time. Every inch that the passage gained in diameter was a step closer to doom for everyone I loved.

With a racing heart and a parched throat, I tried to swallow my panic. I knew I said I'd stop Damarion, but I had no idea how. I didn't think they'd ever taught us how to close the gaping hole of Absolute Good and Evil in school.

Use your logic. Fleur's musical voice was like bells over a waterfall, so tranquil it was almost painful for my chaotic mind to process.

Alright, if anger and fear had opened the tunnel, then the opposite of them should close it, right?

Problem was, negative feelings had a way of getting ahead of a person. In my case, my anger had burst out of me and my cardboard prison and taken on the physical form of a relentless force of nature. Though it was no longer in my body, my anxiety was still feeding it. The throne room became a wind tunnel, if wind could be scorching against the cheek like we were at ground zero of an intense forest fire.

Rationally I knew Grandma hadn't betrayed me, so I couldn't be mad at her anymore. But I'd gotten so angry I had an almost painful need to *stay* angry. So I shifted my wrath towards Damarion, Dan, and the other monks. The tsunami of my emotions trapped them and crashed them against each other as if they were nothing but turned over boats lost at sea. They deserved it, for what they'd done to me, were still doing to me. Those assholes were not leaving until I said they were leaving. I wanted them and everyone associated with that blasted secret society to pay.

The worst thing about being angry was how angry it made me feel, and my inability to control myself only pissed me off more.

I wanted the pounding in my head, which intensified along with the humming, to stop. I squeezed my hands on my thighs, willing the tingling feeling in my fingertips to go away. I wanted to hit something, *anything*, if it would take the pain away. I wondered if this was what going insane felt like. Calmness seemed so far away, it might as well have never existed in my life.

Visualize.

Screw you!

Despite my defiant words, the note of alarm in Fleur's voice got through to me. *I cannot, cannot mess up. This is too important.*

Alright, let's see. The opposite of anger and fear...

Love.

Esme, her concern for me apparent. To her, I was a confounding puzzle, in everything from my love-hate relationship with chocolate to being the poster child for unpopularity. She could've acted high and mighty just like Cousin Fred did, but she stood by me.

My parents. Mom could've disappeared after giving birth to me, as it was in the nature of her race to do so, but she'd stayed. Dad could've been promoted to senior arch demon by now, if he'd hidden his new family from polite vengeance society, but he was proud of us.

He was proud of *me*.

The air around me cooled by several degrees. I continued to visualize.

My pain-in-the-ass half-brothers, who might be wild and crazy, but always shared their new inventions with me generously.

Grandma, whom I'd doubted all my life, whom I'd doubted again just now. I wanted to make up some quality time with her. I wondered if in her private life she was a chocolate fiend, like me.

And last but not least, me. My fun-loving and much-neglected trickery side. Come to think of it, much of my passion and warmth came from that part of me. I couldn't wait to get to know myself more, to see what kind of woman I'd turn out to be. If anything, Fleur and her vengeance demon friend showed me just how important it was to embrace both sides of myself.

By the time I finished counting out all the things I had going for me, my elevated heart rate slowed down. The humming and pounding in my head faded. Exhausted, I slumped against the inner wall of my cardboard prison and struggled to catch my breath, as if I'd just run a full marathon. In a way, I had.

I opened my eyes, which I hadn't even realized I'd closed until now.

From my cutout window, I could see Esme dueling with Damarion. A small fireworks display of spells was dancing at their feet. At one point, while I was struggling to get myself under control, she must've broken free of her restraints and taken on our enemy alone.

And he was winning.

And that wasn't my only problem. I might've stopped the humming, the driving force behind the opening, but the tunnel created thus far didn't go away. From its depth I could vaguely see two balls of energy, one in red and one in blue, attempting to widen the tunnel on their end.

Desperate to do something to help, my fingers fumbled around the inner top of the cardboard box, hoping to tear my prison apart by pressing my palms up and stretching to stand on my toes. But of course, deep down, I knew better. Strengthened by magic, the box was beyond sturdy for mere cardboard materials.

Then my fingers came across a wide range of round little bumps, some sort of beads that were glued onto the ceiling of the box. Further exploration told me that the beads were all over the inner surfaces of the box except the floor.

Now why hadn't I noticed them before? Perhaps I wasn't meant to.

And wait, they weren't beads. They were pearls. Rows and rows of them. I could feel the residual power pulsing through them. My own power.

So my prison was actually a gigantic amplifier, built to

enhance my agitation, and the resulting dissonance, to the Greys' end. Maybe the table could be turned...

But did I dare? What if I let myself go again, and this time I couldn't stop? I felt like a recovering alcoholic at a social dinner, afraid of having even one sip of the proffered wine.

I couldn't do it. I couldn't afford to go into Carrie territory. Not now.

But Esme needed me.

Damarion was holding a whip made of silvery strands. With the same eerie glow of the silver web that had trapped me before, the whip burned the floor like acid wherever it touched the ground. Damarion pushed Esme back with each deafening crack of the whip, until she was backed against the far wall with nowhere else to go, and it was a struggle to block every strike.

She wouldn't last long. But if I helped, who was to say I wouldn't accidentally kill her myself? I had no faith in my own power. Not vengeance, and definitely not trickery magic.

Fleur's merry laughter rang in my head. "My silly girl, don't you realize it is exactly the trickster part of you that makes you excel at vengeance? Who do you think gave you inspiration for all those good-old ironic twists? Trust your vengeance demon side to anchor you, and embrace all that I stand for."

Alright, since she put it that way...

I let myself go, tapping into my trickery magic, releasing all its creative brilliance until it wrapped around me like a shimmering rainbow. At the same time, I was secure in the knowledge that my level-headed vengeance demon side was holding the other end of the bungee cord. Always grounding me, never failing me.

I concentrated all my will on Damarion and wove in the Moses, a classic trickery spell named after its most famous victim. Lost in the desert for forty years, anyone?

In a trance, Damarion pivoted around and around on the spot as if all of a sudden he couldn't see where Esme was anymore, even though she hadn't moved an inch since my spell had started. I took the opportunity to do a Mirage—another desert-themed spell—and interposed an image of Esme onto the mouth of the tunnel.

Damarion stopped turning and focused on the fake visual of my half-sister. He had unfocused eyes and a relaxed smile often seen on drunks at high noon. "There you are. Where do you think you're going?"

He walked towards the tunnel, pronouncing each step with another crack of his whip. A number of stray strands flew into the tunnel and got themselves caught up by something on the other side. In a blink, the whip pulled Damarion into the tunnel, like an over-stretched elastic band being returned to its original shape.

If Damarion liked the Absolute Good and Evil so much, he could stay with them, for all I cared.

With Damarion and his hypocritical self-righteousness serving as a sealant on the other side, the passage to the two extremes started to destabilize. The tunnel winked out of existence, to my ultimate relief.

But that was before I realized it was sending out a shock wave towards all of us remaining in the throne room.

The shockwave disintegrated my cardboard box jail and tossed me against the wall like a rag doll. What was worse than my physical pain was the mental void the breaking down of the dissonant core left behind. It was as if I'd been balancing on a tiny bicycle on a piece of rope, then the rope got severed and I found myself free falling. For a few agonizing seconds that felt like a lifetime, the deafening lack of vibration brought a high pitched ringing to my ears, and I cried out in pain.

Then the mental void was filled with an outpouring of my half-sister's concern, and the pain was lessened.

"Megan!" Esme ran to my side. "Are you alright?"

I nodded weakly and looked around. Dan Pillar was caught in a magical full-body bind-slash-protective barrier, which I assumed was courtesy of Esme, but other than the three of us, nobody else was in the near-empty throne room.

"Where are the other monks? Dan's henchmen?" Had they escaped? I would find them and bring them before the Council as witnesses to tonight's event. Even the most stubborn of old guards would have to listen in the face of hard evidence. Well, those who weren't part of the plot anyway.

"The monks jumped planes, and the henchmen, being fragile humans, all got vaporized by the shockwave. I barely had time to shield this one." Esme pointed at Dan, then at the ceiling, which was rumbling ominously. "We'll track the monks down later. But we gotta go now. This whole place is going to cave in a few minutes."

The ceiling started crumbling, raining large rocks down on our heads. Looked like we had even less time than we thought. Well, at least I still had one captive to take with me. I grabbed Dan and flew him through the portal Esme just opened out of thin air.

Esme and I threw ourselves into the portal right before the whole throne room went to hell.

Well, not literally. Having such concrete evidence of the Greys' existence delivered right to Hell would've been too easy for me.

I rolled out of what appeared to be a fireplace, the momentum of the collapse smacking me right into the opposite wall. I hoped this whole wall-kissing thing didn't become a habit.

"Ouch." I groaned as my back made contact with Esme's elbow when we both dropped to the ground like beat-up bowling pins.

"We're on the human plane. Hart House again, from the looks of it," Esme stated. And not the bootlegged one, either. The feel of the wall, as I'd learned from firsthand experience, was too solid for a non-real plane.

Since Dan had a history of getting away from me, my eyes went searching for him the moment I steadied myself. While I'd been rolling, I'd caught a glimpse of him on the cream-colored carpet in the center of the room.

He wasn't there anymore.

A strange sense of sleepiness threatened to take me under. My muscles relaxed involuntarily, and my legs turned to jelly. One look at Esme, who was barely holding her upper body from the ground with her elbow, told me she was feeling the same strange lethargy as I was. I tried to force myself to panic, to be alarmed, but all I could feel was a sense of utter complacency and laziness. I made my heavier-by-the-minute head turn from side to side, trying to see if Dan was responsible for this. It could be the surviving monks, for all I knew.

At the corner of the room to my right stood Dan; looked like the portal had disabled his full-body bind. He was holding a small baby bottle, the type the shelter used to hand-feed newborn kittens. But instead of milk or formula, there was maroon-colored faery dust in it. With each shake of the bottle, Dan sprinkled a dash of magical adrenaline suppressant on Esme and me, rendering our bodies weak and useless. It couldn't kill us, but it would slow us down. A lot. The crystal-like dust sparkled eerily in the dark room, matching the dread that was now spreading across my system.

"You have three choices." I tried to keep the panic out of my voice and ignored the lead-like feeling in my body.

"Oh?" Dan raised his eyebrow as he put away the baby bottle, confident that he had us. And he was right.

"You can make a run for it, or you can kill us, *then* make a run for it. I wouldn't recommend the second option, as we vengeance demons are pretty hard to kill. Might slow you down, you know."

"More the reason I should stop listening to your babbling and get gone." Dan turned towards the door.

"But you really should listen to my third choice," I said quietly, trying my best not to ruin the dramatic effect by slurring my words. "The health, happiness, and freedom of your grandson depends on it."

He spun around. "Are you threatening to hurt him?"

"No, I'm threatening to hurt you through him." I might not have had the heart to do it before, but tonight's events transcended sympathy and kindness. Dan was my only non-blood-related witness for Damarion's actions. Not to mention, he was a treasure trove of who-was-working-for-whom across the planes. He needed to be questioned, then brought to trial in front of the Council. I owed it to the safety of all the planes to do whatever it took to take him in. "You know enough about me to know I mean business."

"No." For the first time, other than arrogance and self-centeredness, there was real emotion in Dan's voice. Genuine concern and fear for his grandchild. Dan took out a nasty-looking knife. "Then I'll just have to kill you now."

"Too late. Five seconds ago I finished sending a mental call to arms to all my vengeance brethren on the public psych link. They might not like me, but they will avenge me. If they don't hear back from me in fifteen minutes, Will's going to get it. You can't gut me and reach him in time. Go quietly, and I'll call it off."

Call it blackmail. Call it ruthlessness. I intended to get the job done.

Dan stopped in his track—not leaving, yet not stepping forward to gut me, either. We were at an impasse.

But time was not on my side.

With my eyes almost closed and my eyelids weighing a ton on my face, I knew I didn't have long before losing consciousness.

I had one last trick up my sleeve.

I used the last of my strength to reach up and touch my pearl pendant, remembering the cute little burp it had given off when it had absorbed the anti-magic balm on its surface. I silently commanded it to do the same for the faery dust on my person. I wasn't sure if I was using my vengeance or trickery magic, and in a way, it really didn't matter anymore. I was using Megan magic, which had a flavor all of its own.

Dan watched as I stood slowly and stretched, and he

didn't run, though he still could've. I willed my pearl to work on Esme. In no time, she opened her eyes and looked around. Her alertness had made a full return.

Satisfied with her condition, I turned to Dan. Keeping my eyes on him, I took out my cell phone and dialed a number I'd never called before but had memorized since my first week at Vengeance U.

It was picked up after a single ring. "Hello, this is Reapers 'R' Us. How may I help you?"

My eyes didn't leave Dan's face as I answered, "I'd like to call in a pick-up. Code Silver."

"I'll send a dispatch ASAP."

Dan dropped the faery dust bottle with a defeated slump to his shoulder, looking a decade older than he had at the beginning of this evening. Code silver meant he'd be escorted by reapers under maximum security, as this was a special case if there ever was one. He was not technically dead yet, but based on his role in the crimes against the Cosmic Balance, he'd most likely be after the trial.

But not before he coughed out some names. A lot of names. And if I found out the likes of Madeleine or Cousin Fred were indeed involved with the Greys, then Hell had no fury like, well, me.

In under a minute, a trio of senior-level reapers materialized in front of us. With a little more backbone than I'd given him credit for, Dan walked up to them with arms at his sides. I noticed the reapers didn't bother to cuff him, not just because Dan had nowhere to run, but also out of respect for his lack of resistance. I gave them the information to retrieve Guillermo after they were done delivering Dan.

Dan turned toward me. "You'll stop the call to arms right

away."

I nodded. "Already done."

He curved his lips slightly, in mockery or maybe even self-deprecation. "They're going to get it out of me anyway, so here goes. Eight."

"Huh?"

"The Greys are divided into eight sects. I headed one, Enid another."

"You mean there are still six of them out there?"

"Yes, and they won't stop. Good luck." Dan's eyes glinted. Was that a fair warning or a taunt? I knew not.

In a flash they were gone, prisoner and soul collectors.

There was just Esme and me left. I collapsed against the wall, and Esme rushed to support my elbow. "Hey, you alright?"

"Just give me a minute."

"There is no such thing as a public psych link, is there?" Esme bit her lip.

"Believe it or not, there is. I picked that one up when I shared minds with Grandma."

"Oh." She seemed surprised at that.

"But you have to be arch demons or above to use it, let alone call arms. So I did lie." Despite knowing it had been the only way to get Dan to turn himself in, I still felt kinda crappy about threatening to hurt an innocent who was his grandson. Well, not crappy enough to not give my inner trickster the thumbs up. I guess part of growing up, and growing into the career that I'd chosen, was to understand that there was no such thing as a perfect vengeance.

"We'll hunt down the other cells." Esme placed her hand on mine, letting her warmth and comfort flood through me.

"As soon as my suspension gets lifted." I nodded.

"It was just a matter of time, even before tonight. Now you won't have any problem at all."

And I had a favor to return to Gregory. Damn if a part of me wasn't looking forward to that. Later, I'd lie to myself and say that my motivation was purely for Serafina's sake, but not at this moment.

I'd gotten Esme back, completed my first co-op assignment, and I'd discovered my grandma's love. Not bad for a day's work.

But most of all, I'd found myself.

I was a proud vengeance demon and an equally proud trickster. Heaven—and Hell—help anyone who'd been up to no good.

THE END

THIS IS WHERE THE AUTHOR SHAMELESSLY BEGS YOU TO LEAVE A REVIEW...

Did you enjoy VENGEANCE BE MINE? If so, I would really appreciate it if you could write a review on Goodreads and/or your online retailer!

WANT MORE VENGEANCE?

Sign up for my mailing list on my website to receive VENGEANCE BE MINE, VENGEANCE 101, and the VENGEANCE WORK KIT for free. You'll also receive semi-regular updates regarding my latest release and offers, but you're free to unsubscribe anytime.

VENGEANCE BE MINE is the story of a young woman, Megan, who struggles with her identity as a vengeance demon and trickster hybrid, but ultimately realizes how her two sides balance her.

VENGEANCE 101 (exclusive to newsletter subscribers) details Megan's adventure as a freshman at her vengeance university, and explores her motivation behind wanting to become a vengeance demon.

VENGEANCE WORK KIT (also exclusive to newsletter subscribers) is a fun collection full of interesting tidbits about the vengeance world, including a sample vengeance work order and a guide to a successful vengeance!

About the Author

Louisa Lo lives in Toronto, Canada with her husband,
an aristocratic cat, and more cardboard boxes than she
cares to unpack. She decided to write about vigilantes,
because it seems like a better life choice than trying to
become one and landing herself in jail. She just has that
kind of luck.

Visit Louisa's website at **www.LouisaLo.com** where
you'll find her social media links.

Discover the Changeling World—and the Fae Prince— that Serafina Left Behind

What if everything you've ever known, down to what you are, was a lie?

Growing up in the enchanted kingdom of Dualsing, seventeen-year-old Lady Serafina has always known she's different. Her fae power never manifested itself during puberty, and her parents treated her like a tolerated houseguest rather than family. Even her childhood sweetheart, Crown Prince Eldon, distanced himself the moment he was old enough to know the secret about Serafina that everyone in their world seems to know—except her.

Now her upcoming birthday is being treated as a national holiday by the very people who have neglected her and Serafina is developing abilities that feel terrifyingly right, but aren't fae power at all.

As she starts to investigate her origin, Serafina has no idea she will be setting in motion events that will have far-reaching consequences not just for herself, but for all the planes.

BEFORE VENGEANCE, a prequel of VENGEANCE BE MINE, is available at your favorite online retailers.

Recommended reading sequence

THE VENGEANCE DEMONS SERIES

Vengeance 101 (exclusive to newsletter subscribers)

Vengeance Be Mine

Vengeance Work Kit (exclusive to newsletter subscribers)

Before Vengeance

Vengeance Unclaimed

A Good Vengeance

Vengeance For Hire

Hell Hath No Vengeance

Vengeance Delayed (Coming Soon)

Note: Check out the Vengeance Demons Boxset—it's an excellent deal!

THE LADY SLAYALOT SERIES

A Royal Apocalypse

The Slayer Queen (Coming Soon)

BE A VENGEFUL VIXEN!

I'd love to have you join my Facebook reader group!
Search "Vengeful Vixens Louisa Lo" on Facebook.

www.ingramcontent.com/pod-product-compliance
Lightning Source LLC
Chambersburg PA
CBHW020252200626
46816CB00001BA/260